S0-CKH-038

KILLED
by
SCANDAL
SIMON NASH

Also available in Perennial Library
by Simon Nash:

DEATH OVER DEEP WATER

KILLED by SCANDAL

SIMON NASH

PERENNIAL LIBRARY
Harper & Row, Publishers
New York, Cambridge, Philadelphia, San Francisco
London, Mexico City, São Paulo, Singapore, Sydney

This book is fiction
All characters and incidents
are entirely imaginary

A hardcover edition of this book was published by Geoffrey Bles in England and by Garland Publishing, Inc., in the United States. It is here reprinted by arrangement with the author.

 For information address Harper & Row, Publishers, Inc., 10 East 53rd Street, New York, N.Y. 10022. Published simultaneously in Canada by Fitzhenry & Whiteside Limited, Toronto.

First PERENNIAL LIBRARY edition published 1985.

Library of Congress Cataloging in Publication Data

———

Killed by scandal.

"Perennial Library."

I. Title.

PR6005.H323K54 1985 823'.914 84-48185
ISBN 0-06-080741-5 (pbk.)

---

85 86 87 88 89 10 9 8 7 6 5 4 3 2 1

CONTENTS

St. Edmund's Church Hall — Haleham Green

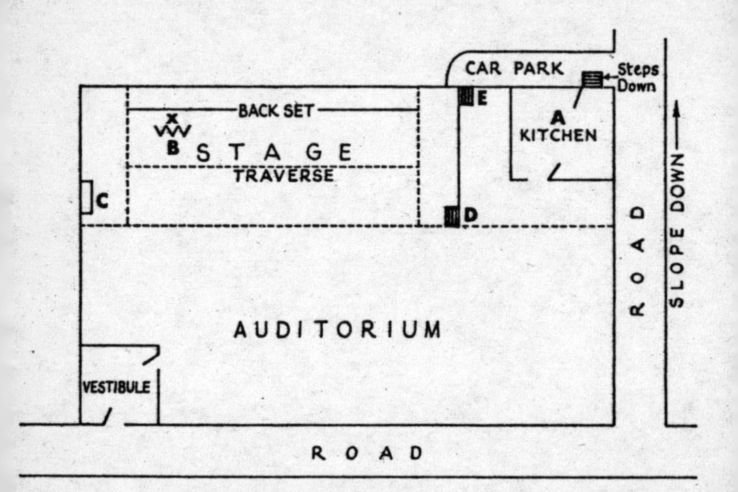

A – where Bould sat
B – where Bould's body was found
C – switchboard where Seward stood
D – steps up to stage
E – steps down to dressing-room under stage
------ curtains

CHAPTER ONE

Ludlow Goes on Stage

Adam Ludlow had just finished his first lecture of the Lent Term when he was seized by the Professor of Applied Mathematics.

"You're just the man," said the professor, taking him by the arm and guiding him along a corridor when he had no wish to go. Ludlow, who kept up a happy feud with everything which he collectively described as 'science', muttered something which might have mentioned the Greeks bearing gifts. The professor went on undeterred.

"The thing is this; I've got a sort of interest in the people who get up amateur theatricals in the bit of a suburb where I live——"

"Really? I'd no idea that we shared any common interests, but if you want to talk about drama——"

"Well, I don't actually. They got me to become a vice-president or something. I give them a subscription, but I don't often go to see them. Not that I mind doing a show if the family wants an evening out. But you know how it is—these fellows like to get a few names on their notepaper, and there's an idea going round that we university types are intellectuals, and all that."

"Most amusing error, no doubt," said Ludlow, "but I still don't know where I come in. Do you want me to tell them the truth?"

"Jolly good! But to come to the point. These people are putting on a play, quite soon I believe, and they asked me if I could find someone to give them a bit of a talk about it. You know—background, and that sort of stuff."

"What play is it?"

"Now, the secretary did tell me. She's a nice person, the secretary; you'll like her. What was it—something about a scandal——"

"*The School for Scandal*?"

"That's it! Clever of you to guess. Who wrote it?"

"Sheridan."

"That's right."

"I know it is."

"So the point is, will you go and talk to them about this Sheridan?"

"It isn't my best period," Ludlow said, taking refuge in the academic's finest excuse for not doing something. "Why not ask Hardacre?" Hardacre, the Professor of English, was the head of Ludlow's department.

"I did, but he wouldn't look at it. He's frightfully busy with his book."

"He has been for twelve years, to my knowledge," said Ludlow who had no expectation of further promotion and was also protected by a small private income from the need to be polite about professors. As he really never minded speaking on any subject, he said that he would do his best to think up something about Sheridan.

"That's grand," said the Professor of Applied Mathematics. He had now reached the door of his own room and was willing to release Ludlow at last.

"Provided somebody writes to tell me exactly what is wanted, and remembers to tell me when and where they want it," said Ludlow as he gathered his gown and his bruised dignity around him.

He did in fact receive a clear and explicit letter from the secretary of the Haleham Green Thespians, whose name turned out to be June Morland, asking him to speak at the

St. Edmund's Church Hall at 8 p.m. on a date two weeks ahead. All of which explains why he was driving his ancient Austin in a north-westerly direction on an evening late in January, in opposition to a wind that was coming out of the north-west at a speed which suggested that it was trying to escape from something particularly unpleasant.

There is nothing notably unpleasant about Haleham Green nor is there anything to encourage a light-hearted visit. The site of the old village is commemorated by the High Street, which now contains no building more than thirty years old. The green, after having bits cut off and enclosed for several hundred years, eventually gave up the struggle and became part of a housing-estate. The inhabitants of this estate, and of the few older houses which hang around the fringes of the district, claim to live in London when they want to impress acquaintances they meet on holidays. When the L.C.C. threatens them, however, they are strong for their membership of Middlesex. The shops have the familiar names that have spread so far that they no longer tell the traveller what part of the country he has reached.

Ludlow prided himself on his ability to find anywhere that could remotely be considered as part of London. He reached the High Street of Haleham Green in spite of discouragement from the fugitive wind, but was unable to find any trace of a church and still less of a church hall. The street was empty and showed no ambition to be anything else. On his third crawl along it, Ludlow saw a young man come out from a door beside a chemist's shop — one of the few that bore a private name. Being unfamiliar with Ludlow and his moods, the young man was startled to be hailed in these words:

"Good evening, you're a stranger in these parts yourself, and you've never heard of any Thespians and you don't known where St. Edmund's Church Hall is."

The other recovered himself quickly and smiled as he approached the car. "As a matter of fact," he said, "I'm a Thespian and I'm just going to the hall. I was afraid I was going to be late, so if you give me a lift I'll show you the way."

He got in beside Ludlow, showing himself to be of medium height, with a slim build which at first made him look a little younger than he was. He was sharp-featured, intelligent-looking, but somehow not entirely at ease in what he was doing at present.

"My name's Donald Hedge," he explained as Ludlow jerked back into motion through the well-worn gears. "I keep the chemist's, there where you picked me up, and I live over the shop. You must be Professor Ludlow."

Ludlow made a polite noise that allowed him to accept the title without open deceit.

"It's very decent of you to come and talk to us. I hope there'll be a good crowd."

"So do I," said Ludlow, "especially after the trouble Cleopatra and I have had to find the place."

"Who's Cleopatra?" asked Donald Hedge, peering round at the back seat.

"My car, who is even now waiting for guidance."

"Oh, sorry — yes, you turn right just after the next lamp. Why is it — she — called Cleopatra?"

"Because age cannot wither her, nor custom stale her infinite variety. It doesn't matter," he added, seeing a well-known look of mingled wonder and alarm on the other's face. He changed the subject and asked, "Are you in the play?"

"Yes, I'm Joseph Surface."

"An interesting part. It needs some skill in an actor to bring out Sheridan's parody of the earlier sentimental comedy, while at the same time making the character credible within the logic of the play."

"Yes. Quite. I'm not much good really, but one gets dragged into these things, and they're always short of men. Terry said I looked all right for the part anyway."

"Who's Terry?"

"Terry Colbert, the producer. He's a teacher at the Grammar School, but he gives nearly all his spare time to the Thespians. He's terribly good, though he does get very worked up at rehearsals."

"Producers often do. So you had other motives for becoming a—Thespian?" Ludlow uttered the word with distaste.

Donald Hedge made a noise that was almost a giggle, and then said, "Turn left at the next corner, and we're there."

"There" was a squat and gloomy building, awkwardly placed on a slope away from the road. Under Hedge's direction, Ludlow parked Cleopatra in a yard at the back and was then taken round to the main door. The wind was now very angry with everyone and seemed to regard the presence of St. Edmund's Church Hall as an insult that should be removed as soon as possible. They came into a small vestibule, where the wind collapsed into a flat cold. The pervading atmosphere of damp, stale smoke and wet overcoats suggested that the hall was in frequent, if not joyful, use. Hedge pushed open a swing-door and said to no one in particular, "Here's Professor Ludlow."

The auditorium, if it could be dignified by such a name, seemed even colder than the vestibule. A few people—they looked very few to Ludlow's anxious glance—were sitting in two rows on those steel and canvas chairs which can be so usefully stacked in piles and have nothing else whatever to commend them. A lot of other chairs were performing their proper function by remaining stacked at the back of the hall, from which place the caretaker had clearly not thought it worth disturbing more than two dozen of them. The audience, such as it was, sat facing a curtain that had once been purple but had in recent years nearly fulfilled an ambition to be brown. Ludlow's spirits, always liable to a quick rise and fall, were very low. They rose slightly when a young woman appeared in front of him, and said:

"Good evening, Dr. Ludlow, so good of you to come. I'm June Morland."

June Morland was pretty enough for Ludlow not to mind yet another misapplied title. She was small, but had a grace of poise and movement which made most people think her to be taller. Her hair was not red, but it was too red to be described as merely brown. Her nose, a thought too long for the roundness of her face, turned the least bit upwards and rescued her from conventional and unmemorable prettiness. Ludlow looked at her and said:

"Lady Teazle, I presume."

"That's right, how did you guess?"

"No producer who knew his job could fail to cast you for it." This brief but pleasant exchange was shattered by a little man, no taller than June, who thrust himself between them and announced:

"Glad to meet you, Ludlow; I'm bold."

Ludlow was wondering what to say about this obvious self-revelation, when June Morland saved him by explaining:

"Mr. Bould is our Chairman."

Ludlow's height and gaunt face give him an appearance of severity which he does not always try to soften. He found something extremely repellent in the aggressive little figure who was now shaking his hand. Bould had a skin of the type which always appears slightly dirty, however well washed its possessor may be. He was about fifty, nearly bald but with a good deal of hair at the back of his neck to compensate for what had slipped away from his head. He wore old-fashioned eyeglasses on a black silk ribbon; his teeth paraded both their expense and their falsity whenever he spoke.

"There aren't many people here," said Ludlow sternly.

"It's a cold night," Bould replied, in a tone that suggested a great nobility on the part of those who had come. "Most of the cast are here anyway. And my wife and daughter, too. My daughter's in the play, so I hope she'll learn something."

Bould abruptly walked away as if he could bear the sight of Ludlow no longer. In fact he appeared to be collecting his family. Mrs. Bould was sitting at the far end of the second row, protected by so many shapes and layers of wool that the needles which she held might have been knitting her into yet another garment or unknitting one of those that she already had on. When she got up in acknowledgement of a bark from her husband, she showed herself to be several inches taller than he was. Her grey hair was mostly piled on top of her head, with a few rebel strands which conducted a harassing action into her eyes and across the bridge of her sharp nose. She went meekly after Bould, who was now bearing down on a pretty girl and a well-built man who were deep in quiet conversation by one of the two radiators. Detaching the girl, Bould returned to Ludlow and announced, "My wife and daughter."

"Maria," said Ludlow, looking at the girl.

"No, no, her name's Frances," Bould replied testily.

"He means in the play, Daddy," said the girl, "how clever of him to guess."

"Oh, you know the play, do you?" said Mrs. Bould, with an air of surprise that anyone outside Haleham Green should have heard of it. She collected a knitting-needle that had got caught up in her outermost layer of wool.

"Considering that I've come to lecture about it — oh, yes, I have read it a few times."

"Time to start," Bould announced, pulling out a pocket-watch. "You were a bit late getting here, I think."

"It wasn't very easy to find the place."

"When I'm in a strange town, I always carry a map. Are you ready?"

"Quite, thank you."

As Ludlow followed Bould across the hall, he saw that June Morland was looking angrily at the chairman. Ludlow had got well into his forties without marriage, from a variety of causes in which laziness and a love of personal freedom stood high. He was by no means unsusceptible, however, and he hoped that June's annoyance was caused by the discourtesy which he had received from Bould. But there was something else, a kind of disgust, tinged with fear, which made him regretfully dismiss the idea. He had no time for conjecture, for Bould plunged behind the curtain and into a dusty gloom through which a short flight of steps was faintly visible. Climbing these behind his guide, Ludlow struck his head on the top of an opening which the shorter man had passed unscathed, and found himself on the stage.

"Curtain and lights," Bould shouted, "come on, Seward, we're waiting."

"All right, Mr. Bould, I'm coming."

A figure unidentifiable in the semi-darkness hastened up the steps and across the stage, muttering maledictions. The curtains parted and a strong light revealed Ludlow pulling out his notes with one hand and straightening his errant tie with the other.

"Not the spot, Arthur," called another voice from the back of the hall, "just battens. I'll look after the house lights."

"Right you are, Terry."

Ludlow found himself slightly less illuminated, and able to see that a table and two chairs stood before him. Seward reappeared, jumped over the footlights and entered the darkness which had now descended on the body of the hall. Bould ushered Ludlow to one of the chairs and stood in front of the other.

"Fellow Thespians," he began, "I'm not much of a one for lectures, and I don't expect any of you are. But some of us thought it would be a good thing to know a bit more about this chap who wrote the play that we have been so busily engaged in. So we got Mr. Ludlow, who's a teacher at London University, to come and say a few words to us. He works under Professor Haddock, who as you know is one of our honorary vice-presidents and a good friend of the Thespians. So I'm sure we are in for an intellectual treat, and I'll ask you to give your attention to Mr. Ludlow, who's going to tell us all about Sheridan."

Ludlow got up and put his notes back in another pocket, where they peeped out pathetically asking to be used all through the lecture. He was too experienced to be put off by chairmen and their inaccuracies. He also knew that there are basically two ways of giving a lecture. If you have an audience which knows nothing about say, Sheridan, and is anxious to learn, it is best to begin by telling them when he was born. If the purpose of the lecture is not to instruct the audience but to impress them with how much the lecturer knows, a recommended opening would be five to ten minutes on the civilisation of the Incas. You can then get round to the fact that Sheridan wrote a poor and little-known play called *Pizarro*, and your reputation is made. On this occasion, Ludlow peered into the darkness and announced, "Richard Brinsley Sheridan was born in 1751."

The next forty-five minutes passed without incident. Ludlow kept to the point fairly well and went into only one of his famous digressions. The restrictions on the theatre in the eighteenth century led him to an attack on all governments, and the present one in particular, for failing to encourage the arts.

"The National Theatre," he railed, "has been on the Statute-book since 1948. But is it opened? Is it even begun? The dreary guardians of our destiny wail that we can't afford it. But if anybody wants to do something destructive with an atom, our every pleasure is taxed——" He got back to Sheridan within eight minutes.

At the end, Bould gave something which might have been a waking snore, but which Ludlow hoped was a grunt of approval. He suggested that the house lights should be put on, so that they could all see each other in case anybody wanted to ask any questions. In the awful silence which followed, Ludlow was able to look at his audience collectively. There were about thirty people in the hall, more than he had noticed at first. Frances Bould had gone back to her previous companion, and was clearly more interested in him than in anything Ludlow had been saying. After Ludlow had had time to smoke half a cigarette, June Morland dutifully asked whether there was any connection between Sheridan and Goldsmith, which took ten minutes to answer. Another silence, and an intelligent-looking young man took up a point which Ludlow had made. When this was dealt with, a large man with a red face, who had been opening and shutting his mouth for some time, got up and knocked over his chair as he did so. He announced that he was Charles Surface — in the play of course, ha, ha — and he thought it ought to be played for laughs right through. But Terry — indicating the young man who had just spoken, told him to make it more sympathetic, like. Who was right? Ludlow talked about sentiment and conventional morality, and the two traditions in the early novel, until no one knew who was right about anything. Bould then made sure that there would be no more, by thanking the speaker for his interesting talk which was so full of facts about seventeenth-century writers like Golding, and then hurried off the stage. Ludlow, following him, again failed to duck and emerged from behind the curtain rubbing his head. Now that he was literally on their level, the audience lost their shyness and surrounded him.

"Would you like some tea?" said June Morland, holding out a cup filled with a strange liquid of a deep orange colour. Ludlow accepted it with thanks, and tried to listen to several people who were asking him how their parts ought to be played. It appeared that Frances Bould's friend, whose name was Tony Dexter, was Sir Peter Teazle. The red-faced man who was Charles Surface introduced himself as Clifford Fielding. There were other names and faces which Ludlow made no attempt to remember. His digression into the National Theatre question brought him into a mild political argument, in which several of the Thespians obviously regarded him as a dangerous revolutionary who was capable of saying unkind things about the dear Prime Minister.

As he swallowed his repellent tea and tried to keep up some degree of politeness, he became increasingly aware that this was not altogether a happy society. A certain asperity in the conversation, a tightening of lips and raising of eyebrows at apparently casual remarks, a tendency for couples to retire into corners for prolonged muttering, all suggested that the normal undercurrents of amateur drama were swelling into a tidal wave. The increasing coldness of the hall, whose radiators had by now stopped trying to cope with the unfair opposition, could not be blamed for all the sense of discomfort. However, another half-hour passed pleasantly enough for Ludlow, who never minded being the centre of interest. At last he managed to move towards the door, where Bould extended an unconvincing hand and thanked him for coming.

"I hope you'll come and see the play itself," he said.

"Well, I don't know," said Ludlow, feeling even colder than before at the thought, "I'm rather busy in the evenings."

"Do come, Mr. Ludlow," said June Morland who had come up to them, "we should love to see you again."

Slightly moved by this, but still hoping to escape, Ludlow asked when the play was to be.

"Tuesday to Saturday, the week after next," June replied.

"What a pity; I'm engaged every evening that week, except Monday."

"Then come to the dress rehearsal — that's on Monday."

"Perhaps the producer wouldn't like strangers to be there," said Ludlow in a last despairing effort.

"He wouldn't mind a bit, would you, Terry?"

"I'd be honoured," said Terry Colbert. "As a rule, I don't let anybody in except the cast; it's rather off-putting to have all the families getting a free show and giggling about it, but I'd very much value any comments you might make."

So it came about that Adam Ludlow was cajoled and flattered into a promise that was destined to take up much more of his time than one evening. On asking whether anybody wanted a lift in the direction of London, he got a polite acceptance from Terry Colbert. After being left out in the cold for so long, Cleopatra was naturally sulking and refused to start. Ludlow sighed and reached for the starting-handle.

"I'll turn her over for you," said Colbert. His pale, thin face with high cheekbones at the corners of blue eyes, was lit by the headlamps as he bent to the task. His fair hair, a little too long, fell forward. Between them they made Cleopatra wake up, cough a few times and then roar with disapproving energy. On their way, Colbert became talkative.

"That was a jolly good lecture," he said. "One misses that sort of thing now. You're at North London, aren't you?"

"Yes. Are you familiar with the college?"

"Not really; I was at Queen Adelaide's. I read English there."

"Ah yes, under Pigeon. I never knew a man with such a passion for the wrong poets."

"He was very hot on Spenser, I remember."

"Precisely."

They drove on in silence for a short time; then Colbert said:

"I envy you your job. It's a different world from mine."

"I suppose teaching has its rewards everywhere."

"Not in Haleham Green Grammar School. It's pure hell. I'd get out if I had more courage."

"How long have you been there now?"

"Nearly two years. It feels like a life sentence already."

"Still, you must find some pleasure in the — ah — Thespians."

"Oh yes, it's great fun. I used to do a lot when I was a student, and I've never been able to keep away from it since. Old Pigeon was always dropping pointed remarks about 'other young men who had wasted their time on amateur theatricals.' I think he resented the fact that drama was written for the stage and not the study."

"A lot of my colleagues do. But you seem to be doing a good job here."

"They're a decent crowd, though it's the very devil to persuade them to try a period play, even one as hackneyed as this."

"*The School for Scandal* never fails if it's done with reasonable competence. I suppose the tearing down of reputations has a perennial appeal. Not perhaps in a peaceful place like this," Ludlow added, probing.

Colbert laughed. "Don't you believe it," he said. "There's enough scandal going on in that society to keep a dramatist busy for years. It's these dull suburban places that really have the fun and games. You've got to do something if you're going to keep sane here."

"Yes, I've often thought that sheer boredom is at the root of a lot of queer things. Possibly the witch-cult in the middle ages started that way. However. Yes, I must admit that I seemed to detect a certain tension here and there this evening."

"Well, you met Bould for one, and you probably saw that his daughter has her claws deep into Tony Dexter."

"Sir Peter Teazle? Yes, I thought there was something there. She seemed a pleasant enough girl."

"Oh, she's all right. Anyway, Daddy doesn't approve and he's making life hell for both of them."

"What's wrong with Dexter?"

"Nothing, except stupidity. He's about fifteen years older than her and there's some sort of trouble in his past which Bould has dug up. Trust him," he added savagely.

"You don't care for the chairman of the society?"

"Nobody does. He's got pots of money and he's a bit of a power locally, so we put up with him."

"What does he do?"

"Interferes with everybody's business — oh, I see what you mean. I don't know. Some kind of clothing business I think. He's semi-retired now, made a packet in the war out of uniforms and things. He still goes to town two or three days a week, and spends the rest of the time making trouble He's a J.P., local councillor and all that — and a governor of my school."

"And that perhaps is where you came to dislike him?" Ludlow asked.

"Yes, though his normal manners are enough to put anyone's back up. I'll tell you about it another time, because my place is just here. If you'll be so kind as to drop me on the corner. Would you like to come in for coffee?"

"No, thank you, I really must get back."

"Perhaps after the dress rehearsal then. I shall look forward to seeing you. And thanks again for coming tonight."

Colbert swung his legs gracefully out of the car and disappeared with a final wave of the hand up a dark side street. Ludlow got into gear again and headed for the distant warmth of his flat, against the wind which had now turned round and was trying to blow him right back to Haleham Green.

CHAPTER TWO

Dress Rehearsal

"How did you enjoy my little talk?" Ludlow asked Professor Haddock when he saw him next day.

"Well, old man, I'm afraid I couldn't get there, actually."

"Yes, I found it rather a difficult approach on a windy night."

"Well, what I mean to say is, I had something else on. I was most frightfully sorry to miss it."

"No doubt you will go to the play?"

"Depends. I've got rather a lot to do in the evenings just now."

After this brief exchange with their respected but absent vice-president, Ludlow might have put the Haleham Green Thespians out of his mind for ever. But on the Friday before the dress rehearsal he received a letter from June Morland reminding him of his promise and hoping *'very much indeed'*, underlined twice, that he was still able to come. One sentence in her letter went somewhat beyond the formal terms of a renewed invitation. *'At this stage of rehearsals,'* she wrote, *'tempers get a little strained, and it would be so valuable to have a neutral person present.'* So Ludlow decided to sacrifice Monday evening, moved by an old-fashioned conscience about keeping promises, an innate curiosity, and perhaps by the memory of an attractively tilted female nose.

Apart from being a Monday, the day of the rehearsal turned out to be particularly trying in other ways. The morning was occupied by a succession of students, some of whom had forgotten to write their appointed essays, while others had unfortunately remembered. In the afternoon there was a meeting of the Board of Examiners, already sharpening their knives for the vivisection of students in the summer. The paper in which Ludlow was one of the two examiners was roughly handled, ending in the excision of a question of which he had been rather proud. As a climax, he managed to knock over his cup of tea in the Senior Common Room, emptying most of it over the Principal's shoes. It was with little love in his heart that he once more took the road and directed Cleopatra's aged bonnet towards Haleham Green. The night was even colder than on his last visit and the thought of two hours or more on one of those peculiar chairs was a grim prospect. It must be admitted also that Ludlow is not at his best on occasions when he is expected to sit and listen, instead of having people listen to him.

This time he found the hall with no trouble. The icy air that greeted him might have been kept in cold storage ever since his last visit. In spite of the gratifying attention which he received on entering, including the reward of a smile from June Morland, he could tell that the strain of relationships had not improved in two weeks. The tendency to get into small groups was even more marked, and the fact that most of the people were now in eighteenth-century costumes and wigs made identification difficult. For a moment Ludlow thought that Frances Bould had now attached herself to Clifford Fielding, but after more scrutiny he realised that it was Dexter's florid make-up as Sir Peter Teazle which had caused the confusion. Fielding himself had lost ten years by the same process and was deep in conversation with his stage-brother, Donald Hedge. Bould and his wife seemed to be the only two not taking part in the play, except for the producer and a girl with long black hair, round glasses and prominent teeth.

Bould merely waved coldly at Ludlow and did not get up

from his chair by the radiator. Opposite him, as if they were at their own chilly fireside, his wife had turned her attention from knitting to writing letters. Colbert, however, immediately came over and shook Ludlow by the hand.

"It's grand to see you again," he said, "especially as everything seems to be going wrong."

"You mean that I am a suitable messenger to announce the tragic climax?" Ludlow asked.

"Oh dear, no — only it's a relief to see someone who isn't so desperately involved."

This was so like what June Morland had written to him, that Ludlow could not help looking inquiringly at Terry Colbert.

"I mean," the lattter went on, "dress rehearsal is bad enough at any time, but when half the cast want to cut each other's throats——"

"That's fairly normal at this stage too," Ludlow said encouragingly. "And perhaps it'll help to create a suitable atmosphere for the play."

"It's supposed to be a comedy. Oh well, we must hope for the best. Sorry to keep you waiting, but we should be able to start soon. How's it going, Arthur?" he called to the blank curtain.

Some dishevelled light-brown hair with a sallow face under it came round the edge of the curtain.

"It's still sticking at this end," said the face, and disappeared.

"Curtain's not working properly," Colbert explained. "That's Arthur Seward, who does our lighting and general stage-management. He's a marvellous electrician, but a bit awkward to handle sometimes. Did you meet him when you were here before?"

"I think I just saw his back."

"I'd better give him a hand, if you'll excuse me. Monica, come and look after Mr. Ludlow."

The long-haired girl trotted over, clearly more pleased at being asked to do something for Terry Colbert than at looking after Ludlow.

"Monica Stafford," Colbert introduced her. "She holds the prompt-book, and does most of the make-up as well. She's the Secretary at my school, and she's a real treasure, aren't you, Monica?"

With this line, which seemed to be delivered with more of a sneer than a compliment, Colbert hurried away and left Monica to giggle at Ludlow.

"I hope your work for the evening is over," Ludlow said.

"I doubt it. They practically all wanted prompts last Friday. And now everything seems to be going wrong before we start. Still, a bad dress rehearsal means a good performance, doesn't it?"

"So it is commonly believed."

"Poor Terry gets so upset if everything isn't perfect. He's ever so sensitive."

Ludlow made a non-committal noise, but Monica was quite happy to expound the merits of Terry Colbert without any conversational exchange. Ludlow looked round the hall, while she continued to chatter. Bould and his wife remained crouched by their radiator. A group surrounded the second radiator, mostly young people whom Ludlow did not remember seeing at his lecture. Frances Bould and Dexter stayed in their corner; June had now joined Hedge and Fielding down by the stage. Nobody was speaking very loudly. The way in which glances were cast from Bould to Dexter and back again made it clear where trouble was expected. Ludlow realised that Monica was asking him a question.

"Don't you think so?" she said, evidently for the second time, her glasses flashing curiosity at him.

"I don't think I have enough information to give an

opinion," he said, hoping that this academic answer would cover all possibilities. It did not, for Monica looked at him with mingled surprise and exasperation. He never knew what the question had been, for the curtains suddenly opened with a cantankerous swish, and Terry Colbert stood in the middle of the stage.

"All right, first scene," he said. "No, Monica, you stay out front with me tonight in case I want you to write down any last-minute changes."

"I'm not having any more changes in my part," Clifford Fielding said. "You've mucked me around enough already."

"We'll see how it goes. Beginners on stage. Close the curtains, Arthur, and light for the first scene. The rest of you sit down and keep quiet until you come on. And don't be late for your entrances tonight. Can you find a chair, Mr. Ludlow?"

Ludlow found a chair and sat on it. Monica Stafford sat in the middle of the hall, with the prompt-book importantly open on her knees. The rehearsal began. It was no better and little worse than the dozens of amateur performances which Ludlow had seen. June Morland and Tony Dexter had some talent, but most of the others showed little but enthusiasm. However, enthusiasm is a good quality for the amateur who is willing to be taught, and it was clear that Colbert had done well with unpromising material. He was the kind of producer whose work is never finished, who wrings the last effort out of himself and his cast during the dress rehearsal and then suffers through every performance. The dress rehearsal under this direction may leave everyone so exhausted that the first night is an anti-climax, and it seemed as if the Haleham Green Thespians were going to suffer this very fate. Terry Colbert ran from one side of the hall to the other, shouting instructions to the harassed Seward at the lights, correcting positions and interrupting much too often. Yet there was no doubt that he knew his business;

and when he was content to stand quietly with Monica Stafford and let the play go along, there were moments of quality. On balance, Ludlow was not enjoying himself. As he shivered on his uncomfortable chair, he thought sadly of the many bright and warm places where he might have been.

At last Colbert called for an interval. He came over to Ludlow and said, "What do you think of it?"

"Some interesting interpretations," Ludlow said cautiously.

"Do you think the balance between the two Surface brothers is right? I mean, is the contrast brought out without making either of them a caricature?"

"Oh yes, I'm sure — you've made good use of your material there."

"Neither of them is much good, I know. At least Hedge is docile and does what he's told — but always forgets it by next time. Fielding thinks he's one of nature's comedians. He overplays everything and takes no notice of what I say. But it's almost impossible to get a cast together in a place like this. It's all very difficult," Colbert said sadly, brushing back his hair out of his eyes.

"The set is very good," Ludlow said, trying to find a bit of comfort for him.

"Not bad, is it. Seward and another chap made it from sketches I drew for them. You can see how we keep the wooden flat for the main scenes — with the books painted on it, it's Joseph Surface's library, and with a few hangings it can be another interior. Then we've got the traverse and movable props for shorter scenes."

He was cut short by the appearance of the inevitable tea.

"Thank you," Ludlow said to June Morland, who had brought it. "Do you make this here yourselves?" It should be explained that he was stupid with cold and that his mind was still running on scenery.

"Oh yes — there's a little kitchen at the back with a gas stove. It's about the warmest place in the hall."

"I'm looking forward to seeing your next scene: it comes just after this, I think," said Ludlow, trying to sound more intelligent and gallant than he had before.

"You won't see much of me — I'm behind the screen most of the time."

"I shall look at the stage only when your moment of revelation comes."

"Never mind, it's a lovely screen so you can look at that instead. I feel quite cosy behind it; one night I shall just be discovered asleep when it's knocked over."

"Did you hire it specially for the play?"

"No," June said, "Mr. Bould kindly lent it to us. He has a lot of nice things in his house." The way she said it seemed to be a condemnation of Bould and all his works.

"Yes, and the way he carries on about it, you'd think it was gold-plated," Colbert added. "I wish we *had* hired one, and then we wouldn't have him shouting to be careful with it in the middle of a scene."

At this point Bould did in fact shout, as if having his own private rehearsal for what Terry Colbert objected to. What he said, however, had no relation to the screen or to any part of the play. It was unmistakably:

"Frances, for God's sake stop chattering to that fellow and come and help your mother to find what she's looking for."

There was silence, as everyone turned to look at Bould who was glaring at Frances and Tony Dexter, alone in their own corner. Mrs. Bould, fishing in her handbag, looked embarrassed.

"It doesn't matter," she said, "later will do."

"She can come now." Bould made no effort to lower his voice. "You said she might know where you'd put it. She can give some attention to her parents instead of hanging on to Dexter and making herself a laughing-stock."

"There's no need to shout at her, Mr. Bould," Dexter said. He was trembling a little and it was probable that he had gone pale under his dark make-up.

"You keep out of this. It's none of your business."

"Excuse me, but it is. If I'm going to marry Frances——"

"You know what I think of that, Dexter. You've heard what I've got to say on that subject, and you know why. And if she's fool enough to think she'd enjoy living on your miserable little clerk's wages — because there won't be a penny from me——"

"Oh, wrap up!" It was Clifford Fielding.

"What did you say, Fielding?" Bould was strangely, perhaps dangerously, quiet.

"I said, wrap up. We don't want to hear your family quarrels. Give it a rest."

Bould moved towards him, slow and threatening, thrusting his hands deep into his coat pockets.

"I should have thought, Fielding, that you would be the last person here who would dare to speak to me like that."

"What the devil do you mean?" said Fielding, obviously frightened.

"You know what I mean. Do you want all the others to hear it?"

The others were looking very anxious to hear it, but they were disappointed by a diversion from Frances, who burst into tears and said:

"I'm going home."

"Now look what you've done," said Terry Colbert.

"All right, Terry, I'll take her." Tony Dexter assumed a protective role.

"You do nothing of the kind. It's time to start again. Oh stop it, Frances, you'll ruin your make-up."

"She's not on for a bit," said Monica Stafford, in a comforting tone that was directed to Terry and not to the weeping Frances.

"Act four, scene three. Joseph and servant on stage. Lady Teazle ready. Quiet in the hall."

There was a power to command in Terry Colbert. The sobs of Frances began to subside and Bould went sullenly back to his wife by the radiator. Ludlow, feeling most embarrassed, returned to his uncomfortable chair. The cups were collected and the house lights went out. The famous scene in the library went well enough, but Terry Colbert became increasingly frantic. Donald Hedge, in particular, could do nothing right, and he was not aided in his dialogue with Tony Dexter by the fact that the latter was still too clearly furious about what had happened in the interval. Fielding too had not recovered from his words with Bould and only June Morland acted with any composure. While she was behind the screen — a very large and handsome screen which was spread across one corner of the stage — the scene flagged and Colbert leapt about shrieking like a mad hare out of season. Somehow they got to the end of the scene; as the curtains closed, Bould got up and said:

"I'm going to sit in the kitchen and put the stove on. I don't see why I should be frozen to death as well as bored to death."

There was silence, broken only by an angry hiss from Monica Stafford.

"Why not go home, dear, if you're tired?" said Mrs. Bould feebly.

"I didn't say anything about being tired. No, I'm waiting to see that Frances comes back in decent time tonight, not staying out to all hours with that fellow."

"I'll see she gets back."

"Since when have you been able to drive the car? God knows where the two of you would end up if I didn't watch you. And, Colbert, try to speed it up; we don't want to be here all night."

With this final admonition, Bould stamped out and disappeared behind the curtain. There was a kind of collective sigh from everybody. Dexter, who had just come forward in time to hear Bould's last words said:

"I'm sorry, Terry, but I can't do any more tonight. There are limits to what a man can take."

"We must go on," said Colbert, forcing a smile and looking like a child who is trying not to cry. "I know it's beastly, but the show must go on, and all that. A real actor never lets his private worries interfere with the show, isn't that right, Mr. Ludlow?"

"Yes, undoubtedly," said Ludlow, wishing more than ever that he had not come. "Is there anything I can do, or perhaps I ought to leave——"

"No, please stay, if you don't mind." It was Donald Hedge, who had taken off his wig and put it back at a crooked angle. "It's a great help to have somebody to play to, who hasn't seen it all for weeks."

Ludlow, it must be admitted, rather hoped to hear a word from June Morland in support of this plea, but she had vanished since the end of the last scene. However, he settled down as comfortably as circumstances allowed and smiled encouragingly through the gloom. The next scene was fairly short, but it was not allowed to finish without interruption. After a few speeches, Ludlow saw June slip through the curtain that cut off the wings and the kitchen from the rest of the hall and come to sit near him. Even in the semi-darkness, he could see that her lips were tight and that she was deeply troubled. Perhaps because she had carried the weight of the evening so well until that time, the sudden sob that broke from her was the more disconcerting. The action on stage faltered and stopped. Ludlow got up, making encouraging noises, and most of the unoccupied members of the cast fussed around her. Ludlow took out his handkerchief, realised that it was not as clean as it might be and put it back.

"Please go on," June said, "I'm all right, really. Just tired."

"Can I get you anything?" Ludlow asked, though it was difficult to think what could conveniently be got at that time and place.

"No, thank you. Please leave me alone. I'm so sorry — go on with the rehearsal."

The little crowd dispersed again and the scene continued, even more shakily than before. Donald Hedge forgot his words twice but was allowed to go on unrebuked until almost the end of the scene. Then Colbert shrieked:

"For God's sake, Donald, what are you standing there for?"

Hedge peered indignantly into the darkness of the hall and said:

"It's where I was last time."

"No, you're out of position again. You should be more downstage."

Colbert appeared through the wings and thrust Hedge towards the footlights.

"I'll be over the front soon," Hedge said with what dignity he could summon to his help.

"You've got plenty of room. You must open up the stage. And try to get some life into it when you are given the letter. You look as if it was a circular."

"I'm sorry you aren't satisfied. But you make it extremely difficult when you keep interrupting. Nor is it usual at a dress rehearsal. If you can't let us alone at this stage, we may as well go home. And that's where I'm going if I have to put up with any more of this."

He looked as if he meant it. Everybody waited for the explosion, but Colbert was no fool and knew when he had driven his people too hard.

"All right," he said, "you're doing your best, I know, and it isn't too bad. Let's see if we can get through to the end without any more interruptions."

He came forward, jumped down the front of the stage and went to stand quietly by Monica Stafford. The rehearsal continued, and somehow the last few scenes were played without trouble, if without distinction. Bould did not come back, and Ludlow found himself thinking wistfully of the gas-stove which he was monopolising. The end came at last and there was a rustle of relief as the lights came on in the hall.

"All on stage," shouted Colbert, "we must organise the curtain-call before we finish."

"I don't expect there'll be one," said Tony Dexter who had taken off his wig and showed no desire to put it on again.

"Nonsense, it wasn't too bad at all," Colbert said cheerfully. "We don't want everyone dodging about aimlessly at the end, so get in your places now and try to remember them. Open the curtains, Arthur. It doesn't matter about lights — just leave them as they were in the last scene."

The cast grumbled its way back on the stage and were commanded into a sullen semicircle.

"Sir Peter and Lady Teazle in the middle — Charles on their right, with Maria — Joseph on Lady Teazle's left — Joseph! Donald, where are you?"

Others took up the call, and in a moment Donald Hedge hurried into view.

"Sorry," he said, "I'd just gone out for a drink of water. I thought we'd finished."

"We must get this curtain-call right, and then I'm going through one or two scenes again."

There was a concerted wail of protest at this, but Terry Colbert remained inflexible.

"One or two bits are still appalling," he said. "If we can

tidy those up, the play will be in fairly good shape for tomorrow. It's worth a bit of extra effort, isn't it?"

Several people audibly said, "No." However, they resigned themselves and came down to the floor to wait for orders. Mrs. Bould, tucking her impedimenta into various folds of her garments, said that she would go and sit with her husband until Frances was released. She trotted out, Colbert promising not to keep anybody for long.

"You won't want me any more, will you?" asked Hedge with more desire than hope in his voice.

"Yes, I certainly will. We'll do the library scene with Lady Teazle behind the screen again."

It was Clifford Fielding who protested this time.

"No, no, no!" he shouted, "I will not go through that blasted scene again for anybody. I'm sick of it."

"It's terribly important, and it was dragging badly towards the end," Colbert said. "We needn't do the whole thing, just from page eighty-three, when Charles enters."

"Oh, so it's me you're getting at is it? The scene gets bad as soon as I come on?"

"Really, Cliff, you are an idiot," said Donald Hedge. "It's I've been getting it all the evening. What are you grumbling about?"

"Come on, let's get it over," said June and went through the curtains to the stage.

"All right, page eighty-three," Colbert said as if no one had raised any objection. "Lady Teazle is behind the screen — she's gone, good girl. Sir Peter is hiding on the other side, Joseph is on stage, centre, and Charles is ready to come on. All right back there, Arthur?"

Seward's voice assured him that it was all right. Fielding, Dexter and Hedge went through the curtain and a few moments later the action began. Despite a distinct sense of strain, all went tolerably well and Colbert restrained himself from interfering. At last came the point when Fielding had to throw down the screen and reveal Lady Teazle hidden behind it. He took hold of it with a vigour that was born of the evening's annoyances and threw it aside, exclaiming as he did so:

"Lady Teazle, by all that's wonderful."

Dexter should have followed with, "Lady Teazle, by all that's damnable." But the only sound he gave was a gasp. For there was no Lady Teazle behind the screen. Instead, Fielding had revealed the crumpled figure of Bould.

CHAPTER THREE

Enter Two Policemen

It is not often that anybody actually stamps his foot, except in children's stories, but that is precisely what Clifford Fielding did.

"Look at him," he shouted, "what does he think he's playing at now? All we want to do is to get home out of this, and Bould has to come and spoil the scene——"

He was interrupted by the sound of Terry Colbert retching, and by a simultaneous scream from Frances. Donald Hedge, who had entered on his cue at the moment the screen was thrown down, was kneeling by Bould.

"I'm pretty sure he's dead," he said after a quick examination. "Help me to move him, Tony, so that I can get a better look at him."

"Leave him where he is." It was Ludlow, who had been forgotten in the excitement but now hurried up on the stage with an agility far removed from his usual comfortable pace. Hedge ignored him and, seeing that he could expect no help from either Fielding or Dexter who had recoiled from the body in horror, he called into the wings:

"Arthur, come here quickly, please!"

Arthur came from his side of the stage, opposite the one which gave access to and from the rest of the hall, and Ludlow saw him clearly for the first time. He was fairly tall, lean and grey-faced, with thin brown hair plastered flatly on his skull. His arms were long in proportion to the rest of his body; at the moment he was rubbing the right one with his left hand.

"What's up now?" he demanded. "How much longer is this lark going on?"

"Mr. Bould's been hurt—I think he's dead. Help me with him."

"I've hurt me arm on that ruddy curtain. I can't move nobody."

"You really must leave everything as it is," Ludlow said importantly, coming to the middle of the stage. "I know procedure in cases like this: I have worked with members of the C.I.D." He omitted to mention that on that occasion he had himself been rebuked for interfering with evidence.

"What the devil have the police got to do with this?" asked Fielding.

"That remains to be seen. But Mr. Bould seemed quite healthy a few minutes ago. If he's dead now, there will be a lot of questions to answer. Especially as he turns up in a place where we had every reason to expect to find Miss Morland."

"Good Lord, where's June?" Hedge forgot everything as he rushed off the stage and down the steps at the side. Here he collided with June Morland coming out of the kitchen.

"What's happening here?" she asked calmly.

"That's what I want to know." Terry Colbert, pale but recovered from the first shock, was elbowing everybody aside. "Where have you been? It's not like you to miss an entrance——"

"Shut up," said Hedge roughly, "this is more important than the play."

"If you're going to take that attitude, Hedge, the prospects for tomorrow are unexciting."

"There won't *be* any tomorrow — I mean, there won't be any performance, by the look of things. Are you all right, June?"

"Yes, of course I am. I'm sorry I wasn't ready. Shall we go on?"

"Don't go up there," Ludlow restrained her as she moved towards the stage. "There's been — Mr. Bould is hurt, badly."

"Is he dead?" The directness of the question was startling.

"I think so."

"I wondered why he wasn't in the kitchen." She seemed to dismiss the whole thing as a minor puzzle, now solved. Ludlow found himself troubled, almost shocked.

"But where have you been?" Colbert asked again.

"I went into the kitchen, to wash up the teacups."

"What on earth for?"

"I just thought I would. I didn't feel like going on again."

Nobody seemed to know what to do. Ludlow, Colbert, Hedge and Fielding were gathered round June. Dexter had gone to look after Frances, the others were all huddled together staring at the bright stage where Seward stood alone, looking at Bould's body with an expression that might have meant several things, none of them pleasant. Colbert was the first to show any practical sense of what had happened.

"Where's his wife?" he asked.

"She went out to sit in their car, when he wasn't in the kitchen," June said.

"Somebody must fetch her."

"I'll go," said Monica Stafford, which she did.

"Why don't you get a doctor?" asked Frances, "It may still not be too late."

"I'm afraid it is," Ludlow said gently. "But certainly a doctor should come at once. And the police must be told."

"I wish you wouldn't keep on about the police," said Dexter with his arm around Frances. "It's in extremely bad taste."

"So is murder," said Ludlow.

Murder. Now that it had been said everyone looked almost relieved, though several voices broke into automatic protest. Fielding alone accepted the truth of what Ludlow said, and offered to go at once.

"I think," Ludlow said very deliberately, "it had better be somebody who hasn't — ah — had words, with Mr. Bould recently."

"What the devil do you mean by that?" asked Fielding.

"It's reasonable, Cliff," Colbert said. "If it is murder, there are a good few of us who didn't exactly love Bould. I'm sorry, Frances, but that's the truth of it."

"I know. But a quarrel is a different thing from wanting to — to kill someone. Isn't it?" Frances said, almost defiantly, looking only at Dexter as she spoke.

"Of course, darling. But Mr. Ludlow's right."

"You keep out of it, Dexter," Fielding said. "Or perhaps you want to show how little you're worried? After all, you're probably number one suspect, if it is murder."

"Would you care to repeat that outside?" asked Dexter, as he relinquished Frances and advanced on Fielding.

"It seems to me, from what little I've seen, that there are a number of potential suspects," Ludlow said in the voice he usually keeps for his most recalcitrant students. "And the longer you delay, the more heavily suspicion is going to fall."

At this, both Fielding and Dexter seemed ready to turn on Ludlow, but the tension was broken by the return of Monica supporting Mrs. Bould, who was displaying a marked preference for walking unsupported. All fell back respectfully and Frances ran to her mother.

"It's no good pretending I'm surprised," Mrs. Bould said as calmly as if one of her knitting-patterns had turned out badly. "I've fully expected this for a long time. A natural sorrow doesn't prevent me from saying quite categorically that he simply asked to be murdered. Not that it's the right thing to do, of course, under any circumstances. Where is he?"

"On the stage," Ludlow murmured, torn between surprise and respect for the expression of an honest opinion.

"I wondered where he'd got to, when he wasn't in the kitchen and hadn't taken the car. What did he go there for? And why didn't we all see him go there?"

"Those are questions to be decided," Ludlow said, "and it's time that we started doing something towards deciding them. You two, go together and bring the first policeman you can lay your hands on." He pointed at two startled youths, of about undergraduate age, who had minor roles in the play.

"We can't go out like this," one of them said with a broad gesture around his eighteenth-century costume.

"Nonsense, boy. It has been painfully clear to me for some time that young people today have no regard for their appearance," Ludlow said, looking complacent in his shapeless tweeds and crumpled shirt. "At least you appear to be moderately clean, or if not the make-up conceals it. Run along. Unless there's a telephone anywhere in this building?"

Heads were shaken, and the two embarrassed young men were propelled out of the hall by a jab of Ludlow's bony fingers. The remainder all drifted to the back of the hall, turning away from the stage. Nobody spoke, nobody looked another in the eyes. Ludlow returned to the stage, where Seward was still standing silently. He looked carefully at Bould's body, then went to join the others, giving Seward a sign to follow him, which was obeyed. He went and spoke to Hedge.

"How do you think it happened?" he asked abruptly.

"Well, I'm not any more expert than you are in these things, Mr. Ludlow. I'm a chemist, not a doctor, you know. But it looks to me as if his neck had been broken."

"I agree," Ludlow said with a glance at Mrs. Bould and Frances. They still seemed comparatively unaffected, though Frances was crying quietly. It was June who reacted.

"Good gracious, are you sure? Donald, is this true?"

"I think so, but I'd rather wait for the doctor."

June looked as if she might laugh or cry at any moment. There was a look of almost relief that passed as soon as it had come. Nobody spoke again, and it was not long before Ludlow's two unwilling messengers returned with a young policeman whose bicycle-clips showed that he had just been collected from his cold round of the area.

"Ah, Felton," said Hedge, "how's that toe of yours?"

"Much better, thank you, Mr. Hedge. That stuff you give me took all the stiffness out. But what's going on here? Fancy dress party?"

"We have been rehearsing a play," Colbert said sternly.

"What for did you tell me there'd been a murder?" asked the constable, turning on one of his young informants. "Just play-acting is it?"

"I'm afraid not," said Ludlow. "Will you turn your attention to the stage for a moment?"

The constable did so, then ran forward and started trying to clamber over the footlights. Ludlow directed him to the stairs at the side, and in a moment he appeared under the lights like a stray bit of chorus from *The Pirates of Penzance* who had got into the wrong theatre. He knelt down and said:

"Gorblimey, it's Mr. Bould. Who did this?"

"That is what we are just bursting with desire to learn," said Colbert sarcastically.

"But he's a magistrate," said Felton, as if so important a person should not have the added indignity of an anonymous murder. Then he pulled himself together, remembered bits of the training-course that had long been submerged under cases of lightless cars and unlicensed dogs, and said:

"Has anybody left these premises since this occurred?"

"Nobody, except our two young friends who returned with you," said Ludlow.

"Right. Now this may be a case of murder. I'm not saying it is, mind you, and I'm not saying it isn't. But in my opinion, it's a job for the Inspector himself. Have you got a phone handy," he asked as if someone might have a spare telephone concealed in his costume. On being told that they had not, he thought for a while and then asked them all to stand still while he counted them. This arithmetic over, he hurried to the door with the parting words:

"Now you've all been counted, see? And if anybody is short when the Inspector comes, his absence will be regarded as a fact he will be called upon to give an explanation of."

With this admirable exit-line he withdrew. Monica Stafford burst into tears, accompanying the action with a dive for the comfort of Terry Colbert's thick sweater.

"Why can't we go home?" she demanded. "Why is everybody making us stay here? Terry, do take me home."

"Because, my dear girl," Colbert said, disentangling himself as gently as he could, "it is regrettably obvious even to the local constabulary that one of us is a murderer."

Donald Hedge, with a complete loss of his usual mildness, seized Colbert by a large fold of his sweater and glared into his face.

"What right have you got to say that?" he demanded, ignoring a light counter-attack from Monica on his right flank. "What do you know?"

"Merely that, the geography of this hall being what it is," there is very little possibility of anybody having got in from outside. Now will you please return your hands to the awkward position they usually hold when you are on the stage."

Hedge released him and walked away, his head drooping

as if he had just received a dreadful shock. The pause that followed was the most unpleasant yet. Ludlow reflected that his first impression, that this was not a happy society, was being too abundantly proved. He thought sadly about hot whisky and lemon and his own shabby dressing-gown by the fire. Dexter was the first to break the silence.

"June," he said, "why did you go straight out to the kitchen instead of going on stage?"

"I just thought I would."

"You must have had a reason, surely."

"I was so tired; I didn't feel like going through the scene again."

"You were the only one who seemed keen when Terry suggested it."

"I changed my mind, that's all."

"Leave her alone," said Hedge turning to a new attack. "It's no business of yours."

"It's quite a lot of my business now," Dexter said deliberately. "I have the right to look after the interests of the family. He would have been my father-in-law——"

"There didn't seem to be much chance of that earlier this evening."

"No, there didn't," Clifford Fielding broke in. "You remember what I said before, Dexter, and I'm prepared to say it again. You had a very good reason for killing Bould, didn't you? I daresay he'll carve up for a nice amount, which you'd never have smelt if Frances had married you without his consent."

"And I remember something else," Dexter said, surprisingly taking no notice of Fielding's insinuations. "Bould made it pretty clear that you had cause to be afraid of him. So what were you doing in the kitchen after he'd gone there?"

"I was never in the kitchen the whole evening."

"My dear fellow, don't bother to deny it. I saw you

when I was going on the stage. You slipped in looking furtive, and that's a bit of information that can be passed on to the police with my compliments."

"I — I was going for a bit of fresh air outside."

The amiable conversation was interrupted by the return of Constable Felton with a very large Inspector who ignored everybody and went straight to the stage.

"I'm treating this as a case of murder," he said to nobody in particular. "Has anything been moved?"

"I just sort of straightened him out, to have a look at him," said Donald Hedge, "but nobody's touched anything since."

"Very good," said the Inspector, apparently to the top of the proscenium arch. "Who was the first to discover the body?"

"I was," said Dexter, Hedge and Fielding all together.

"You all came upon it at the same time?"

"Well, we were all on the stage," Dexter said. "It was during the play. He was behind a screen."

"Indeed?" The Inspector turned his attention to the footlights. "What gave you reason to suppose that there was anything behind the screen?"

"We didn't," Fielding took up the story. "I had to pull it down. There was supposed to be a woman behind it."

"A woman," said the Inspector, as if the word confirmed all his suspicions. "And may I ask what play this was?"

"*The School for Scandal*," said several voices.

"Ah! And may I ask further if this is perhaps a play which contains a certain amount of indecency?"

"It's a classic!" Monica Stafford's voice rose shrill and indignant.

"So," said the Inspector, still not looking at anybody, "it's a classic." He looked like a man whose brilliant theory has suddenly been shattered. He bowed his head, whether in respect to the corpse or the memory of the man who wrote classics, then pulled himself together and came down from the stage. During this inquisition, Felton was trying to count everyone again and get the same total as before.

"Now I must tell you something," the Inspector said earnestly to a stack of chairs in the corner of the hall. "I am a man who knows his limitations. I am also a man with a great deal on his plate at the moment. I am therefore going to avail myself of the highest resources of the Metropolitan Police to which I have the honour to belong. Felton, stop running about. I am going to put this case into the best pair of hands at Scotland Yard. That is if the said pair of hands is empty at the moment. I must therefore ask you all to remain here."

There was a concerted wail of protest.

"It's so cold," said June.

"I am not responsible for the climate, madam," the Inspector said in the voice of a man who was going to be responsible for nothing that was not laid down in the regulations.

"Can't we go and change?" asked one of the young men in the cast. "These costumes are so jolly cold round the legs."

"You should have thought of that before you started dressing up," said the Inspector, investing the phrase with massive disapproval. "No, I'm afraid that you must all remain here under supervision until such time as Inspector Montero has seen you and allows you to leave."

"I beg your pardon," said Ludlow, aroused from the stupor of cold and misery. "Did you say Montero?"

The Inspector's eyes switched from their distant contemplation and looked straight at Ludlow.

"I did," he said. "And may I ask whether you have any objection?"

"By no means. Inspector Montero is an old friend of mine."

In fact. Ludlow had come to know Montero through a case involving a student, and the two had met once or twice since then for a quiet drink. The Inspector was impressed and became more human at once.

"Fancy that now," he said. "Why, Montero and I were on the beat together, more years ago than either of us wants to remember now. He was always the clever one, though. He went into plain clothes and he's made quite a name for himself. I only hope he'll be free to come out and handle this. Now if this had happened two miles farther up the road, it'd be the business of the County Police — we're just on the Metropolitan limit here. And that lot over there would probably try to handle it themselves — and get into no end of bother with it. I say, it's a wise man who knows his own limitations, Where's that doctor?"

"I've no idea," said Ludlow, as the question seemed to follow from the previous confidences, but Constable Felton rightly assumed that it was addressed to him.

"He was out on a case, sir," he said. "I left a message."

"Very pious man is Doctor Slattery," the Inspector said. "Don't let him convert you to anything. But he's a good doctor."

At this moment the pious doctor arrived, erupting into the hall with a force that seemed strange with his rotund figure and white hair.

"Here we are," he announced. "What have you got for me this time?"

"It looks like a murder, doctor."

"Dear me, dear me, it's a wicked world. And I've just come straight from a maternity case. In the midst of life. Who is it now?"

"It's Mr. Bould — he's up there on the stage. There's been some kind of playacting going on here."

"My old grandmother," said Doctor Slattery as he steamed cheerfully towards the stage, "would never enter a theatre. She said it was the Devil's playground. A good phrase, and I'm not so sure she was wrong. No good is likely to come of pretending to be what you're not." His voice passed behind the curtain and a moment later he came on the stage, still talking.

"So it's Bould, is it? Poor fellow, I wish I could think he was in a fit state to meet his death." He busied himself for a few minutes and then, with a sense which nobody else had displayed, dragged a piece of cloth out of the wings and covered Bould's body.

There was a whispered consultation with the Inspector, from which Ludlow's sharp ears caught occasional phrases — "Neck broken — accident most improbable — base of skull — not more than half an hour." The doctor then broke away, advanced on Mrs. Bould and Frances and said:

"I'm sorry that you've had this trouble come upon you. We are all under judgement, you know. Swallow these." He produced a small box from his bag and thrust pills at them in spite of their protests. "That will help when the delayed shock comes to you," he explained encouragingly. "Do you want me any more, Inspector?"

"I'm getting a man from the Yard. He might want to see you."

"He can come and see me at home. The temperature of this hall is most unhealthy. Don't blame me if you all develop pleurisy. Good-night."

Nobody felt any happier for this, and when the Inspector went to telephone it was a very disconsolate flock that huddled round the inefficient radiators under the eye of Felton.

"I've got a wonderful idea," Monica Stafford chirped suddenly. "Professor Ludlow can give us a lecture about something, just to pass the time."

But probably for the first time in his life, Ludlow did not feel like talking. So they huddled together miserably until it seemed as if time itself had stopped there in the hall, while outside the world went on its way and forgot about them. The sun might have risen and set again without its warmth ever reaching into the hall. In fact, it was a creditably short time before a car stopped outside and the Inspector returned with two men in plain clothes. The first was of little more than medium height, neat and unremarkable in his appearance, with a fair moustache as unpretentious as the rest of him. Only his blue eyes, deceptively mild most of the time, could flash into chilling shrewdness. He was followed by a taller man with a lean, anxious-looking face. The two of them had evidently been told of Ludlow's presence, and they greeted him affably.

"Not you again!" Inspector Montero said as he shook Ludlow's hand. "How on earth have you managed to get mixed up in this? You remember Jack Springer, don't you?"

"You're getting a proper glutton for murders, Mr. Ludlow," said Detective-Sergeant Springer.

"You've met Inspector Belling of the local division already, I think," Montero went on.

"Indeed I have," said Ludlow, feeling happier now that he saw some familiar faces, and was himself again the centre of attention.

Two detective-constables, carrying mysterious bits of equipment, came in and disrupted the social occasion.

"We'd better get to work," Montero said. "I don't want to keep these ladies and gentlemen hanging around longer than necessary. Let's have a look at the body first."

Ludlow was determined not to be left out of anything after suffering in silence for so long, and he walked with Montero as the detectives made their way behind the scenes. Nobody stopped him, and he felt quite at home when he slipped behind the curtain once again. They stood in a narrow passage between the outside wall of the building and the side of the stage. Straight ahead was a half-open door.

A short flight of steps led to the stage, and another staircase on the left went down out of sight.

"Get a rough sketch of all this, Jack," Montero said. "Let's have a look in here first."

He pushed the door fully open and looked into a little dingy room with a single unshaded bulb hanging from the ceiling. Another door, open enough to let in a taste of the cold outside, was in the far wall. The shorter wall, to the right of where he stood, was taken up by a gas stove, a sink and a draining-board on which a number of clean cups and saucers were stacked. A wall-cupboard, a table and two very nasty chairs made the rest of the furniture.

"Don't go in," Montero said as the others crowded behind him. "Is this where he went?"

"It's where he said he was going," Ludlow answered.

"And that was the last time you saw him alive? And then he turns up on the stage. A jolly piece of acrobatics by somebody. Let's have a stroll up there ourselves."

He shepherded them back into the passage and up the steps, passing unscathed through the stage entrance. Ludlow and Springer both hit their heads; Ludlow swore under his breath, Springer aloud and picturesquely. Montero gave only a cursory examination of the body, then signalled to his photographer to go to work. He himself seemed more interested in the structure of the stage and settings. A wooden flat, eight feet high, had been erected across the back of the stage and extended a little way towards the footlights. At its ends, narrow curtains masked the entrances. A traverse curtain which could divide the stage in half lengthways was now bunched up on its horizontal wire, out of sight of the imaginary audience. The famous screen lay where it had fallen in front of Bould's body. The entrance through which they had come gave the only access from the hall or the places backstage. As so often happens in amateur productions, those who were supposed to enter from the other side had either to be in position before the scene began or to make their way along the narrow space between the wooden flat and the back wall. Seward's switchboard, a surprisingly efficient and elaborate piece of mechanism, was on this far side of the stage.

Having completed his tour, Montero left the stage again and led the way down the stairs just outside the kitchen. The damp air which greeted their descent dispelled any thought that the air in the hall was as cold as air could possibly be. A low lintel brought further disasters to the taller members of the group and admitted them to a semi-basement room which seemed to run the whole length of the building. The clothes hanging on the walls, abandoned as if their owners had flown back to disappear into another and more colourful century, showed that this was the cast's dressing-room. There was no way in or out except the narrow stairs down which they had come, unless a thin athlete could have got through one of the two small windows high up in the outside wall — a fact which made Inspector Belling mutter darkly about fire-regulations. He also looked with distaste at the open boxes of make-up on the single trestle-table that occupied the centre of the room.

"Is that the stuff they've all got on their faces?" he demanded, apparently of the long looking-glass on the opposite wall.

"Indeed it is," said Ludlow, in whom the smell of grease-paint had revived some happy youthful memories.

Belling said something which sounded rather like 'pansy'. However, Montero did not detain him long in this cellar of vice, but asked him to get the body moved to the mortuary.

"When our chaps have finished on the stage," he added, to Springer, "tell them to go to work on that little kitchen. Meanwhile we'll do our questioning down here."

"We'll catch our deaths, sir," said Springer sadly, but he

went about his task and soon returned with his notebook poised for action.

"We might as well get your story first, Mr. Ludlow," Montero said as the three of them drew their chairs close to a rusty pipe that ran for no obvious purpose along the bottom of the wall. Ludlow told them how he came to be in Thespian circles, from his first arrival to lecture to them up to the discovery of Bould's body that evening.

"So you had the whole thing pretty well in view all the time did you?" Montero asked when he had finished.

"I did, but remember that the lights were out in the hall and it wasn't easy to see much detail there. Although the shadows flitting to and fro were about as entertaining as most of what was happening on the stage."

"But you have got a pretty good idea of who left the hall during the period that we're interested in?"

"Mostly from hearsay or from their own admissions. I don't know any of them well, and the costumes make it much harder to be certain of anybody in the darkness. Look, here's a programme someone gave me just before the wretched thing started. Perhaps you'd like to work through that."

"Thank you, that'll be a help." Montero studied the folded yellow sheet which Ludlow handed to him, and visibly disapproved of the quality of its printing. "Does this include everybody who was present this evening?" he asked.

"Yes, except for Bould and his wife — and myself, of course. The producer's name is there, and the stage-manager; oh, and the assistant stage-manager, in other words the prompter."

"Do you think we can eliminate anybody at all — I mean can you be sure of anybody not going out alone after Bould did?"

"As I say, I haven't learnt the names of many of them. I'm assuming they were all there, because there were no gaps in the cast during the rehearsal. But I think you'll find when you question them that a large group of them stuck together all the time, except when they had to go on stage. They monopolised one of the radiators — though really refrigerator would be a more suitable——"

"Yes, quite so. Now, from what you've told me, it seems that this chap Hedge said he'd been out for a drink of water, so he must have gone into the kitchen. Did he say anything about Bould being there or not?"

"Nothing. He was more concerned about being late for the curtain-call than anything else."

"But he did seem concerned about something then?"

"He hadn't been at ease all the evening. I did notice that, because I'd had a bit of a talk with him the first time I came here, and his manner certainly seemed different tonight."

"We'll have a look at this Mr. Hedge later. Now, Dexter, in your hearing, accused Fielding of going into the kitchen at an earlier time, which Fielding at first denied and then admitted."

"Yes, he said he was going for what he described as fresh air. We had quite enough air where we were, even if it could hardly be described as fresh. But some people would throw open all the windows of an igloo, if there were any."

"Why didn't he go to the main entrance if he wanted some air?"

"I was not really in a position to do your interrogating for you, was I?"

"I was just thinking aloud, Mr. Ludlow. Now did anyone else enter or leave the hall during the period that we're interested in?"

"Well," Ludlow said rather reluctantly, "Miss Morland went out soon after Bould."

"Alone?"

"Yes."

"Did she go into the kitchen? Well, of course you can't

know that. But presumably she didn't go on the stage, or you wouldn't think it worth mentioning."

"No, she didn't have an entrance then."

"Was she out long?"

"A few minutes. I'm not sure. I don't think you need start suspecting her though. She's certainly not the sort of girl to commit murder."

At this, Springer gave an ironical chuckle and turned it into a cough when Montero glared at him. He looked back through his notes and put in a question on his own behalf.

"This is the same lady who ought to have been behind the screen at the time the body was discovered, but who then appeared from the kitchen and said she had been washing up?"

"Yes."

"Has she shown any hostility towards the murdered man?"

"Nobody seemed to like him, and I'm not surprised. He was a most ill-mannered fellow, and also stupid. He didn't attend to my lecture properly."

"Is that a reasonable cause for murder?" Montero asked with a smile.

"If it was, the lecture-rooms would be littered with the bodies of students." Ludlow was glad to turn the conversation away from June, though he had seen Montero in action before and knew that the subject would not be left alone indefinitely.

"Well I think that's all we need from you for the moment. It's very useful to have an impartial witness."

"That's practically what has already been said to me by two members of the company, before anything happened."

"You think they were expecting trouble?"

"The atmosphere was certainly unpleasant, and I don't refer only to the cold. I think you may uncover quite a lot of scandals here before you finish."

"How very appropriate. All right, you'd better go back upstairs with the others. I'm sorry we have to keep you hanging about."

"Not so sorry as I am. Can I stay and listen while you talk to the others?" Ludlow showed such a child-like eagerness not to be left out that Montero had to suppress a smile.

"No, I'm afraid it wouldn't do. There'd be a fuss if any of them complained about it afterwards. But I'm not going to deny that I'll be glad of your help. I haven't forgotten how you cleared up that case before — of course we'd have solved it, but you did take a few short-cuts that we couldn't."

"Yes, you nearly solved it by suspecting the wrong man. Are you sure you don't suspect me of this one?"

"Oh, run along and translate some Anglo-Saxon poetry."

"I prefer to call it Old English," Ludlow said.

"Never mind, I was brought up common. You might send Mrs. Bould down to us, please. I don't want to keep her and the daughter any longer than I can help."

Their previous acquaintance had taught Ludlow that he could not easily get the better of Montero in academic badinage. He went quietly.

CHAPTER FOUR

Some Unrehearsed Dialogue

Although the two detectives rose and put on expressions suitable for condolence with a widow, they were both aware that Mrs. Bould did not look particularly distressed as she came down the narrow stairs into the dressing-room. A certain redness around the nose and eyes seemed to be attributable more to the cold than to sorrow, for she moved with composure to a chair which Springer put for her and looked ready to answer anything. Her expression suggested that she was thinking, 'I know we've got to keep up certain conventions, and I shall do my part, but you needn't waste any of your sympathy.' Montero did his part as well.

"I know how painful for you this must be, Mrs. Bould," he said "and I shall keep you only for a very short time. I am sure that you are as anxious as we are to have the murderer of your husband discovered, and you may be able to tell us something that will help us."

"It is murder then?" The question was direct, curious but not shocked.

"I'm afraid so. From what the doctor told the local Inspector, and from our own observations, there can be no way in which he met his death accidentally. I'm very sorry."

"So it's come at last. I'm not very surprised."

Montero showed no obvious reaction, but anyone who knew him well would have seen the kindly blue of his eyes turn to steel for an instant.

"Now, Mrs. Bould," he said gently, "I've been told that you said something of the sort soon after your husband's body was discovered. Can you give me any idea of what you meant?"

"I meant just what I said, Inspector. My husband made himself objectionable to a great many people. He had so many enemies that I imagine you'll have a hard job finding who did it. Now can I go home?"

"Just a few more questions, please. Did any of the people present this evening have particular cause to dislike your husband?"

"Most of them, I should think. No doubt your friend Mr. Ludlow will have told you what passed during the rehearsal."

'This woman looks like a simple and ineffective creature,' Montero thought, 'but she's shrewd, and as hard as nails. We shan't get much out of her.' Aloud he said:

"Do you suspect anybody in particular?"

"No." That was that.

"May I ask you something about your own movements this evening. You were with your husband the whole time until he left the hall and went to sit in the kitchen?"

"I was and there are plenty of witnesses to prove it."

"After he left the hall, did you go out at any time before the end of the rehearsal?"

"I sat and knitted until what I thought was the end. Then young Colbert wanted to do some more. I couldn't stand the cold any longer, so I decided to sit with Bartholomew where it would be at least a little warmer."

Springer muttered "Bartholomew Bould" like a man uttering a powerful charm. Montero looked severely at him and returned to the questioning.

"Was there anybody at all in the kitchen?"

"No. The gas-cooker was lit and the oven-door was open. It's the only way of getting warm in this place. But there was no sign of Bartholomew."

"What did you do then?"

"I turned off the gas and shut the oven door, as there was

no point in wasting it. I thought he might have gone home, so I looked out but the car was still there——"

"Forgive my interrupting, but where exactly was your husband's car?"

"There's a small yard at the back, down the slope. You must have noticed how this hall is built — the ground at the back where we are now is lower than at the front. He keeps the car there."

"So that bit of ground is on a level with the floor where we are now sitting, though you have to come downstairs from the hall itself?"

"Yes. Does it matter?"

"Probably not, but we must get all the information we can. Now, was there any other car — any vehicle of any kind — on this piece of ground at the back, when you looked out?"

"There was Fielding's car, and a couple of bicycles that belong to people in the play. And a dirty old car I hadn't seen before."

"That will have been Mr. Ludlow's."

"He ought to know better."

"No doubt. What happened then?"

"I went out to see if Bartholomew was in the car. He wasn't, but I thought he couldn't have gone far without it. He hates — hated — walking. So I got in, and I waited, until that silly girl Monica Stafford came out saying that he had been killed."

"Did she actually say that?"

"I think she said, 'Your husband's had an accident'. She was quite hysterical."

"Is the back door normally locked?"

"Yes, it is. I think it's supposed to be a fire-exit or something, so that the key is kept in the lock inside."

"Was it locked when you first went into the kitchen?"

"I suppose so. Yes, it was. I had to turn the key to get out."

"So your husband couldn't have gone out that way?"

"I—well, no, but I didn't think of that at the time."

"Quite understandable. Now, are you quite sure that nobody left or entered the kitchen while you were there?"

"I didn't say that—you didn't ask me. June Morland came in, when I was looking to see if the car was outside. I asked her if it was over already, and she said it wasn't but she was going to wash up the teacups."

"Didn't it seem odd to you that she wasn't on the stage?"

"I can never remember who's supposed to be on the stage. It's a difficult play to follow. I liked it much better in October when they did *Quiet Wedding*."

'And that sudden lapse into simplicity doesn't convince me any longer', thought Montero. 'She's tough enough for a direct attack'. He got up, went to the looking-glass on the wall and seemed to be admiring his reflection. He suddenly turned and said sharply:

"Mrs. Bould, how did you get on with your husband?"

"I disliked him very much. I had reason to, but they are not reasons which concern you, or this present business." She spoke without passion or resentment.

"Forgive me," said Montero, "but was there any question of a divorce or separation being discussed?"

"Certainly not." She seemed to react strongly for the first time. "People of our sort don't do things like that. Besides, one has made one's bed, and one must lie on it. Don't you know the hatred that there is in most homes?"

Montero, who had a very comfortable and affectionate wife awaiting him at home said nothing to this. Springer put in a question.

"What do you think of this chap—er, Dexter, who's your daughter's young man?"

"I take no objection to him?"

"But your husband did, I think."

"I have already told you that my husband made many enemies."

There was nothing more to be gained here. Montero dismissed her, and asked that Frances should come for a few minutes. At the foot of the stairs, Mrs. Bould turned and looked at them with what might have been malice, or even triumph.

"I didn't kill him, you know," she said.

"And I wouldn't be too sure of that," said Springer as soon as she had gone.

"I agree that that woman is capable of more than would appear at first. But she couldn't break a man's neck. She's the sort who might well put weedkiller in his tea rather than have the scandal of a divorce, but she just wouldn't have the strength to kill him as he has been killed."

Springer never left a theory alone until he had shaken it in his teeth and worried it to death.

"Well, I went on a course once," he said, "and there was a bloke who gave us a talk on the stat — stattie — figures of murders this century. And do you know how many were done by the wife or husband?"

"I've no idea. How many were there?"

"Ah, now, I don't exactly recall offhand, but it was the hell of a lot. And another thing, sir — you were just talking about poison; well, what about those teacups?"

Montero was prevented from answering by the appearance of Frances Bould, looking more distressed than her mother had done, though not prostrated with grief. In spite of her swollen eyes and the blotches on her make-up, she was very pretty in the simple costume which her part in the play required. After further condolences, Montero soon established that she had not left the hall the whole evening, except when she had to go on the stage. Most of the time she had been with Dexter.

"I don't want you to trouble yourself at this time," Montero said, "but can you give me any idea of who might have disliked your father enough to want to kill him?"

"Daddy wasn't popular," Frances said without hesitation. "He used such an aggressive sort of manner to people. And sometimes he could be downright rude. But he could be kind too, you know. He was very good to me, though he used to lose his temper and say horrid things."

"So he probably had a number of enemies in this district?"

"I expect so. I mean, he'd quarrel with anybody when he was in a bad mood. Why, he even had rows with Tony — oh!" She clapped her hand to her mouth in a schoolgirl's gesture that Montero found very appealing.

"Don't worry," he said. "No innocent man has anything to fear from the truth, so let's have it. Your father disapproved of your friendship with Mr. Dexter, and they had words about it. Is that right?"

"Yes. We got engaged before Christmas, but Daddy carried on terribly and threatened things."

"What kind of things?"

"About money, and his will. I didn't care. I wanted to marry Tony, and I wouldn't care if he had nothing to live on at all."

'You soon would care, my child', Montero thought.

"Mr. Dexter then is not a rich man?" he went on.

"He works in an office in the City."

"Did he at any time or in any way make threats of his own, to your father?"

"Never. He was always polite and patient."

"Why was there so much disapproval of him?"

"I don't know. Because he was older than me. But what does it matter? Thirty-eight is not really old."

"Certainly not," said Montero, being ten years older. "However, there were quarrels?"

"Yes, but they were nothing really. You ought to have heard the things Daddy said to Mr. Fielding."

"Really? Tell me about them."

"Well, he lives next door to us, and there's been a bit of bother about a fence or something. Then one day Clifford Fielding's dog came into our garden, and scratched up some plants, and Daddy was furious. He was shouting about his solicitor, and Mr. Fielding was shouting back. It was horrid."

"It must have been. Thank you very much, Miss Bould. I don't think I need ask you or your mother to stay any longer. Go home and try to get some sleep."

"Please," Frances turned as she reached the foot of the stairs, "can you let Tony go as well, so that he can take us home?"

"Ask Mr. Dexter to come down here now, and I'll let him go as soon as I can."

Dexter came in looking like an eighteenth-century rake after a hard night. He had taken off his wig and his own fair hair stood up in damp spikes. His florid make-up as Sir Peter Teazle was blotchy. Montero plunged straight into the attack almost before Dexter had sat down.

"You didn't like your future father-in-law, did you?" he demanded.

"Frankly no." Dexter seemed unperturbed. "He didn't like me either."

"Why was that?"

"He thought I wasn't good enough for Frances. I'm not, but if she thinks I am, that ought to be all right. We're not living a hundred years ago, are we?"

"No, indeed," answered Montero, weaving a pleasant fantasy in his mind around this unquestionable piece of chronology combined with the costumes which were being worn. Springer recalled him to the present duty by putting in a question.

"Between the time that Mr. Bould went out and the time his body was discovered, did you go into the kitchen at all?"

"No. Why should I?"

"Can you account for your movements all through that time?"

"Well, let me see. Bould went out after the scene at the end of the fourth act — that's the one with the screen that we went through again at the end. I came off the stage then, and I was with Frances all the time, until I had to go on again. After that scene I went back to Frances, and we had an entrance together in the last scene. Then everybody went back into the hall, and Terry made us do some more — and you know what we found."

"In the second of these scenes you have just mentioned," Montero took up the question, "were you alone when you went to make your entry?"

"Yes. The others came on from the other side of the stage, and they had to be there before the scene started. I just went and waited in the wings by myself."

"How long were you there?"

"I don't know. Perhaps a minute, perhaps two. Terry gets furious if anyone's late for an entrance, so we always give it plenty of time."

"And you did not go into the kitchen."

"I've told you, no. I'm not accustomed to having my word doubted."

"At the moment, we find it healthier to doubt everybody, sir. We only want to get things cleared up. Did you see anybody enter or leave the kitchen during that time?"

"Clifford Fielding went in, looking furtive, just as I was on the steps for my entrance."

"What do you mean by furtive?"

"Well, he was looking as if he didn't want to be seen, and he slipped into the kitchen, and shut the door very quietly behind him."

"Surely it was natural for him to move quietly when the rehearsal was on?"

"I suppose so. But he usually stamps about regardless."

"You didn't hear any conversation from the kitchen after he went in?"

"No, but I was on the stage by then, and anyway it's quite a solid door."

"Do you know when he came out?"

"He was ready for his entrance in the last scene, that's all I can tell you."

"You don't like Mr. Fielding, do you?" Springer asked.

"We don't hit it off very well. He's just not my type, I suppose. And tempers get a bit frayed at this stage in a play."

Dexter winced suddenly and rubbed his leg.

"Rheumatism?" Montero asked sympathetically.

"It's nothing, just a spot where I once carried a piece of shrapnel around for a time. It plays me up when it gets cold — like now, with these silly stockings."

"Bad luck. Where did you get it?"

"Normandy. A Commando raid, just before the big party in '44."

"Well, you can get back into trousers now. I won't keep you any longer."

"Can I take my clothes? They're hanging up here."

"Good Lord, we're stopping everyone from changing. Still, there's nowhere else."

"What about on the stage?"

So Montero and Springer removed themselves to a couple of fake antique chairs behind the closed curtain for their next interrogation. Following up what Ludlow had told them, they worked through most of the minor members of the cast, who all seemed to be safely eliminated from suspicion. Each of them had been in company with at least one other during the whole of the critical period, and nobody had seen anything that might be helpful. It was getting late by the time Montero ticked off the crumpled programme again and looked wearily at the remaining names. He took Monica Stafford next, who was clearly prepared to talk all night if necessary. To her disappointment, she was asked only to confirm what had been established already. Nobody had missed an entrance, though Hedge had been late for the curtain-call. Terry Colbert had been in the hall the whole time, except for his brief appearance on the stage when he had trouble with Hedge. Bould was unpopular with everyone.

"The trouble is," Montero said to his sergeant when they were alone again, "that nice people seldom get murdered. If Bould had been a philanthropist loved by all in the parish except for one wicked poacher, we might be finished by now. Ah, well. Let's see who's left — Morland, Hedge, Fielding, Colbert, Seward. Let's have the lady next."

Unlike Monica, June Morland was not inclined to talk. She took the offered chair calmly enough, but her pert nose and pretty lips told a different story from her eyes. Montero was gentle.

"Will you tell me," he said, "whether you left the hall during the evening, except to go on the stage?"

"I went to the kitchen, twice." She silently defied him to find out more.

"When was the first time?"

"At the beginning of Act Five in the book — though we've placed our intervals a bit differently."

"That must have been at the same time as Mr. Bould went?"

"I followed him there."

"Why did you do that?"

"Because I wanted to talk to him, privately."

"About what?"

"I said it was private."

"I see. You had your talk, and came back to the hall, leaving him in the kitchen?"

"Yes. I was with him a few minutes."

"Did anybody else come in during that time?"

"No."

"Mr. Bould was alive and well when you left him?"
"Of course."
"I hope so. Now please tell me what happened after the rehearsal proper, when Mr. Colbert decided to do some more."
"Everyone was a bit annoyed and there was an argument. I decided we might as well get it over. Then I changed my mind and went to wash up the cups we'd used for tea during the interval. I stayed in the kitchen until Donald Hedge came in and told me what had happened. That's all."
"I don't think it is all, Miss Morland. Why did you go to wash these cups?"
"I just thought I would."
"You changed your mind about going on with the rehearsal, during the very few seconds that it took you to go from the hall to the side of the stage?"
"I did. Isn't it a woman's privilege to change her mind?" she added with a smile that went no farther than her mouth.
"Let me see if I can remember my Sheridan," Montero said as if he were prepared to let it go at that. "In this scene, Lady Teazle has called to see Joseph Surface and is with him when her husband Sir Peter is announced. Joseph hides her behind a screen, and after some talk with Sir Peter there is a visit from Joseph's rakish brother Charles. Sir Peter hides and hears what passes between them, eventually revealing himself and being reconciled with Charles. Then, while Joseph is out of the room, Charles throws down the screen in the belief that Joseph has a 'Little French milliner' hidden there, and Lady Teazle is revealed to her husband. Right?"
"Very good, Inspector. I congratulate you on your memory."
"He's a proper caution for poetry and plays and things," said Springer enthusiastically. "Ask him anything you like — go on, ask him——"
"All right, Sergeant, I'm not doing it for a living in a music hall. The point of all this, Miss Morland, is that you

ought to have gone on the stage for the second run-through of that scene and hidden behind the screen. Instead you went and washed up in the kitchen. I ask you again, why?"

"And I tell you again, because I thought I would."

"Who usually washes up the cups?"

"We leave them for the caretaker, next morning."

"Weren't you afraid of getting marks on that beautiful costume you're wearing?"

"I didn't think of it."

"Was Mrs. Bould in the kitchen when you went to wash up?"

"She was standing in the doorway, looking out."

"You mean, the outside door was open, and she was there?"

"Yes. As soon as I came, she said she was going to wait for her husband in the car. And she went."

"Nothing else was said?"

"No. I just started to wash up."

"Was the gas stove lit when you went in?"

"I don't think so. No, I'm sure it wasn't. It was lit when I went to see Mr. Bould the first time, because he had the oven door open and was warming himself."

"Did you lock the outside door after Mrs. Bould had gone out?"

"No."

"All right. Now are you sure you can't give me a better reason for going and washing up instead of carrying on with the rehearsal?"

"I've said all I'm going to say. You can't make me tell you anything at all."

"That's perfectly true. But our experience is that people who are unwilling to answer questions usually have something to hide. For instance, it might make me think that the reason you didn't go on the stage was that you knew perfectly well what was hidden behind the screen by that time."

"That's ridiculous."

"I hope it is. Miss Morland, what are you frightened about?"

"Nothing. I'm not frightened. Do you wonder if I'm upset, with this terrible thing happening?"

"Not at all. You'd better go home now."

June was obviously surprised that Montero let her go without further questioning, but she gathered her long skirt gracefully and went off the stage as if she was making an exit in the play. At the edge, she paused and looked back, perhaps with the thought of returning, but then she turned again and went. Montero and Springer looked at each other for quite a long time before speaking.

"Well, Jack," said Montero at last.

"She knows something all right. And she's dead scared too."

"Of us, of the murderer, of the dead man?"

"I don't know, sir. And this washing-up business. If this was a case of poisoning — but it isn't."

"We shall know that after the post-mortem. Perhaps the murderer was making doubly sure."

"Maybe there was something in the tea to drug him, and then the murderer got him up to the stage when he was unconscious."

"Maybe. I'm sure of only one thing at present, and that is that June Morland could tell us a lot more than she has. Well, let's get on. Joseph Surface — Donald Hedge. Fetch him up."

Donald Hedge was only too willing to be fetched. In fact he was already at the foot of the stairs when Springer went for him, and he pushed the Sergeant aside in his eagerness to confront Montero.

"What have you been doing to Miss Morland?" he demanded.

"Sit down, sir. Asking her questions, as I'd now like to do with you if you please."

"She's very upset," said Donald as he sat down.

"Isn't that natural in the circumstances?"

"What the devil do you mean by that?"

"Come now, Mr. Hedge. Don't you find violent death upsetting? I do, in spite of a certain familiarity, and so does Sergeant Springer here."

"Yes, I see what you mean."

"What did you think I meant? No answer? Well, let me put it another way. What is your relationship with Miss Morland?"

"We are friends."

"Nothing more?"

"You are impertinent."

"I'm so sorry. Let me remind you that, as Miss Morland has just truly remarked, you are not obliged to answer any questions if you don't want to."

"I've nothing to hide. I'll answer anything that is relevant."

"Very good. Then tell me where you went at the end of the rehearsal—I mean the main rehearsal, not the repeated scene."

"I went to the little kitchen at the back. My throat was dry and I wanted a drink of water."

"Were the teacups that had been used during the interval still unwashed?"

"Yes, they were in the sink. I got a clean one from the cupboard."

"I understand that you were late getting back from the kitchen for the arrangements for the curtain-call. You took rather a long time over a cup of water, didn't you?"

"I stayed in the kitchen for a minute or two. I was rather upset and I wanted to be alone."

"What had upset you?"

"Nothing special. It had been a trying sort of rehearsal, and I'd had a bit of a row with Terry Colbert at one point."

"Was that unusual?"

"I'm always getting told off at rehearsals. I know I deserve it, and he's a jolly good producer, so I generally don't mind a bit. It just seemed to get on top of me tonight."

"So you wanted a few minutes by yourself. Quite understandable. But," Montero went on as if he was pouncing on his prey, "you had the company of Mr. Bould while you were in the kitchen."

"No," Hedge answered, looking genuinely surprised, "he wasn't there. I assumed he'd gone home."

"Was the outside door locked?"

"It was shut, certainly. I didn't try whether it was locked."

"Did you like Mr. Bould?"

"Not specially, few people did. I didn't see much of him."

"We're getting the time narrowed down a bit," Springer said cheerfully after Hedge had been dismissed. "That is, *if* they're all telling the truth, which I doubt."

"So do I. Bring — what's his name — oh yes, Clifford Fielding, and let's see if he can narrow it down a bit more."

Fielding was in a blustering mood and inclined to take a very high-handed attitude. Montero, who was well known in Scotland Yard for his ability to deflate people without being rude, soon got the interrogation on the level that he wanted. Fielding agreed that he had gone into the kitchen at the point when Dexter claimed to have seen him.

"But why did you deny this at first when Mr. Dexter mentioned it, before we came?" Montero asked.

"I was annoyed at him interfering. He's too fond of poking his nose into things. Ever since he got off with Bould's daughter, he's been lording it over everybody. Well, I suppose he'll come in for a good packet now, and none too soon if you ask me. Bould was the sort to cut them both off with a shilling. He's the one you want to suspect, not blokes like me who hadn't anything to gain from killing him."

"Nobody is being suspected yet, Mr. Fielding. Or if you prefer, everybody is. So the best thing you can do to establish your innocence is to answer my questions truthfully. Why did you go into the kitchen at that moment?"

"I had a few pages between scenes."

"That is not what I meant. What did you want out there?"

"I went to get a bit of fresh air."

"Was it very warm in the hall?" Springer asked innocently.

"It was damned cold, and you know it, so don't try to trap me that way. But the air's foul and stale, I can't bear a stuffy place — and don't tell me that a place can't be stuffy and cold at the same time, because it can."

"Just like a police station," Springer murmured to his notes.

"But why," Montero took up the questioning again, "did you go through to the kitchen instead of to the main door of the hall?"

"The main door makes a noise when it's opened. I didn't want to disturb the rehearsal."

"Very commendable. So you got your — er, fresh air, at the back?"

"I didn't get it at all. Bould was in there warming himself by the stove, and I knew he'd kick up a fuss if I opened the door."

"What was he doing?"

"I tell you, sitting by the stove."

"Did you speak to him?"

"I had to say something, so I said I'd come in for a warm too."

"Surely you knew that he'd already gone there, before you?"

"I'd forgotten. Otherwise I wouldn't have gone near the place. We didn't get on terribly well. I mean, you know what next-door neighbours are like, and we had a few words only last week."

"What was that about."

"Carlos — that's my dog — went into his garden, and he said he was damaging his beds, as if there was anything to damage at this time of year. And he called him dangerous when he wouldn't hurt a fly."

Montero correctly apportioned this flood of pronouns between man and dog.

"Was there an open quarrel about this?" he asked.

"We shouted at each other over the fence a bit. And that's another thing — who owns the fence? Now if the supports are on his side, I say he's responsible for the upkeep. Am I right?"

"I really don't know, I'm a policeman, not a solicitor. Was this quarrel renewed in the kitchen tonight?"

"Oh no, we just talked about this and that for a few minutes. He never did have much to say."

"So you state that you did not open the back door at any time, and that you left Mr. Bould in the kitchen, apparently in good health?"

"That's right. Is there anything else you want to ask me, or shall I sign my statement now?"

"There's nothing to sign, Mr. Fielding. We haven't asked for a formal statement and have no intention of doing so at present. If we do, you will be cautioned in the proper manner. That is all for tonight, thank you."

Fielding's exit from the stage on this occasion was a great deal less confident than his entrance. Montero and Springer looked well pleased with their work, though Springer had something on his mind.

"I thought you'd ask him about the row he had with Bould during the interval, sir?" he said.

"So did he. Now he doesn't know how much we've got on him, and a worried man is likely to do something to commit himself a bit further."

"Do you think he's the one, then?"

"I've no idea at present, but I'm sure he didn't go to the kitchen for air, fresh or stale. And he knew perfectly well that Bould was there. Come on, let's have the lad who produces, before we're all frozen speechless."

After the trail of dishevelled eighteenth-century figures, there was a refreshing look of reality about Tony Colbert, even though he was clad in a sweater that was much too big for him and jeans that must have caused him considerable anguish when he sat down at Montero's request. He looked really miserable, and Montero was enough of a psychologist to direct the vanguard of his interrogation with the right placing of sympathy.

"It's an unfortunate end to all the hard work you must have put in on this play," he began.

"The whole thing has been doomed, absolutely doomed, from the start," Terry drew his hands through his hair so that it flopped in two depressed swathes over his ears.

"I'm sorry to hear that. What went wrong?"

"First, there was a lot of opposition to doing a costume play at all, from morons on the Committee who can think of nothing better than the nice comedy they saw when Aunt Edith came to stay five years ago. Then my Joseph Surface got a job in Birmingham, and I had simply nobody for it but Donald Hedge, who's a nice fellow but has very little idea of acting. All through the rehearsals, Bould was hanging around and upsetting Frances and Tony Dexter. Now he spoils everything by getting himself killed. We can't possibly open tomorrow now."

Montero nodded sympathetically.

"I expect you want to get away and forget about it," he said, "but if you can answer a few questions first it may be a great help to us in our investigations. You see, you have the chance of seeing the rehearsal as a whole, whereas the others are concerned only with their own bits of it. I suppose you were in the main body of the hall during the whole of the time we have to consider — that is to say, from the time Mr. Bould left it until his body was discovered."

"Yes, of course. I can't say that I was in any one place, because I'm afraid I'm rather a peripatetic type of producer. I mean, I run about a lot," he explained kindly to Springer, who was taking notes.

"You didn't leave the hall even for a moment?"

"No."

"Not even to go on the stage?"

"Oh well, yes, I did get so worked up at one point that I went up just to put Donald Hedge in the right position. He took it rather badly, and actually he was right. I do tend to break in a bit too much — but they're so slow to remember, you've no idea. Anyway, after he'd blown up, I thought I'd let the last few scenes take their course and then tidy up some of the worst bits at the end. That was how he came to be discovered, of course."

"If Miss Morland had gone on then as you directed, she would have been the first to find the body."

"I suppose she would. It's not like June to miss an entrance either. She's usually pretty unflappable, but something seemed to be eating her this evening. She got in a state about something a bit earlier."

"Yes, I know about that. Did anyone else miss an appearance?"

"No, they were all right on cue. I'm pretty fussy about that and they get drilled to it. Donald Hedge was missing when I came to arrange the curtain-call, but that didn't matter too much."

"All right. Now this screen, which played such a part in the action, both rehearsed and unrehearsed — this is it, I suppose?" Montero said pointing to the screen which still lay where it had fallen.

"Yes, you see, this is supposed to be in Joseph Surface's library, and Lady Teazle——"

"All right, thank you, I know the play. You got this screen from Mr. Bould did you?"

"Yes, he lent it, and he made such a fuss——"

"Will you please put the screen in the position it occupied when Bould's body was discovered."

Colbert heaved the screen upright in the corner of the stage. Montero walked round, went behind it and then emerged and studied it from every angle.

"It's a substantial piece of furniture," he said at last. "No difficulty in hiding a body behind that. What I want to know is, what chance the murderer had of getting to it unseen. Now I believe that Mr. Bould went out immediately after the scene in which Lady Teazle is discovered. At that point, the screen would be lying flat on the stage where it was thrown down. Am I right?"

"Exactly, Inspector. Now it's interesting that you used the phrase 'thrown down', because the original stage-direction says, *Charles Surface throws down the screen*. And that's what I insisted on having, though in many modern productions he simply draws it gently aside. But surely Charles is the kind of character who would act on a strong impulse, and show a clear physical manifestation of his feelings."

"Certainly," said Montero, interested, "and that of course would help to point the contrast with his brother Joseph, whose very actions are slow and subtle, like his motives."

"But what happens to the screen then?" Springer asked pointedly, bringing his chief back from the world of literature to more immediate business.

"Arthur Seward picks it up and sets it where it was before for the next scene," Colbert explained.

"The next scene is the same?"

"Yes, still the library. Seward just draws the curtain for a moment to show that time passes and then we go straight on."

"So, except for a few seconds, the screen is in full view of everybody in the hall from the time Lady Teazle is discovered until the end of the next scene. What happens then?'

"The next scene is in Sir Peter Teazle's house, and we play it in front of the traverse curtain."

"That's the curtain drawn up in the corner over there?" asked Montero, going and looking at it.

"Yes. It runs freely on that wire just above the middle of the stage, and Seward pulls it across between scenes when it's needed. After the scene in Sir Peter's house, we're back in Joseph's library for the last scene of the play which is done with the traverse open like the two before."

"Therefore, if I've understood you rightly, the only chance for getting something behind the screen was during one scene, or in the brief pauses between scenes. But surely this chap Seward would have had his eyes on the stage the whole time?"

"He can't see anything from where he stands by his switchboard — he takes all his cues by sound."

"Did he miss any this evening?"

"Not one, though he had a bit of difficulty with the front curtain at the beginning. He's a first-rate stage manager; he works at an electrical sort of shop in the High Street. Do you know, he made that switchboard himself in his spare time. Come and look at this dimmer——"

"What about Mr. Bould?" asked Springer, who saw his chief's attention being distracted by frivolities again. "How did you get on with him?"

"Not awfully well, I'm afraid," Colbert replied, unwillingly coming back to sordid reality. "He wasn't an easy man to get on with. As far as I was concerned, he was a perfect nuisance — always turning up at rehearsals, and criticising and complaining in a loud voice. He had no manners; I thought he was very rude when Mr. Ludlow gave us that splendid lecture a couple of weeks ago. And look at this evening — he upset half the cast in one way or another. I suppose I shouldn't go on like this now he's dead, though."

"I shouldn't worry," said Montero, "it only confirms what we've heard several times before. But what surprises me is that you tolerated him here."

Terry Colbert grimaced and made an expressive mime of counting money.

"He was a pretty rich man," he said, "and he forked out a good donation for us several times. That's why we made him president of course. He paid for the materials for Arthur's switchboard, for one thing."

"He must have had a real interest in the art of the theatre then."

"He had a real interest in the art of being a big fish in all the local ponds. His daughter's very keen, and I think he came to rehearsals partly to keep an eye on her and Dexter."

"Why did he disapprove of Mr. Dexter?"

"I haven't a clue, unless it's that he's so much older than Frances. To give him his posthumous due, old Bould was genuinely fond of her, I think, though he treated her pretty rudely in public sometimes."

"You've been a great help, Mr. Colbert. We ought to be able to narrow down the time of the murder now. By the way, if you hadn't decided to go through that scene again, when would Bould's body have been found?"

"When the caretaker came in tomorrow morning, I suppose."

"Would he have gone and explored the stage?"

"No — in fact, he'd definitely been told not to, once the sets for the play were up. Good Lord! We mightn't have known until the performance!"

"That would have shaken the audience," said Springer.

"Your theatrical tastes begin and end with Grand Guignol, Sergeant. Mr. Colbert, who had a key to the hall?"

"Well, I have — I come to open up for rehearsals, and there's a terrible fuss if I leave them waiting in the cold for five minutes. The caretaker has one of course — he's the verger of the church as well. I suppose the Vicar has — I don't know who else."

"So you are always the last to leave the hall, as well as the first to arrive."

"Not necessarily; it's a yale lock and the last one just pulls it after him."

"What about the back door?"

"That's never used, but I always see that it's locked before I go, It's an old mortice lock, and the key stays inside because it's supposed to be a fire exit."

"Apart from his being a nuisance at rehearsals, did you have any personal reason for disliking Mr. Bould?"

"Not really. He got me into a bit of a row at my school — he's on the Governors, but it soon blew over."

"All right, thank you. I'm sorry the play is spoiled, but perhaps you'll have better luck with the next one. If you'd be so kind as to send your stage-manager up, we needn't keep you any longer."

"What about all this?" Terry asked with a sweeping gesture around the stage. "Are you going to tear it down, looking for clues?"

"Not tonight anyway. We'll tell you before we disturb anything."

"It does get into them, this acting lark," Springer said thoughtfully when Terry had gone. "Fancy thinking about his bits of scenery after all this. I never had anything to do with it myself, but I did go and sell programmes once. I had a young lady who used to do play-acting, down in Norwood. That was before I met Mrs. Springer of course."

"Well, spare me the details of your pre-marital adventures,

Jack, because we've got another man to deal with and I can hear him coming."

Arthur Seward's feet were heavy on the steps that led to the stage, and his voice was harsh with cold and indignation. He sat down, rubbing his arm, and looked angrily at the two detectives.

"What have you done to your arm?" Montero asked.

"Strained it trying to unstick that curtain. And that was just the beginning of it. Start badly and you'll end badly, that's what I always say. Here I am hanging about in this ruddy hall, kept till the last because I'm of no account. Let me tell you, I've got work to do tomorrow——"

"So have we. If you'll answer a few questions, we shall finish all the sooner. Did you leave the stage at all after the interval this evening?"

"How could I?"

"I'm not asking you how you could. Did you?"

"I did not. I stood by my switchboard the whole time, except for putting the stage right between scenes. Ask Terry Colbert whether I was late on a single cue."

"Can you see the stage from where you stand?"

"Not a thing. That flat's eight feet high, and I stand with my back to it. Go and try it if you don't believe me."

"So your duties are to open and close the curtain, which you do from where you stand, to control the lights and to put the stage in order at the end of each scene. It's a lot for one man, isn't it?"

"I like to work on my own. Some plays, I want help with the scene-changes, but for this one it's only a matter of opening and closing the traverse and moving a few chairs."

"Did you go and pick up the screen after the scene in which Lady Teazle is discovered behind it?"

"Of course I did. It was there all right for the next scene, wasn't it?"

"Did you, either then or at any other time during the rehearsal, see or hear anything that struck you as unusual?"

"Can't say I did. It was the usual organised chaos, like any other dress rehearsal I've ever seen."

"Now think carefully. Sometimes the characters have to make their way around the back of the wooden flat, in order to enter from your side. Is that right?"

"It is."

"Did anybody come round the back this evening?"

"I don't think they did. They usually come across the stage before the curtain opens. I think they all did this evening."

"Would you know if anybody came round the back, without having an entrance to make?"

"I think I would. Not if I had a tricky bit of lighting, so I'm not swearing to anything."

"I'm not asking you to at present. What did you think of Mr. Bould?"

"Same as everybody else, that he was a mean old devil."

"Did you have anything special against him?"

"He got me in trouble with Mr. Ramage — that's my boss. Made a complaint about me. But it didn't do no good — I'm worth too much to get the sack for the sake of Bould, rich though he might be."

"I see. So you didn't kill him, then?"

"No, I didn't. You've no call to be making accusations——"

"I didn't, I asked you a question. And it's the last one for the time being. You can go home now, Mr. Seward. Come on, Jack, let's go and thaw ourselves and see what we've got so far. We might dig Mr. Ludlow out of his private iceberg as well."

CHAPTER FIVE

Who Plays the Villain?

Ludlow was not frozen into immobility, however. He was sitting by one of the radiators, making sketches on the back of an envelope. Montero came up quietly and peered over his shoulder.

"I think I ought to charge you with being in possession of drawings of a military installation," he said.

"This," Ludlow answered with dignity, "is a sketch of the stage and the room at the back. I've been trying to work things out."

"It doesn't look much like it to me."

"I have an impressionistic technique for drawing maps."

"Well, come and work things out with us. Everybody's been allowed to go, so nobody will write any letters to *The Times* if I let you know what's been going on."

They went through to the kitchen, where the two Detective-Constables had finished their work. The contents of Bould's pockets were laid out on a small table. One of the men was fondly packing up his large camera, while the other checked the labels on an assortment of sealed envelopes. Montero went to the back door, opened it and stood shivering in the cold. As Mrs. Bould had said, the path sloped down to an open yard that was really only a widening of the side road. He shut the door and then went and lit the gas stove before saying anything.

"Any luck, Parker?" he asked.

"I'm not too hopeful, sir," replied the detective with the camera. "The door handle was too smeared to give a decent set of prints. There are only two things that might be any use, as far as I can see. I've got a lovely impression of two hands flat on the floor—on that bit of lino there by the sink that doesn't match with the rest. And there are hairs and possibly a bit of skin on this thing."

He pointed to a flat-iron, delicately tied up in a plastic bag as if for a presentation.

"Any prints on that?" Montero asked.

"Nothing, sir. Whoever used it must have had gloves or held it with a handkerchief. Of course, if he had his hand clenched round the handle, his fingertips would probably be pressed against the base of his own hand anyway."

"Good man, Parker, we'll make a detective of you yet. Right, just scout round the rest of the hall and see what you can pick up — though I doubt whether there'll be anything.

"I emptied his pockets before they took him away," said the detective with the envelope. "It's all on the table there."

"We'll take a look at that later."

The two men left with their equipment. Montero, Springer and Ludlow sat down, close to the stove. After a nod from Montero, Springer pushed his notebook over to Ludlow, who ran through it with the speed of a practised reader. Montero folded his hands comfortably and looked as if he had just taken the chair at a committee meeting of no great importance.

"I think," he said, "we can assume for the moment that Bould was attacked here in the kitchen. It may be that those prints on the floor are not his, and it may be that the hairs on the iron have a perfectly innocent explanation. But, adding the probabilities to what the doctor told us, I take it that the murderer came in here, struck down Bould by a blow at the back of the head from that iron and then exerted pressure in some way to break his neck. He then took his opportunity to carry the body behind the screen on the stage, where in the ordinary way it wouldn't have been found until to-morrow. The scene in which the screen is thrown down was over before Bould left the hall, and there was no reason to suppose that it would be repeated, since this was a dress rehearsal. If it wasn't for a fussy producer, the murder would still be undiscovered."

"But his wife and daughter would have missed him, and made a commotion," said Springer.

"Of course, but would they have thought of looking on the stage — a place where Bould had no reason to go? Remember that when his wife didn't find him in the kitchen, she assumed that he had gone home. Even if a search had been made, the murderer would have had a good deal of time at his disposal, to destroy clues perhaps. In any case, it's always wise to get as much time as possible between committing a crime and having it discovered, for the simple reason that people forget very quickly. The chance of really incriminating testimony decreases with every hour that passes, as all criminals know."

"Do you think he might have been lured up on to the stage and killed up there?" Springer asked.

"It's very unlikely, though if those prints don't fit, we may have to think again. But it seems almost impossible that a murder could have been done without people on the rest of the stage hearing it. At present, it doesn't matter too much. The most important fact before us is that Bould, dead or alive, was got behind that screen without anyone seeing him. So it must have been during the brief pauses in between scenes, or during the time when that curtain was drawn half-way across the stage."

"The traverse curtain," Ludlow said.

"That's right. I couldn't remember the technical term."

"I used to do a good deal of acting at one time," said Ludlow.

"What did you enact?"

"I did enact Julius Caesar: I was killed in the Capitol; Brutus killed me."

"It was a brute part of him to kill so capital a calf there."

The two men laughed, and Springer, who always feared for his chief's sanity during these outbreaks, returned them to business.

"He needn't have taken the body straight from the kitchen to the screen," he said. "He could have gone and waited behind that wooden wall arrangement they've got until he had a chance to get on the stage itself."

"Why should he take that extra risk? People were likely to use that narrow passage at the back for their entrances, though admittedly Seward has said that nobody seems to have used it this evening. No, there was plenty of opportunity to slip through behind the traverse from the steps at the side of the stage. It wouldn't present too much difficulty for a person who knew the arrangements for the different scenes, unless he had bad luck and ran into somebody, which he didn't."

"It's bound to be a man," said Ludlow rather hopefully, "and a strong one. It must take a lot of strength to break someone's neck."

"Not nearly as much as you might think, Mr. Ludlow, provided the victim is made unconscious first as he seems to have been. It's more a knack than sheer strength—if I got my right arm round the side of your neck now——"

"I'll take your word for it. He had to carry the body to the stage afterwards."

"Bould wasn't a big man, was he? That wouldn't be any great problem, especially to a man who was desperate enough to do a murder. I agree, though, that it doesn't look like a woman's crime. Now, let's see what we've got. This is the dull part of a detective's work, Mr. Ludlow. We don't get the sort of cases you read about in books, where a murder is committed by some inexplicable means. It's usually only too clear how it's been done. The question is, why and who. There seem to be plenty of motives in this case. Have you any ideas yourself?"

"My two visits here made it abundantly clear that Bould was generally, and I must say deservedly, disliked," Ludlow said. "From a quick reading of the Sergeant's excellent notes — I wish I could persuade my students to write as clearly and in such good order. How are we expected to teach a special academic discipline to minds that are not trained in the logical processes of thought? Where was I? Yes, from those notes, it seems that four people have admitted going into the kitchen after Bould left the hall, and two others might have done so, but deny it. The rest seem to be eliminated, thanks to their way of herding together and giggling in corners at all times when they were not in view on the stage."

"I agree," Montero said. "Let's go through the possibilities, and compare their movements with the state of the curtains. Young Colbert has told us how things ran in the last scene, and you will be able to confirm it, Mr. Ludlow. Now, the first one to leave was Miss June Morland, who went to the kitchen specifically for the purpose of talking to Bould, on what she describes as a private matter. Did you happen to notice her going and coming back?"

"I saw her come back," Ludlow said. "She seemed upset about something — indeed, the rehearsal was interrupted for a few minutes while we all tried to — ah — comfort her."

"How long was she out?"

"If she went immediately after Bould, perhaps five minutes."

"And during that scene, the screen was exposed to view. There was, however, presumably a short period between scenes when the front curtain was closed."

"According to what Seward said," put in Springer, "he

was on the stage some of that time, putting the screen back."

"Fair enough. So it doesn't look as if she could have done much during her first visit. But she went to the kitchen again, and did some washing-up, at a time when she ought to have been on the stage. Whether the washing-up itself is significant probably depends on the result of the post-mortem. But it does look very much as if she knew quite well what was behind that screen, and didn't want to go near it. We'll be seeing her again."

"The next to go out, on my reckoning, was Dexter," Springer said. "He was alone at the side of the stage, says he never went into the kitchen, but has nobody to confirm it."

"And during that scene, the traverse was drawn across the stage. He could have done it, but it would have needed very quick work to be in time for his own entrance. Did he seem at all agitated when he came on?"

"No," replied Ludlow. "He is one of the few members of this ill-fated company with any talent. He carried his part with reasonable competence all the evening."

"Still, we can't leave him out. It's hard to see how he had time to do it — but we do know that he was on bad terms with Bould over his engagement to the daughter. If she was coming in for some money, and was in danger of losing it — well, we shall learn that in due course too."

"There's one other thing," said Springer. "Do you remember, sir, how he let fall about having been in the Commandos?"

"I do indeed, Jack. And I can read your innocent mind. Advanced instruction in unarmed combat: how to break a man's neck before he can give the alarm. I know, we teach a generation to kill and then we wail about the crime-wave while we're preparing a new war for the next lot. Never mind, we're just plain coppers and we have to leave that sort of thing to our betters. Yes, Dexter could have done it. Who was next?"

"Clifford Fielding, seen by Dexter to go into the kitchen, and himself admitted it. Tells a very thin story about not knowing Bould was in there, and going for a bit of fresh air. We don't know how long he was there, but certainly that there traverse thing was drawn some of the time. He's a powerful sort of fellow, seems quick-tempered. Admits a quarrel with Bould, which is confirmed by Bould's daughter. Mr. Ludlow tells us of a spot or trouble this evening, during which Bould uttered what seemed to be a threat."

"Very succinct, Jack. And after him?"

"Donald Hedge was missing when this producer fellow wanted them all on the stage. Says he went for a drink of water, and stayed a long time because he was upset. Did he strike you as being upset, Mr. Ludlow?"

"Yes, he did. He's an appallingly bad actor at the best of times I should think, but this evening he was very shaky in every way. Also I had a brief talk with him the first time I came here, and he seemed quite an agreeable and balanced young man. Something was troubling him, something more than the cold and the chaotic nature of the rehearsal."

"What chance did he have of getting behind that screen?"

"Very little," Ludlow said. "The front curtain was closed and everyone came down into the hall, but then Colbert ordered them back on the stage. He could have done it then, if he'd watched his opportunity, but it would have needed careful timing."

"And there was the risk of running into Seward, who thought the rehearsal was over and would be coming down too." Montero was beginning to look discouraged. "Then Mrs. Bould goes out, and the curtain remains closed for some time while they are arguing about whether to go on. She wouldn't be capable — physically capable, I mean — of doing it, but she could have let in somebody. She certainly had that back door open."

"With the irascible husband sitting there calmly, waiting to be murdered? I don't see it at all." Ludlow got up and paced about as he often did when he was thinking, though the dimensions of the kitchen limited his movements. "Of course, she might have let somebody *out*."

"You mean, the murderer was hidden in the kitchen all the time?" Montero was interested by this. "But where? There's no room here, and Hedge or Fielding would certainly have seen him."

"He might have been in the dressing-room. He could have watched for his chance and taken it. Then Mrs. Bould could have come to let him out and lock the door after him so that it would seem as if nobody could have gone that way. But Miss Morland came before she could lock the door, and she lost her head and ran out to the car."

"I don't think much of that, sir, if I may say so," Springer said.

"Neither do I." Ludlow sat down again. "I feel pretty certain it was somebody inside the hall from the beginning."

"That Miss Morland had a second chance when she went out to wash up," said Springer with a sly glance at Ludlow.

"No, the curtain was opened almost as soon as she had gone," Ludlow answered. "Besides Bould had already disappeared by then, unless both Hedge and Mrs. Bould are lying."

"And Mrs. Bould is clear unless Hedge is lying, which he may be," Montero said. "He has a bit more to explain yet."

"Motive?" asked Springer.

"None, so far as we know. Bother!"

"What's more, sir," Springer said retrieving his notes and looking at them, "I think we ought to concentrate on Fielding. He says that Bould was alive when he went for this fresh air of his. If he's telling the truth, that lets out

Dexter and Miss Morland as well as himself, and means that Hedge has got a lot to answer for. If he's lying, then he's our man."

"The fallacy in your logic, Sergeant, is the assumption that murderers are the only people who ever tell lies," said Ludlow. "There is a dismal game called 'Murder' in which the murderer is the only one allowed to lie when questioned by the temporary detective, while the others have to tell the truth. Even then, it is sometimes hard to discover the murderer's identity. In the present situation, all the witnesses may be lying, for different reasons. I agree that Fielding's testimony is significant."

"Let's finish as soon as we can," said Montero. "Who else did we see?"

"Monica Stafford," said Springer, turning back his notes. "Never left the hall. Anyway, no motive except a general dislike of the man, and looks physically incapable of it. Terry Colbert, the producer, also never left the hall, unless you count going on the stage. Could he have nipped round to the back and done it, Mr. Ludlow?"

"No," Ludlow said, "he called out to Donald Hedge and then got straight up on the stage. He came back over the footlights, and didn't move again. Hedge's reaction seemed to quieten him, and he stood quite still by that silly girl who was prompting."

"During the scene when he intervened on the stage, the screen was exposed to view wasn't it?" Montero asked.

"Yes, so that seems conclusive, as he certainly didn't budge at any time when either the traverse or the front curtain was closed."

"Fair enough. Who else? Oh yes, Seward. What about him, Jack?"

"If he was crafty, he could easily have done it during the scene with that traverse. He admits that the lighting wasn't very tricky, and he must have been able to reckon the length of every scene pretty accurately, with the number of times he's been through it. Also has strained his arm in some way, which he says is by pulling the curtain. Dislike of Bould who had tried to make mischief with his employer."

"But one doesn't murder people for that," said Ludlow. "I mean, if one of the more unsavoury of my colleagues were to go to the Principal——"

"You'd be surprised what people will do. Although," Montero said, "I don't see how he could have done it during that particular scene, if Fielding is telling the truth about finding Bould alive. And there was certainly no time between scenes, as Seward was responsible for opening and shutting the curtain, and there were apparently no exceptionally long waits. This, I can see, is another of those cases where nobody could possibly have done it. But somebody did. I think we'd better pack it in for tonight."

"I'm ready, sir," said Springer looking at his watch. "It's past the witching hour."

"Well done, Jack, a quotation at last."

"Is that one of them quotations?" said Springer, pleased. "I never knew that before."

"We'd better look through these things before we go." Montero went over to where the contents of Bould's pockets were spread out on a small table in the corner. Ludlow looked at the little collection. Two hours earlier, every object there had played its part in a man's life, precious to him for itself or for what it represented. Each had had its purpose in the plans of a brain that had feared no sudden ending. Now there was nothing but the beginning of corruption, waiting for the pathologist's knife, insensible to the alien hands which had descended on those prized possessions. Ludlow shivered a little, these fragments of the affluent society recalling the old and inescapable mystery of death. Montero, perhaps no less sensitive, was more accustomed to the ritual. He handled each object carefully but with thoroughness, checking with the list which the Detective-Constable had made.

"Keys, comb in case, fountain-pen, loose change, pocket diary — we'll go through that later — matches, cigar-case with three cigars, wallet. Check the contents of the wallet, which seems well stuffed. Driving licence, book of stamps, credit card, cheque-book, a large number of banknotes, which we'll count later, a receipted garage bill, hullo, what's this?"

He drew out a sheet of writing-paper, folded across, and opened it with care. It was an ordinary enough type, light blue and without any printed heading. On it was written, "Donald Hedge, 5, 9, 25."

"Anybody going to guess what that means?" Montero asked. "No? Well, I don't blame you, because I haven't a clue and I think it's too late for sudden inspirations. But it does suggest that Mr. Donald Hedge may bear a bit more investigation. We'll keep quiet about this for the time being. That's the lot. One more look round and we'll call it a day, or rather a night."

He led the way down into the dressing-room again. This time his attention was held by what seemed to be a cupboard at the far end. He opened the door, and revealed an ancient and depressed-looking boiler.

"So that's what's responsible for the cold," Ludlow said.

"Apparently. No way in here. I wonder where the coke is brought from."

"Nowhere, I should think."

"That can wait, anyway. What about those windows?"

Springer climbed on a chair and examined the two small windows.

"Thick with rust," he reported. "They haven't had these open for years, I should think."

"I can't say I blame them. Up on the stage, and then we're finished."

The stage was still brightly lit, Seward evidently having thought that his duty for the evening was more than fulfilled. Their fresh examination revealed nothing of any interest. Springer went to the switchboard, and produced a number of futuristic lighting effects before managing to get everything switched off. The three men stumbled wearily across the hall, Ludlow completing his discomfort by hitting his shin on one of the metal chairs. At the main door, a cold group of men in raincoats were cajoling the two Detective-Constables. They brightened up at the sight of Montero, and grasped their pencils with numb fingers.

"Anything for the Press?" asked one of them.

Montero shook his head. "Nothing tonight, boys," he answered. "You'll get a hand-out from the Yard tomorrow if you want it. For the moment, you can just say that Bartholomew Bould, a prominent local resident, was found dead at a rehearsal of the Haleham Green Thespians in St. Edmund's Church Hall, Haleham Green."

"Give us a break, Inspector. Any suspects?"

"You'll get a break for libel and contempt if you're not careful, Harry."

"Not even a description of some man you want to interview?"

"We've done enough interviewing for one night."

The disappointed reporters dispersed. Ludlow and the detectives stood bracing themselves for the plunge into the cold outside.

"We'll try to get the inquest for the day after tomorrow," Montero said, "and ask for an adjournment. There shouldn't be any difficulty about that. Will you be coming along then, Mr. Ludlow?"

"Let me see — Wednesday — I can if it's in the afternoon."

"It probably will be. Then you can let us know if you have any ideas, because frankly this thing's got me stumped so far. We'll get hold of Bould's solicitor and have the will read too, if there is one. That may give us something to go on. There's nothing more to be done tonight."

He pulled the heavy door after them and they made their way round to the yard at the back of the hall. Bould's car remained in its place, lost and meaningless as the contents of his pockets. A black police car sneered silently at the patient Cleopatra.

"Would you like a lift back in a real car?" Montero asked with a smile.

"No, thank you, I prefer not to be seen in bad company," Ludlow replied.

However, it ended with Cleopatra being pushed out of the yard by all four detectives before she would consent to wake up. Ludlow sailed away towards the main road with much dignity as if she had just won the prize for the best-kept car.

CHAPTER SIX

A Twist in the Plot

Ludlow's previous experience of criminal investigation had taught him that violence, mystery and other people's misfortunes are a perpetual source of interesting conversation. This being added to the fact that students would rather talk about anything than the subject on which they are supposed to be working, the events of the night cast some long shadows into the day. He arrived in College extremely tired and with an irritation at the back of his nose which warned him that a cold was certainly on its way. His stomach was not at its best, and on the whole he wished he had never heard of Haleham Green and its Thespians. The stimulus of teaching, which he always enjoyed even in its more frustrating moments, revived him slightly. It may have been his physical tiredness, or it may have been his extraordinary talent for digression, which let him fall into the trap of one of his second-year students, a fair youth with huge blue eyes which lent an undeserved appearance of innocence. Ludlow was trying to find out what the boy had learnt about *Macbeth*, a set play.

"How do you account for the different reactions after the murder?" he asked.

"I suppose everybody would react differently to murder," said the student. Then, hopefully, "Did I see something about you in the paper this morning, sir?"

In spite of Montero's reticence, the morning papers had picked up a good deal of information and had not failed to print it.

"I've no idea what you saw in the paper. I do not possess the power of thought-transference, and if I did it would seem that your brain would have very little to offer in exchange, judging by your efforts this morning. Now, without looking at the text, why did Lennox suspect the grooms of the murder of Duncan?"

"Because — oh yes — they had the bloodstained daggers by them, and blood on their faces. So he was trying to do some detective work, but he went wrong. It must be very easy to pick up false clues after a murder."

"Indeed it is. I remember very well — however, how had these false clues been planted?"

"By Lady Macbeth after her husband was afraid to go back to the room. But they couldn't have been very hot on detection in Shakespeare's time, so it was easy to fool them."

"Never underestimate the men of the English Renaissance. Because they didn't have washing-machines, or indeed much washing of any kind, and went about the world at a comfortable pace instead of trying to go faster than light, or do I mean sound? However, the point is that they were extremely shrewd and intelligent. If you look at that excellent play *Arden of Feversham*, you will find a most interesting piece of criminal detection. The victim was murdered in the house and his body taken away, but one of the rushes from the floor caught in his shoe — let me see, I've got the play here somewhere."

So another hour was lost, but perhaps not wasted.

Professor Haddock, after his long neglect of Thespian activities, was now tenderly concerned about what had happened and seemed inclined to blame Ludlow for disrupting the peace of Haleham Green. Ludlow tried to get some information from him, but he knew nothing about any of the persons concerned and was able to report only that Bould had not seemed to be much liked. As events had already made this fact too clear, Ludlow was glad to make his escape as quickly as he could. The day's work over, he returned to his bachelor flat with a number of essays to be marked. Here he prepared himself a remarkable dish, consisting mainly of rice with the addition of several improbable flavours. Thus fortified, he prepared for a quiet evening correcting the errors of his tutorial flock. Yet somehow he seemed to find himself drawing plans of the stage at St. Edmund's Church Hall and writing lists of names and times which he compared with a copy of *The School for Scandal.* The result was that he got very little work done, and slept badly in spite of his lateness on the previous night. Nevertheless, when the time came on the following afternoon to take the road for Haleham Green again, he was looking thoughtful and by no means depressed.

It was still very cold, but a doubtful sun was slanting across the road as Cleopatra puffed bravely along, and Ludlow was able to forget for a while the further development of regrettable symptoms at the back of his nose and throat. The inquest, Montero had telephoned to tell him, was to be held in the offices of the Urban District Council, a squat red building which looked as if it had been set up in wet clay and then squashed out of proportion by an angry giant before it had had time to set. However unpopular Bould had been locally, he had been well-known enough to attract a fair crowd after he had been put beyond the reach of dislike. The double row of chairs which stood for the public gallery was almost full when Ludlow arrived and he had to push his bony way past shopping-baskets before he could find a seat. Montero and Springer were seated, more exclusively but not more comfortably, at the side of the room, together with the local Inspector.

The Coroner, a middle-aged doctor with a moustache which he seemed to be trying to bite in an ill-tempered way when ever he spoke, took his place punctually at three o'clock. Mrs. Bould, wearing a long black coat whose bulges suggested that her assortment of woollen garments still prevailed underneath, gave evidence of identification. Frances, looking very charming in black, was not called. Constable Felton gave evidence of being called to the hall and finding Bould's body there, and Inspector Belling told how he in turn had come and made his examination.

"I don't want to anticipate any investigations that may be going on elsewhere," the Coroner said with a savage bite at the left tip of his moustache. "But I imagine we have all read our newspapers. Did you, Inspector, have reason to believe that the body was discovered in somewhat unusual circumstances?"

"I did, sir. There seem to have been a number of witnesses to that occurrence, though I was hoping that it would not be necessary to have them questioned here today."

"I take it that this death is likely to be the subject of a criminal investigation?"

"It is, sir. I may go so far as to say that I have already enlisted the help of a very distinguished officer from Scotland Yard. I should therefore like to ask for this inquest to be adjourned at this stage."

"I have no objection to an adjournment, but perhaps we should hear the medical evidence first. Doctor Slattery, please."

Doctor Slattery took his place as if he were about to begin a sermon.

"You are Doctor William Slattery?" asked the Coroner, who had been playing golf with him two days before.

"I am."

"You act as police surgeon for this district?"

"Indeed I do." Slattery seemed to regret the admission.

"Did you receive a call from the police on Monday evening this week, at about ten o'clock?"

"It must have been a little later, by the time I got the message. You see, I was out on a maternity case——"

"We needn't bother about the exact time. Were you asked to go to St. Edmund's Church Hall?"

"Yes, I was."

"Please describe what happened on your arrival there."

"I was taken to the stage at the end of the hall, where I found the body of a man I knew as Bartholomew Bould. He had been dead for not more than an hour, probably less. I made an examination of the body, as well as I could under those circumstances."

"What did you discover?"

"Bruising and abrasions at the back of the head, caused by a blow which had fractured the base of the skull. There was also a fracture of the upper cervical vertebrae,"

"Would either of those been sufficient to cause death?"

"The damage to the base of the skull would have caused death if medical attention had not soon been given. The fracture of the vertebrae would certainly be fatal."

"Did you form any conclusion about these wounds? I mean, could they have been self-inflicted, or the result of an accident?"

"Neither could have been self-inflicted. The blow on the head could possibly have been accidental, but the fracture of the vertebrae was caused by pressure at the side of the neck, with concurrent twisting. In my opinion, that had been done deliberately by another person."

"Did you form any opinion about which of these injuries was the first to be inflicted?"

"It seemed probable that the blow to the skull had been delivered first and that the neck had been broken immediately afterwards. I was able to confirm this opinion when I made a post-mortem examination of the body next day."

"May I ask a question, sir?" Montero was on his feet and looking at the coroner, who nodded.

"Do you think, Doctor Slattery, that Mr. Bould could

have walked from one place to another between getting hit on the head and having his neck broken?"

"Certainly not," replied the doctor, with a look of distaste at Montero's non-medical language.

"I don't want to seem to be disputing your expert opinion, sir, but one does hear of cases in which a man is hit on the head and then walks for quite a long way without being aware of what he is doing."

"Not with this type of blow. It is true that an injury to certain areas of the brain can cause amnesia, without affecting the locomotive power. But this blow must have caused immediate loss of consciousness and movement."

"One other question, if I may. When you did the post-mortem, did you examine the contents of the stomach?"

"Of course I did. The dead man had had a meal about two hours before death, and had drunk some tea about half an hour before."

"There was no trace of any poison, or drug?"

"None whatever."

"Thank you, sir." Montero bowed to the Coroner and sat down, looking a little discouraged.

"Was the deceased a regular patient of yours?" the Coroner asked.

"He was registered with me, yes."

"Was he in good health up to the time of his death?"

"Perfectly fit, very fit for his age. There was no organic trouble of any sort. He took good care of himself."

"Thank you, Doctor, that will be all." The Coroner took a last bite at his moustache and missed it again. "The inquest is adjourned, *sine die,*" he said as he rose.

Ludlow stretched his cramped legs and looked around the emptying room. Mrs. Bould and Frances looked as if they were coming to speak to him. Also, to his surprise and pleasure, June Morland had come in even later than himself and had been sitting at the back near the door. She smiled in his direction, but at the same time Montero beckoned him to come over. With a sad thought of the many times that duty had overcome pleasure, Ludlow went and joined the police officers.

"We're just going for a cup of tea," Montero said. "Will you join us?"

"Why not all come down to the Station?" said Inspector Belling hospitably. "There's always a cuppa going there."

"We won't take up any more of your time, old man," Montero said, with the look of a man who has had to drink more police station tea than was good for him. "We'll find somewhere, just to fill in time before the next bit of work."

They walked out into the High Street.

"There seems to be two possibilities," said Montero. "There's the Crown at the other end, shut now for serious business unfortunately, but they do teas. Or there's that."

He pointed across the street to where black letters on a pale mauve ground announced "Cath's Café." Lace curtains below threatened rock cakes and dainty sandwiches.

"I don't know," said Ludlow, "whether it is better to be on the fringe of forbidden joys or to plunge straight into hell. But on the whole I think the Crown would be preferable."

"It's a cruel shame," Springer said as they made their way along the street, almost deserted on this early-closing day, "that a working man can't have a pint when he feels like it."

"Come now, Sergeant, surely you must uphold the law."

"Uphold it I may, Mr. Ludlow, but I don't have to agree with all of it. If I had the making of the licensing hours you'd soon see a few changes."

The lounge at the Crown was a pleasant place even at that hour of the afternoon. They ordered tea and sat down by a good coal fire while they waited for it.

"It is pleasant to get out of the smokeless zone occasionally," Ludlow said. "One almost forgets the comfort of a real open fire."

They said little until tea was brought and they were alone. Then Montero took out some notes.

"I'll put you in the picture as far as it goes, Mr. Ludlow," he said, "and then you can tell us if you've had any ideas. First, what we've checked up about the hall and what was found there. The coke is kept out in a little store in that yard at the back, and the caretaker has to carry it down in buckets to the boiler. So it's pretty clear why he doesn't keep up much of a fire. Anyway, there's no possible way in or out of the hall that we don't know about. The hairs and skin on that iron were from Bould's head, and there's no doubt that that was what was used to knock him out. It usually stood on a bracket to the side of the stove, where the murderer could pick it up with his right hand, without having to make any suspicious movement to get it. Bould's diary doesn't give us anything useful. That piece of paper with 'Donald Hedge, 5, 9, 25,' is definitely in Bould's handwriting. All right. That ties up the loose ends, or at least puts them where we can get a good hold on them. Any comment?"

"No, except that you've been busy. You haven't anything that connects Hedge with Bould apart from that bit of writing — no apparent motive for murder?"

"Not a thing, but we've hardly got down to the personalities in the case yet, though one of them has pushed himself forward, so to speak, I'll tell you about that in a minute. To complete the inanimate evidence, or rather lack of it, our men didn't get much out of that kitchen. The only thing that seems to matter is that those prints on the floor were Bould's two hands, spread out flat. So it seems to me a fair assumption that the murderer came quietly into the kitchen, walked across to where Bould was sitting without arousing his suspicions, and hit him suddenly with the flat-iron so that he fell hard on the floor. He then broke his neck — bother these pronouns, but you know what I mean — and carried his body on to the stage and behind the screen at some point when it was hidden from view by one of the two curtains. Anything wrong with that?"

"It sounds all right to me," Ludlow said slowly, "except that it's so difficult to see who had the time and opportunity to do all that. I was going through the text of the play last night, and comparing it with what we know of people's movements."

"So was I, and I didn't come to any conclusions either. But we shall, we shall. As I was saying, the kitchen didn't yield anything else of interest. It was reasonably clean as these places go, and the caretaker said that he had swept it out that morning. Our man picked up a half-smoked cigarette just inside the door, but it doesn't seem likely to help. It's a very common make, crushed as if someone had thrown it down and stepped on it just as he went into the kitchen. It's completely unmarked. From what inquiries we've been able to make, practically everyone in the play seems to smoke to a greater or lesser extent."

"Aren't there saliva tests and things? I understand that you policemen have the marvels of science on your side nowadays."

"We have, but it's not such plain sailing as you might think. You can't just go round demanding samples from unconvicted citizens, or you'll find yourself the subject of a question in the House of Commons. Sometimes I wish for feudal times — provided of course one was on the right side. No, life isn't all the popular science magazines make it out to be."

"Tell me about the man who has pushed himself forward," said Ludlow, feeling quite sorry for the Inspector.

"Ah yes." Montero brightened up. "That's one piece of

luck, though even that was spoiled for us. You remember probably from the questions we asked on Monday that Fielding lives next door to the Boulds. That had been the cause of a quarrel already. Well, our good Inspector Belling posted one of his men to keep an eye on Bould's house for the rest of Monday night. He had a hunch that the murder might have been done for the sake of something which Bould had and that the murderer might try to get it. It looks as if he was on the right lines, because about one o'clock, Fielding came out of his own house, by the back door, and walked round into Bould's garden. There's a gap at the end of the famous fence that caused the dispute, where the dog gets through and where a man can apparently follow. Now here comes the infuriating bit. The local constable, instead of lying low and waiting to see what Fielding was going to do, came right out and challenged him. Fielding, quite self-possessed it would seem, said that he was worried about Mrs. Bould and the girl and was looking to see if they had a light on, so that he could go in and give any help they might want. He said he was delighted to find a policeman was looking after them, said good-night and went home forthwith. From what we know so far about Fielding and his relations with the Bould family, that story just doesn't wash. But there's nothing we can do about it."

"That's the trouble with these country coppers," said Springer with true cockney scorn. "They aren't properly trained."

"And so there's no indication of what he might have been hoping to find, if he'd got in?" Ludlow asked.

"No, but he probably wouldn't have found it. Bould kept most of his papers in the office of his solicitor, which is where we'll be going soon. The will is going to be read at five, not sooner because Dexter insisted on being there, or young Frances insisted for him, and it's the earliest he could get away from work. It must be rather nice to work set hours and know when you've finished for the day," Montero added reflectively.

"You'd hate it, and you know it," Ludlow said. "Who is going to be present at this interesting ceremony?"

"Mrs. Bould and her daughter of course, Dexter, and June Morland."

"Why June Morland?"

"That will probably emerge in the course of things. The solicitor asked her to come along, so I won't offer you very long odds that she's mentioned in the will. I'm hoping that we shall be a good deal farther in our search for motives before very long."

"How much did Bould leave?"

"That's another thing we shall have to wait to learn. That is, if we're not turned out altogether."

"But hasn't the solicitor invited you?"

"He's been quite co-operative. Like all lawyers, he likes having a go at the police, but he's a decent enough fellow and hasn't made any real difficulties. But he said that we'll have to clear out if any of the beneficiaries object to our being there — and that means you too, Mr. Ludlow."

"I never obtrude myself where I'm not welcome," Ludlow said. "But surely the contents of a will are made public?"

"In due course, yes. But I'm hoping to learn something before too long."

"If it comes to that," Ludlow said, "they aren't wasting any time themselves. The unfortunate maker of the will isn't even buried yet."

"They certainly aren't showing any excess of sorrow. I understand that it was Mrs. Bould who was anxious to hear what was coming to her."

"She doesn't know the provisions of the will?"

"Apparently not. Certainly the will's been deposited in the solicitor's office ever since it was drawn up, but it seems incredible that Bould shouldn't have told his wife about it. Still, he was obviously a queer sort of fish."

"If she knows more than she ought to about the murder," Springer said, "and if she's coming in for a good sum, she might think it best to play innocent about the will. We've heard that old Bould used threats about leaving his money to try to break it up between his daughter and Dexter."

"Well, it's time to put some of these conjectures to the test."

Montero got up and led the way out of the lounge. Ludlow cast a wistful look at the fire and followed with the air of a man who is determined not to miss anything. The solicitor's office was not far and they arrived with admirable punctuality just as the church clock was wearily striking five. Like most solicitors, Coram, Coram and Gedge had surrounded themselves with genteel poverty, as if to announce that law was an unprofitable business which they carried on solely for the love of their fellow-men. Equally true to custom, Coram, Coram and Gedge were represented by a Mr. Astbury. The latter was ready for them, and Ludlow recognised him as a man who had sat with Mrs. Bould and Frances at the inquest. He was a fat man, with a look of incurable joviality which had to be suppressed in deference to the occasion. On top of his head was a shining bald patch, which he rubbed with a circular motion of his right hand whenever a difficult question had to be answered. Ludlow found himself wondering whether he had rubbed his hair off by constant friction, or whether he had been born like that and had been proudly polishing the spot ever since.

Mrs. Bould and Frances were already in the office when the detectives and Ludlow came in. Astbury greeted them cheerfully, then seemed to remember the situation halfway through and rapidly drew down the corners of his mouth. He cleared chairs for them, sweeping important-looking papers on to the floor. No-one questioned their being there, indeed there was hardly anything said at all until Dexter arrived, breathless and apologetic five minutes later. He had apparently acquired a respect for Bould in death greater than in life, for he was wearing a decent black overcoat and clutching a new bowler-hat.

"I'm sorry to keep you waiting," he said. "I got time off early from the office, but of course the train had to be late."

"You're not the last Mr. Dexter, certainly not the last," Astbury said with a rub at his bald patch. "We still await Miss Morland."

"June Morland? What's she got to do with this?"

"That's what we want to know, Tony," Frances said with a firm set of her pretty mouth. "A lot of people seem to be taking an unexpected interest in our family affairs."

Ludlow felt sure that this was a cue for his immediate expulsion, but nothing more was said. June Morland did not keep them waiting much longer, but arrived unruffled and smartly dressed in a way that made no pretence at mourning. She ignored everyone except Ludlow, whom she greeted charmingly. When she drew her chair close to his, he found it extremely difficult to keep all his senses alertly fixed on the matter of the will. Astbury cleared his throat, beamed at everyone, then quickly looked sad and gave himself a reassuring rub.

"We are here," he said as if making a great announcement, "to make known the provisions of the will of the late Bartholomew Bould. It is a rather long will, but the bulk of the estate is disposed of in a very simple way."

Mrs. Bould darted a look at June, which might have been triumph or anxiety. June kept her eyes fixed on Astbury. Frances and Dexter looked at each other and then Dexter became interested in the lining of his new hat.

"This being so," Astbury went on, "perhaps it would meet the desire of the present company if I were simply to mention the minor bequests in outline instead of reading the whole document from beginning to end. I have had copies of the will made, so that all interested parties will be able to study it at their leisure. Are you agreeable that I should proceed as I have suggested?"

He rubbed furiously while waiting for objections, but none came.

"Let's get it over," Dexter said at last.

"Quite so, Mr. Dexter, quite so. I'm sure that you don't want to waste your time over minor points." He caught himself half through a smile and hastily unfolded the document which he had been holding.

"'This is the last will and testament of me, Bartholomew Bould,' well, perhaps you'll take my word for it that all is in good legal form. I personally drew up this will at Mr. Bould's direction only a few months ago. I have been handling his affairs for a long time, and I felt it my duty to point out the hazards of dying intestate. Though I never thought that we should come to this moment for many years yet. Dear me."

He sighed and rubbed until the concealed impatience of everyone in the office recalled him.

"I won't trouble you then with the minor bequests. There are quite a lot of them, mostly personal possessions which he willed to various old friends. The Haleham Green Thespians receive fifty pounds. That's good, eh, Miss Morland?"

The temperature in the office dropped several degrees and Astbury, making himself look as severe as he could, went on.

"A number of other local organisations are beneficiaries, for sums ranging from five to fifty pounds. Mr. Bould was very thoughtful, very mindful of his many interests. You'll be able to see all these when I give you copies. Now, there are three main legatees."

Mrs. Bould hissed between her teeth. Springer's eyes were bulging as he clutched his notebook. Montero leaned forward towards the solicitor. Only June still seemed unmoved.

"There is an outright bequest of five thousand pounds to Miss June Morland, provided she is still unmarried at the time of Mr. Bould's death. As that condition seems to be fulfilled, payment will be made in due course. My congratulations, Miss Morland."

Nobody echoed the congratulations. Mrs. Bould, Frances and Dexter were tight-lipped. Montero looked pensive and Springer frankly baffled. Ludlow was full of his own thoughts, which were not taking a pleasant turn. June smiled in acknowledgement of Astbury's words, and the solicitor took refuge from the growing tension by returning to the familiar legal ground of the will.

"The remainder of the estate," he continued, "is to be divided equally between Mr. Bould's widow, and his daughter Frances Mary Bould. Mrs. Bould's share is to include the house which she now occupies."

He laid the will on his desk and permitted a smile to take its natural course without being cut off in the middle. Mrs. Bould was the first to speak, and what she said was unexpected.

"Are you sure there's nobody else?" she asked.

"No other beneficiaries? Not for a large sum, Mrs. Bould. The largest of the minor bequests which I mentioned at the beginning is one hundred pounds. Most of them are quite small."

Mrs. Bould seemed strangely relieved. Dexter opened his mouth, closed it and swallowed and then opened it again to speak.

"How much will Frances get?" he asked.

"It is impossible to state an exact figure," Astbury said with legal caution. "There will be death duties of course. And there are a number of creditors to be met, and a few debts to be called in. All in all, I have quite a lot of work here in front of me." He gestured at the pile of papers on his desk and rubbed his head.

"Can't you give me a rough idea? I mean, Frances ought to know what to expect."

"Ah, a rough idea," Astbury replied cheerfully, "yes, I can do that. So long as you understand that any figure I give you is an approximation only and cannot be held in any way binding. I should say that, when the estate has been properly settled, the residue should amount to something in the region of thirty thousand pounds. In short, and remember this is not to be taken as a precise figure, Mrs. Bould and Miss Frances should each receive about fifteen thousand pounds."

He sat back, secure behind his linguistic safeguards and waited for further comments. What came next was the attack by Mrs. Bould which they had all been expecting since June entered the office. They were prepared for screams, tears, perhaps even a physical assault. The cold, measured tones which in fact emerged were the more disturbing. Gone was the least suggestion of mild vagueness under the grey hair and woollen jumpers. Ludlow thought, as he listened with embarrassed interest, that this was a woman who could do murder.

"So you got your way right up to the end," she said. "You tricked him into this madness, he who would never give away a penny while he was alive, unless it was something that would add to his own glory in the giving. You made sure that you wouldn't suffer, whoever else did. God knows what other wickedness you've done. It will do you no good, nor the next man you get into your clutches. It's money that you've made dirty before you ever got your hands on it."

June was deadly white but she said nothing. Frances began to cry quietly and Dexter made vaguely comforting noises while glaring at all the others impartially. Ludlow felt as if a Victorian melodrama had taken on life and was heading straight for disaster. It was Montero who saved the situation, by a new question spoken in the most casual way.

"Are there any large debts outstanding?" he asked.

"Mostly small items, mostly quite small," said Astbury. "There are one or two larger sums owing, most of them business matters which we shall have settled in no time at all. There is one individual loan of some importance——"

Caution stopped him from saying more, but not before he had pointed unmistakably to a sheet of paper which lay on top of the pile before him. With the speed of which he is capable when he chooses, Ludlow stretched out a long, thin arm and whipped the paper from the desk.

"I say, you mustn't look at that," Astbury said with an ineffective grab at the air. "These are confidential papers, and as the sole executor — oh, do give it back!"

He stretched across the desk, thrusting his bald patch at Ludlow who handed back the paper with every appearance of penitence. The diversion had been welcome, and normal composure was, at least outwardly, restored. Astbury, his hands pressed firmly on his papers to prevent any other flights of curiosity, promised to deal with the estate as quickly as possible. He shook hands with Mrs. Bould, Frances and Dexter, deemed it politic to bow slightly to June and ignored the other three. They all clattered down the stairs and lingered outside for a moment as people do when they want to get away from each other without seeming rude. June looked as if she was going to speak, but she turned suddenly away and left them. In spite of his having disgraced himself in the office, Ludlow received a polite but vague hope that he would be seen one day for tea. When the two groups had gone their separate ways, Montero said to no one in particular:

"What do you think of that little lot?"

"As nice a set of motives as I've seen in my time in the

Force," Springer said cheerfully. "I've had my eye on Mrs. Bould from the start. Oh, I daresay she couldn't have done it herself, sir, but what about hiring somebody? Out of fifteen thousand, you could easy find enough to get a murder done by several gentlemen that you and I know."

"Except, Jack my dear boy, that this was clearly done by someone who knew his way about that hall and stage and knew how the different scenes ran. Still, you can't rule out a widow who's benefited by the death, or a daughter either for that matter."

"And this Miss Morland getting a cool five thousand," Springer added. "There's been some nice fun and games going on in that quarter I'll bet."

"I'm sure there is some very reasonable explanation for Miss Morland's legacy," Ludlow said coldly.

"Reasonable or not, we can't count her out just because you happen to like red hair," Montero said.

"That remark is quite uncalled for, Inspector. And what about Dexter?"

"What about him indeed? Let's see what we've got. Mrs. Bould inherits a good sum, and makes no secret of being on bad terms with her husband. If he was as mean as she makes out, his death puts her better off in more ways than one. The daughter, Frances, also inherits and is free to marry that young man of hers. She seems to have had some affection for her father, and there's no possibility that I can see of her actually having done the killing. Still, there she is. Dexter now has a rich wife in the offing, without any danger of losing her or her money by father's opposition. He seems to be on good enough terms with the mother. He's not well off, and we know him to be physically capable of the murder and to have had an opportunity for it. Then Miss Morland, who has behaved very mysteriously, I'm sorry, Mr. Ludlow, but she has — inherits a sum which isn't a fortune but is worth having. As the Sergeant said, it's a nice set of motives."

"But does it get us any farther?" asked Ludlow.

"Unfortunately not, in the sense that it doesn't introduce any new suspects, and doesn't tell us any more about what happened on Monday evening. Of course, there are more ways than direct inheritance of profiting by a man's death. By the way, that was smart work of yours in grabbing hold of that paper. We'll probably be able to get our hands on Bould's papers after tangling with a bit of red tape, but a short-cut like that is something we daren't take."

"That's why I acted so promptly," Ludlow said, pretending to look modest.

"It's a pity you didn't have it for long enough to read it. Still, it can't be helped."

"Well, as to that, I am rather a quick reader. A trained mind can soon pick out what is important. There are in fact some interesting experiments being done on improved reading techniques——"

"Do you mean, you did read it?" Montero interrupted.

"I was able to see what it was all about."

"What was it?"

"I don't know the technical terms for these things. Lawyers are second only to economists in devising outlandish jargon for familiar objects. I suppose it was a promissory note, or an I.O.U. or something of the sort."

"Never mind what it's called. What did it say?"

"It acknowledged a loan of five hundred pounds from Bartholomew Bould, and promised payment by the twenty-fifth of March, to him or to his heirs and assigns. I particularly noticed that last phrase."

"The devil it did! But you didn't have time to see whose debt it was."

"I was unable to read the document in full. It seems reasonable to suppose that the money was owed by the man who had signed his name, duly witnessed, at the end."

"Mr. Ludlow, stop being infuriating. You're not playing intellectual games with your students now. Who was it?"

"The document was signed by Clifford Fielding."

Montero stopped in the middle of the pavement and stared at Ludlow, while Springer gave a low whistle.

"So now we know why he was prowling round Bould's house on Monday night," Montero said at last. "He thought the paper would be kept there, and he wanted to get his hands on it and destroy it. That's a bit more like the truth than a quarrel over a dog and a fence."

"And that, no doubt, is why Bould said that Fielding was the last person who would dare to abuse him," Ludlow said.

They walked on in silence until they had reached the Council Offices, where their cars had been parked for the inquest.

"It seems that we're in your debt again for a useful bit of information, Mr. Ludlow. Let me know if you unearth anything else, won't you? You know my extension number at the Yard."

"I have my own career to pursue, humble though it may be," Ludlow replied. "The time has come for me to forget that I ever had the misfortune to come to Haleham Green."

It was not long before he realised that he had spoken too soon.

CHAPTER SEVEN

The Plot Thickens

"I may be old-fashioned," Ludlow said, "no doubt I *am* old-fashioned; but I still prefer the conventional spelling of 'psychology' to the whimsical sequence of letters which you have written down here."

He handed the test-paper back to a final year student and looked more benevolent than his words suggested.

"Furthermore," he went on, "you shouldn't talk about Browning's psychology when you mean Browning's religious belief. You don't make hard things easier to explain by putting them in terms which claim a scientific backing. Apart from that, it's not a bad effort. You won't start a new school of criticism, but you ought to get quite a respectable degree in the summer. Do the question on Tennyson for next week, and see if you get through it without using the phrase neo-Romantic. Good morning."

The student removed himself from Ludlow's room, but opened the door again as soon as he had shut it.

"There's a lady in the corridor, sir," he said. "I think she wants to see you."

"So she shall, if she has the wit to read the name on my door. Let's hope she's a lady, anyway."

A shadow continued to hover uncertainly on the glass panel of the door, like a ghost trying to attract attention from the richer world inside, so Ludlow went to admit his unexpected visitor. It was June Morland.

"My dear Miss Morland," said Ludlow, dusting the armchair and scattering unmarked essays with reckless abandon, "this is indeed a pleasure. Do sit down, and enjoy what meagre comfort the college provides."

June sat down, drew the skirt of her black suit demurely over her knees and looked at Ludlow under a ridiculous little hat that seemed to balance most charmingly the gentle tilt of her nose.

"I suppose I ought not to be doing this," she said, as women often do after they have decided to do whatever it is, "but I had to come and talk to you. I hoped to get you to myself yesterday, but you were with that Inspector all the time. And after that ghastly reading of the will, I just couldn't talk to anybody. So I know it's wrong of me to come and bother you at work like this, but I didn't know where else I could find you. And, oh, Mr. Ludlow, I do so need a friend."

She looked vastly different from the pert Lady Teazle of a few days ago, Ludlow thought, as he reflected pleasantly on the idea of June getting him to herself. His critical faculty, nodding but not quite asleep, saw a gleam of something hard in those eyes that were watching him so appealingly. The caution which had served him well in the past now plucked at his mental coat-tails and urged him to choose his words carefully. Raw human nature took caution by the scruff of the neck and pushed it out of sight, but could not quiet its whispering.

"Of course I shall be delighted to help in any way I can, though I am sure you cannot be short of friends. Please don't apologise for coming to see me — it is my privilege that you should want to. But what can I do for you, Miss Morland?"

"Do call me June, Mr. Ludlow."

"Well, well, I shall be delighted. And — ah — my name is Adam."

"Oh, I couldn't, Mr. Ludlow. It would seem so cheeky, when you're a professor."

"I'm not actually a professor, you know. And you'll make me feel old if you won't use my first name."

"No, I don't think you're old at all. But it wouldn't seem right somehow."

As this seemed likely to go on indefinitely, Ludlow performed one of the rapid switches of mood which often surprised himself as much as anybody else. He sat again behind his desk, looked firmly at June and said:

"What exactly is it that you want me to do?"

"I want you to find out who killed Mr. Bould," said June, startled into a direct answer.

"How can I do that? I am not a policeman, and I am not a private detective. Inspector Montero is, as I have reason to know, a very intelligent man. We shall all do much better to leave the investigation with him."

"But, Mr. Ludlow — Adam — I know you're not a detective, but I also know that you were terribly clever about solving a murder that Inspector Montero was working on before. There's been a bit about you in the papers. And everybody can see that the Inspector likes you and trusts you. That awful night when it happened, we were sure you must really be a detective because you went off with him and gave him advice about what to do."

"Well, not exactly; though I have already, I am glad to say, been able to make one or two suggestions about this case——"

"There you are, I knew you'd have started to solve it. So won't you, please, take a special interest in this? It would mean so much to me and it's so little to you — and you've done it all before."

"Murders, of course, are all different. It isn't just a matter of going through the same movements as I did before — and a very time-consuming business that was. Besides, I had a certain personal interest in the result of that investigation."

"Couldn't you find a personal interest in this one?" There was no hardness in her eyes now.

"If I take on this case, which I believe is how a real detective would describe it, I shall have to work closely with the police, as closely as they'll let me. The fact that I know Inspector Montero has nothing to do with it. I may, for instance, require certain information from you——"

"I'll tell you anything, Adam, anything at all."

"Now there are certain circumstances," said Ludlow struggling to keep his head, "in which you might give information without any fear that it would be made further known. Most obviously, if you made confession to a priest. Also if you were professionally consulting a doctor or a lawyer. But any communication you make to me will not be a privileged one, and I may have to pass it on. Is that clear?"

"Of course I understand. I'm not asking you to do anything dishonest, only to help me, because you're so clever."

"Would it not be better to confide directly in Inspector Montero?" asked Ludlow, not sounding or looking as if he thought that it would.

"I'm afraid of him. He looks so hard and unsympathetic."

"He's a very good chap," Ludlow said, thrown back into a cliché by the emotional storm that was raging electrically in his usually peaceful room. "However, I'll certainly do what I can. Perhaps you'd better tell me what you think I ought to know, and then I can ask a few questions, if I may. But remember, I'm not making any promises."

"Thank you so much, Adam. You're very sweet."

This had an alarming effect on Ludlow, who came nearer to blushing than he had for years, but took a bite at a pencil instead.

"First of all, I ought to tell you that I'm engaged to Donald Hedge."

'Told you so, told you so,' said Caution, popping up

gleefully. 'You middle-aged fool,' thought Ludlow. He said, aloud:

"Really? I hadn't noticed any of the usual signs."

June looked, somewhat embarrassed, at her left hand.

"It's been an unofficial engagement," she said. "We decided not to bother with a ring and announcements and things until just a short time before we got married. In a place like Haleham Green, where everybody knows your business, it's better to lead your own life as far as you can. I mean, Donald and I are both fairly well known because of the Thespians, and because he's got a shop in the High Street. And if we announced it, everyone would be giggling and whispering, and making silly remarks every time they met either of us."

"I see. And is it also possible that some ill-disposed person might be able to create — shall we say, not inappropriately, a bit of scandal — if the engagement became too public?"

"How on earth did you know?" June almost snapped the question at him.

"I know nothing except what you've told me. You wanted me to use my deductive powers, such as they are. Hasn't you better tell me some more?"

"I must, though you'll probably hate and despise me for it." She was very feminine and confused again now. "But it's what I came for. I used to be very friendly with Bartholomew Bould."

"We'd better get our terms exact, if we're going to make any progress. Euphemisms lead to vagueness and and false conclusions. Were you his mistress?"

"Yes."

Ludlow got up and went to the window. He did not see the grey quadrangle and the many windows that glowed with all kinds of academic activity. The thoughts and emotions that passed through him were complex, and it must be confessed that they related more to himself than to June. He stood there with his back to the room for two or three minutes, until the jumbled images fell into place. When he sat at his desk again, his manner was dry and efficient. June was crying, or at least was dabbing her eyes with a bit of lace.

"Now I've shocked you," she said.

"A wide reading of English literature leaves one without the capacity for being shocked. I can still be surprised, or I wouldn't be human. Perhaps I'm not, but let it pass. I think it would be better if you put me completely in the picture, as we used to say during the war. Which is something you'll hardly remember."

"You're very kind." June put her handkerchief away and turned her eyes on Ludlow again. "I don't know whether I can make you understand," she said. "I suppose you think I'm the sort that goes sleeping around with any rich man, but I'm not. You saw what kind of man he was, so I'm not going to pretend that I felt any sort of affection for him, though I think he did for me, at first. But when I came to Haleham Green — that was just over two years ago — I didn't know a soul there. I was terribly lonely. My parents both died when I was quite small, and I was brought up by various aunts in turn. Bartholomew had some sort of business connection with one of my uncles. It was he who got me a job in Haleham Green, at one of the small factories that have sprung up just outside — you must have seen them when you drove along the road. It was a good job, as personal assistant to the managing director, a better job, honestly, than I'm qualified for with my meagre secretarial training, though I've managed to hold it down so far. Of course I was very grateful to him, and he invited me to his house once or twice for tea at week-ends. Then he told me about the Thespians. I used to love acting when I was at school — I wanted really to go on the stage, but the aunts wouldn't hear of it. But then of course I was seeing him often, because he always came to rehearsals if he could, though he didn't act himself. Then one night he asked me back for a drink, one night last year when his wife and Frances had gone away for a few days. Suddenly he started telling me how unhappy he was, and how his money didn't mean anything to him because nobody loved him. And I suppose I was just a fool, with too much sense of gratitude, After that it went on, in a horrid, furtive way, for a few months."

Ludlow's lean face looked as if he was about to give a sermon on the perils of theatrical life. Instead he asked, incisively:

"What stopped it?"

"I fell in love with Donald."

"Whom you met as a member of the Thespians also?"

"Not at first. I went into his shop to see if he'd stock some theatrical make-up, because it was such a nuisance having to get it all brought by people who worked in London. Then of course I had to keep going in to tell him new things we needed. Then, this season, he joined the Thespians, and Terry gave him a part in the play. I don't know when we first realised what had happened to us. We got unofficially engaged early in November."

"Did Bould accept the new situation gratefully?"

"Can you imagine him? He kept on pestering me and giving me presents that I wouldn't take. Gradually he saw it wasn't going to be any good."

"And did Donald Hedge know about you and Bould?"

"I didn't know whether to tell him. It used to keep me awake, worrying about what was the right thing to do. I did tell him that there had been another man, and he said he didn't care. In the end, I told him."

"When?"

"Last Monday. That's why he was acting so badly at that

awful dress rehearsal when — when it happened. We met for lunch that day, and I came straight out and told him who it was."

"How did he take it?"

"He was furious — with Bould, not with me. I think we're too much in love for anything to come between us."

Ludlow gnawed a bit of pencil again and decided that he neither liked nor trusted this woman, and that was not merely because of any personal chagrin. Then he thought of Bould's fat little body and mean eyes, and felt a helpless pity for all the loneliness that flies to comfort and finds only what is ugly. He stabbed a mediocre but inoffensive essay that lay in front of him, and was silent so long that June half rose.

"You want me to go," she said.

"I want you to answer some more questions. For one, why are you now so anxious to see Bould's murderer caught and punished?"

"Because I can be saved only if the truth comes out. Don't you realise that I'm the one the police suspect?"

"Come, come, that's nonsense."

"It isn't. If they don't know about what had been going on, they soon will. Wasn't it obvious yesterday, when they heard about the money he left me? I tell you, they suspect me, and I appeal to you to help me. Find the real murderer. Please do it, whatever you think of me."

"I'll find him if I can, though you mustn't expect too much. It's clear that a lot of people are going to be unhappy, in one way or another, until this case is solved. But let me warn you now that, whatever I find out, I must go ahead to the end, whatever it may be. Are you content?"

"Yes, of course. And thank you, thank you so much."

"Let us hope that you'll continue to thank me. Now, this very substantial legacy — did you know about it before?"

"He promised that he'd see I was provided for, if anything happened to him."

"You mean, if he died. Which he has. Did you know about the condition attached to it?"

June seemed to hesitate a little too long before shaking her head.

"All right. Now let us come to the night of the murder. Why did you go to see Bould after he had gone to the kitchen at the back of the stage?"

"To tell him that Donald knew everything, and to try to get him to play fair and leave Donald and I alone."

"Donald and *me*," Ludlow said severely. "Take one thing at a time and we shall make better progress. Who else, besides Bould, knew about this unofficial engagement of yours?"

"Everybody in the society could see how it was, of course."

"Then why so much effort to keep it unofficial?"

"Because people react differently when a couple are just going around together and when they're properly engaged. We weren't ashamed of it, but we didn't want a lot of coy questions and people angling for invitations to the wedding. You know how it is."

"I don't. However — how did Bould respond to your appeal?"

"He just laughed."

"He didn't agree to — play fair?"

"He was in a beastly mood. He tried to make a pass at me even then, and when I pushed him off he said I'd be sorry if married Donald."

"Meaning what?"

"I don't know. I suppose about the will. Anyway, I saw it was hopeless and went back into the hall. I'm afraid I broke down a little."

"Yes, I remember."

"You were very kind then, too."

Ludlow got up and went to the window again, but this time his mind was clearer. He was wondering whether a little bait of information might catch a great deal more. It had started to rain, and the leaky drainpipes on the older buildings across the quadrangle splashed gloomily as a background to his thoughts. A student slipped on the uneven flagstones and sprawled in a damp mess of books, to the uproarious delight of the others who were running for shelter with him. Ludlow turned and swooped.

"Did you know that when Bould was killed he had in his pocket a piece of paper with Donald Hedge's name on it?"

"No!" June's answer was so swift and startled that it was obviously true. "What else?"

"I don't think I ought to tell you more at present, and anyway the rest of it doesn't seem to make sense. Let me go on asking the questions instead. At the dress rehearsal, why did you go and wash up the cups in the kitchen instead of taking your place on the stage when the screen scene was repeated?"

"Because I thought I would."

"So you said before, but I'm afraid it won't do. You must have had some reason — and don't just say that it's a woman's privilege to change her mind."

"I can't give you a better answer. I meant to go on stage, but suddenly I felt so tired and fed up with everything that I just couldn't. Haven't you ever gone and done some routine mechanical job, just to take your mind off things?"

"Yes, but not when I was dressed in a rather elaborate eighteenth-century costume. Did you want to talk to Bould again?"

"But he wasn't there by that time?"

"So you knew that, before you went to the kitchen to wash up."

"No — I just didn't think, but when I got there he wasn't, and Mrs. Bould thought he'd gone out to the car——"

"You'll have to do better than that with the Inspector."

"You think I'm lying?"

"I know that you're concealing something, and I'm sure it would be much better for you if you told the whole truth and not part of it. However, I've promised to look into the matter, and I will. Come and see me again one day next week. Good morning."

Like many visitors before her, June found herself in the doorway, with Ludlow politely holding the door for her, before she fully realised what had happened.

"One other thing," he said as she held out her hand, "did Bould's wife know about your affair with him?"

"I don't know. She never said anything. She may have guessed."

"Her outburst yesterday suggests that she did. Goodbye."

After she had gone, Ludlow sat for a long time looking at nothing. At last he got up, took his hat from the peg and went out to find Cleopatra among the other cars and the multitude of motor-scooters by the entrance gates.

Inspector Montero was also frequently drawn to the window that morning. It offered a more agreeable view than Ludlow's, since his office at Scotland Yard looks out over the river. The Thames was in its most wintry mood, crawling along as if its own greyness was too much of a burden and breaking all over into spitting conflict with the rain. Springer sat with his notebook in front of him, affectionately gauging his chief's reactions like a producer with a brilliant but temperamental actor.

"It's a lovely motive," he said. "All that money going where it's least deserved. Wife and daughter in for a very cosy amount indeed, daughter's boy-friend sitting pretty, Bould's probable girl-friend getting her cut as well. I'd have done him in myself for a share of that lolly."

"You are a natural criminal, Jack, and I can't imagine why I tolerate you. Stop licking your lips and add that Clifford Fielding had a strong negative financial gain from Bould's death, but seems to have slipped up in making sure of it. Answer that and tell him to go to hell if you can."

This last order was caused by the ringing of the telephone, which Springer obediently picked up. Instead of following Montero's second instruction, however, he listened for a moment and then said, "It's that Ludlow — downstairs."

"Let's have him, then. He isn't torn away from his books for nothing."

"You think he's on to something?" asked Springer hopefully.

"He certainly can't be more in the dark than we are; and he's usually worth talking to."

Ludlow did not look very happy when he walked into the office, but he rallied under Montero's chaff and answered with his accustomed turn of sardonic phrase. He told them about June's unexpected visit.

"Thinks she under suspicion, does she?" Springer said. "Well, she's not far out at that, but I'm blowed if I can see how she did it."

"I don't think she did, and I think I know what she's really afraid of," Ludlow said.

"Tell us then," Montero exhorted him.

"Not yet, because I could be wrong."

"That's very modest of you. What else have you found out that you're prepared to share with us?"

"That she was Bould's mistress for a time, and that she is now engaged — unofficially as she put it — to Donald Hedge."

"The first half doesn't surprise me, but the second is very interesting," Montero said. "Hedge had a double motive for murder — he would have been jealous of Bould, and his prospective wife was down for a substantial legacy."

"Provided she was unmarried when the old devil popped off," Springer added.

"Elegantly phrased, Jack, and much to the point. If June was going to get the money, somebody had to act fast before she and Hedge were married. I wonder whether she knew the provisions of the will."

"She told me that she didn't," Ludlow said.

"That may or may not be true. I haven't your touching donnish faith in the absolute innocence of any pretty woman under thirty. At the moment it's Donald Hedge that interests me most. Let's have another look at that piece of paper from Bould's pocket."

Springer passed it over, and Montero read aloud:

"Donald Hedge, 5, 9, 25. Do you know what it means, Mr. Ludlow?"

"I've no idea, but I expect it will come to me sooner or later. It sounds like a date — could it be a date of birth, perhaps?"

"It could, but whose? Hedge must be a bit younger than that date would give him — if it *is* a date; and Bould was much older. Our cipher boys just laughed when I showed it to them, and I must admit you can't expect anyone to do much with three figures. Never mind; we've got enough to keep an eye on young Hedge. If Fielding is speaking the truth, and I've found no reason to doubt it so far, Hedge is definitely the number one suspect. I'm still worried about the time he had to do it in, though."

During these words of Montero's, Ludlow seemed to be distracted from the conversation. He bowed his head as if in thought or some deep grief and took no notice of his companions. Suddenly he looked up and said briskly:

"It's interesting that Arthur Seward should have a conviction for violence."

Montero and Springer stared at him.

"How on earth did you know that?" Montero asked.

"You should be more careful with the papers you leave about on your desk. The art of reading upside down is one that I developed as a schoolboy and perfected in the army. It's served me well at a number of potentially difficult interviews. You have placed right under my nose, albeit facing away from me, a piece of paper which tells me that Seward was fined five pounds for assault causing actual bodily harm, in June 1953."

"You are a proper monkey, aren't you!" Springer said, with more admiration than rancour.

"We dug that out of the records," Montero explained. "There's nothing known about any of the others involved; and that affair of Seward's was only a little argument in a pub that ended in a fellow losing two teeth. Still, it shows that he's a man to be watched."

"Quite so. However, I think it would be as well if you didn't make this conviction of his too public just yet."

Montero looked shocked. "Why, Mr. Ludlow," he said, "we never give notice of past convictions, unless a man is found guilty of another crime and his record is asked for. Why, even if we were to charge Seward with the murder of Bould, and he was brought to trial, we couldn't say a word about it in court. That is, unless defence counsel called his character in evidence, or attacked the character of one of the witnesses——"

"That's all right then," said Ludlow who, like most dons, preferred giving instruction to receiving it. "We don't want to start any false alarms, and we don't want to put any guilty person on his guard." He sniffed loudly, for the cold which had begun in the church hall had not yet run all its damp progress. He looked expectantly at Montero, as if challenging him to make the next move. Montero went back to his window and said nothing.

The rain dripped steadily outside, turning the Embankment into a black mirror of despair over which shiny beetles skated about their errands. The office itself smelt damp. Springer began to whistle softly, then thought better of it and turned his mind to warm slippers and the buttered crumpets that might with luck be waiting for him at the end of the day. Ludlow wondered once again why he should be caught up in this business started by others who were scarcely known to him, and felt ready to curse the things that got named honour and conscience. When Montero spoke, it almost startled the other two, who had gone far from the track which he had never left.

"The trouble with this case," Montero said, "is that we're dealing with such a respectable set of people."

"I wouldn't be too sure of that, sir, from what we know so far," Springer said. "It sounds as if they were getting up to some high old games—and I wouldn't mind betting there's more to come."

"I know that. When I was still on the beat, I learned that if you take the lid off any suburban street you uncover enough to keep our most progressive young dramatists in business for life. But I'm much happier when I'm on the track of real criminals."

"But surely——" for once Ludlow was startled and showed it. "I mean, this is very clearly crime of the worst sort. Bould was clearly a very unsavoury character, but murder——"

"Murder it is, and that's exactly what I mean. A murderer is nearly always a man with a clean criminal record. He strikes once, for some motive of his own; and if we don't catch up with him, he probably goes on living as a pillar of his local society, respected by all as a gentleman and a gentle man. When I'm on a case of large-scale robbery, I've got a great deal more to go by. I can study the method used, and compare it with what we know of the methods of crooks who specialise in that sort of thing. I've got my contacts, who can tip me off if one of the regulars is missing from his usual haunts, or seems to have become very flush all of a sudden. But with murder, it's a different story altogether. Look at this bunch — not one of them known to the police except Seward, and he only for a minor offence that could happen to almost any man of his type. No, give me real crime if you want to spare what's left of my hair from premature loss."

Ludlow got up, as if something interesting had just occurred to him.

"I must get along," he said. "I have a great deal of work to do, which I do not intend to sacrifice to the pursuit of criminals, professional or occasional. Still, I may go out and have another look at Haleham Green. That is, if you have no objection."

"I'd be grateful if you would. I've learned to respect your way of getting to the root of things, though you may use methods that I wouldn't dare to use. So much the better. Let us know if you dig up anything — and thanks for what you've told us this morning."

"You're welcome, as our American friends say. Oh, in passing, what did you think of Mrs. Bould's performance yesterday in the solicitor's office?"

"She reacted as I'd expected in the circumstances," Montero said, looking a little surprised.

"Did she? Ah well, I'm sure you're right. Good morning, gentlemen."

Ludlow ambled out of the room, leaving two detectives with thoughtful faces, and the patter of rain on the window above the river.

CHAPTER EIGHT

Two Domestic Scenes

Tony Dexter and Frances Bould were sitting in the Crown, at the very table in the lounge where Ludlow and Montero had had their tea on the previous day. It was now evening, and the refreshment which a benevolent government allowed its subjects was more varied than tea. The rain which had chased itself dismally all the way from London and back again throughout the day had turned aside and given way to a colder wind which made the large open fire a welcome sight. They sat side by side on a high-backed settle, made ten years ago and blackened with great skill to look like a contemporary of the stage-coach. There was no one else in the lounge, and the small hatch through which drinks were served passed on little sign of life from the saloon bar on the other side. Thursday is a good night for quiet drinkers; the wage-packet has not been delivered, and the football pools demand posting by Friday morning at the latest. Frances clutched a gin and orange without much interest, and Dexter had a firm hold on a pint of bitter with much greater interest. When they spoke, their voices were low, and a stranger who did not know all that had passed in the last few days might have thought that this was some guilty liaison which must be concealed.

"It's no use pretending," said Frances, who had said the same thing in various forms several times already. "I know it looks bad for me to be here, but I think I'd hate myself more if I just went through the motions that everyone expects. Daddy was good to me in his way, and he gave me everything I wanted. But everything didn't quite include the most important thing. He wouldn't let himself be loved; he just wasn't there, when you tried to find something to take hold of and care for. I know he made Mother unhappy. And of course he was beastly to you, darling."

"Which everyone seems to know, including the police." Dexter glared at his pint before taking a comforting gulp. "The fact that he was doing all he could to break us up has been carefully written down in little black notebooks, and will no doubt be used in evidence against me sooner or later. Damn him. I'm sorry, darling, but as you say, it's no use pretending. I wonder whether he'd have succeeded eventually, if this hadn't happened."

"Oh Tony, how can you say that?"

"No, I don't think he would; I'm sure he wouldn't. But it would have made things very unpleasant for you."

"It's all over now."

"Is it? I think he's still chasing us, even now. Look at the will—it's as if even his kindness to you was directed to doing harm to me."

"What on earth do you mean? Tony, darling, haven't you been letting all this get too much on your mind?"

"Do you wonder if I have? Just look at it. Everyone knows I'm on bad terms with your father, because he doesn't want me to marry you. I have a row with him the very evening he's—murdered. There are a few minutes that I can't account for, when I could have done it. His death makes you quite a rich girl. Now do you see why I'm worried?"

"It sounds horrid, all put together like that. But surely——"

"That's how the police will put it together. And there won't be any shortage of people to help them fill out the details. You know how this place is swarming with gossip."

"I know. But after all, you aren't the only one they can

gossip about. I should think half the people in Haleham Green quarrelled with him at some time. And if it comes to that, hasn't June Morland got a lot of explaining to do?"

"After yesterday, I should think she has. I'm afraid there's only one likely explanation for your father's legacy to her."

"I know. Isn't it beastly? I'd half suspected it, but it seemed so impossible. I think Mother knew, and that was what was making her unhappy. Oh, it makes me feel sick."

"Still, it does give the police another person to suspect. And she didn't do herself any good by her odd behaviour at the end of the rehearsal. Also, Donald Hedge is going to be looked at very carefully, if he's as thick with her as everyone thinks. I suppose it's cowardly, but I'm very glad to see any chance of suspicion falling on someone other than myself."

"But, darling, no one could really suspect you. You're so kind, and sweet."

"I'm sure Inspector Montero wouldn't describe me like that. I was fool enough to let him trap me into telling him I'd been in the Commandos, and he probably thinks that puts me in line for being a killer. If he only knew how we all hated it——"

"Go and get yourself another drink, my precious. I don't like to see my boy upsetting himself."

"Frances, would it make any difference to you what I did—I mean, is there enough of me, really me, for you to love whatever happened?"

At this point the conversation became even more subdued, and ceased to be of any interest to students of the murder of Bartholomew Bould.

Meanwhile the few inhabitants of the saloon bar were casting glances at a tall, thin man, in a good but shabby tweed suit and shoes that needed cleaning, who had taken a chair in the corner and stretched his long legs out to the discomfort of lesser men. He puffed at a pipe, made great use of a metal instrument for scraping it, and was making a double whisky last a long time. People came and went. A sprinkling of late commuters on their way up from the station, swallowed a guilty light ale with one hand still grasping the rolled umbrella. Two youths in tight jeans called for gin and drank it with obvious distaste while proclaiming loudly how many they had had before coming there. A very old woman muttered into a glass of stout, stroking her shapeless leather handbag as if it were a cat. Ludlow sat, and watched, and listened.

A big, youngish man in working clothes tramped up to the bar and ordered a pint. Demolishing a third of it in one gulp, he leaned over the bar and demanded of the landlord.

"Where was the favourite in the last race?"

"Third," said the landlord with the grin he applied to all conversations with customers, on whatever topic. The other uttered a short word of Anglo-Saxon origin, the possible literary merits of which had been gravely debated by learned counsel not long ago.

"What won?" he inquired.

"Sunstream, twenty to one."

The disappointed gambler casts doubts on the ancestry of Sunstream.

"Mr. Fielding lost a packet on that," the landlord went on cheerfully. "He was in here a bit earlier on, told me he'd had a good tip but it didn't come off. He seemed fair cut up about it too. He's an unlucky gentleman with the horses. Then there's this nasty business about Mr. Bould, which he's bound to feel, them being neighbours, though some do say that they didn't get on none too well."

"Haven't the police found who done that yet? What do we pay our taxes for, that's what I'd like to know."

"Well Joe, be fair to them now. It's only three nights ago it happened. I reckon there are a power of things you and I wouldn't understand that have to be gone through. I mean, there's clues, and—well, other things."

"It's their job, that's what I say. I do my job, so why don't they do theirs?"

There seemed to be no answer to this, and the saloon bar lapsed back into silence. After a time, Tony Dexter was framed in the small hatch on the lounge side, having at last been released for his second pint. Ludlow got up quickly and carried his glass towards the connecting door. Then, remembering the etiquette and differentials of public houses, he swallowed what was left of his drink, left the glass on the bar and hurried round to reappear and order another from the surprised landlord in the lounge. A moment later, he was looming over Dexter and Frances in their private corner.

"Good heavens," he said with an air of mendacious surprise, "fancy seeing you again. I happened to be passing through here and decided to stop for a drink and a few minutes' warmth. I'm delighted to have come upon you."

Ludlow is not a good liar, but the other two were too concerned with each other and their immediate problems to detect any false note. Rather ungraciously, Dexter invited him to sit down and join them.

For a few minutes, conversation dragged and neither of them seemed inclined to respond to Ludlow's openings. At last Frances glared defiantly at him and said, "I suppose you think I'm wicked to be here tonight."

Ludlow felt a sudden compassion for the youth and innocence of the question, the fear that assumed sophistication could not mask, the bewilderment in the face of evil. He answered her seriously, and gently.

"I do not believe there is any real wickedness in you, Miss Bould. I have never been noted for observing social conventions for their own sake. You are too honest to put on a show of grief that you don't feel. At the same time, you are afraid, and that is something you can't conceal either. Why not tell me about it?"

Dexter shot a look of warning at her.

"You tell me something first," he said. "Are you working for the police."

"No. I am simply following my own curiosity, and a strange old-fashioned desire to see justice done. When I say justice, I'm thinking more of freeing the innocent than condemning the guilty, though I'm afraid one can't be done without the other."

"But you are a sort of detective, aren't you?"

"Not in the way you mean it." Ludlow relapsed into his more usual manner. "I've knocked about a good bit in London, and come up against the shadier side of life. You may think me a sheltered academic, but I have been in a few rough spots that would surprise you." He smiled reminiscently, and it must be confessed, with gross exaggeration. Dexter and Frances were suitably impressed, however, and within a few minutes they had laid all their fears before him. Ludlow nodded encouragingly from time to time, and when they seemed to have finished he pressed his fingertips together and looked at them as if they had been reading him a joint essay.

"We accept then," he said, "that Mr. Dexter here had both motive and opportunity for murder. Means too, since we know that he has had a Commando training and would have no difficulty at all in killing an unarmed man quickly and silently. Miss Bould has no apparent opportunity, and she provides part of Dexter's alibi for a large part of the time. However, she too had motives——"

"Look here," Dexter interrupted, "I won't have Frances brought into this."

"She's in it, isn't she? I was merely thinking aloud, with perfect objectivity. But if you don't want to discuss it any more, I'd better go."

"No, please don't. I'm sorry. I've been in a rotten state for so long now. I'm beginning to feel I'll go round the bend if things aren't straightened out soon. It's not just since Monday, but all the time since I had that awful row with him."

"Tell me about it."

"It must be nearly two weeks ago — yes, it was the Friday evening, two weeks tomorrow. I went round to Frances', and her father came in after I'd been there about an hour. He started going on to me, picked a quarrel in fact, until he said such things that I just had to answer back. That finished it. He could say rotten things himself, but he couldn't stand anyone answering him in the same way. I'm sorry to say it now, but it's true and Frances knows it's true. That time, I just had to come away, and he followed me down the path, shouting after me. Frances came to persuade me to calm down, but I lost my head, and was shouting that I'd do him in. Of course I didn't mean it, but we all shout crazy things like that sometimes, don't we?"

Ludlow mused for a moment over a mental image of himself loudly threatening to do in some of his less agreeable colleagues, but found the picture unconvincing though not unpleasing.

"Did anybody hear all this?" he asked.

"Half the road, I should think. Clifford Fielding must have, and the Daces as well."

"Who are the Daces?"

"Mr. and Mrs. Dace live next door," Frances explained. "They're an old couple — he's a retired bank manager — and they don't miss much that goes on."

"They're nosey," said Dexter.

"So you have Mr. Fielding living on one side of you and these Daces on the other?"

"Yes. The houses are detached, but not very far apart. They must have heard all that happened."

"Most unfortunate." Ludlow made another of his unexpectedly sudden movements, and was out of the bar almost before they could say good night to him.

He was getting familiar with the lay-out of Haleham Green which indeed does not take very long to master, and his glance through the statements which Montero had taken on Monday night had given him a useful list of addresses. Bould's house was not far away. He left Cleopatra parked in the forecourt of the Crown and started off on foot, hoping that the nosey Daces would have some information for him. The road that he sought started with a group of semi-detached houses that huddled in fear of the traffic in the main street near by. In fifty yards it passed from clerks to managers, with houses that had little to commend them except for being separate and set well back from the road. Knowing the name (nothing so common as numbers here) of Bould's house and of Fielding's, even a less acute mind could have deduced that The Cedars must belong to Mr. and Mrs. Dace. No cedars were apparent, but the privet hedge was very neat and the path was kept free of encroaching grass. A light glowed through thick curtains at the side of the house. Thus encouraged, Ludlow reached the front door and knocked quietly. After a couple of minutes he knocked louder, and this produced a faint shriek and a patter of feet that seemed to be going away from the front door. Eventually they pattered back, and a woman's voice from somewhere near Ludlow's waist asked what he wanted, through an opening of not more than six inches.

"I'd like to talk to you for a few minutes if you would be so kind," Ludlow said.

The door opened to nine inches and a face crowned by straggling grey hair peered up at him. Neither spoke, and the situation seemed to have reached an impasse when the door was jerked fully open and a bald man, who reached halfway up Ludlow's chest, stood there with waxed moustaches bristling and looking like a valiant dwarf in a fairy-story.

"Come in, man," he said in a surprisingly deep voice, "and don't stand there making the house cold. Leave your coat here. This way. Sit there. What do you want to know?"

Ludlow found himself obeying orders and sitting down in an overcrowded but pleasant room while his host took the chair opposite him. Mrs. Dace returned calmly to a hard chair away from the fire and took up the knitting which she had dropped on the floor in her first excitement.

"I'm investigating the murder of Bartholomew Bould," Ludlow began.

"The police have been here about it," said Dace.

Ludlow's heart sank at this, and he began to explain about being a friend of Inspector Montero. But Dace clearly spoke from pride and not from annoyance, and was more than ready to be heard all over again.

"I suppose," Ludlow said cautiously, "you must have known Mr. Bould and his family pretty well."

"I'd known him for years, and I hated the sight of him. And don't tell me that I shouldn't speak ill of the dead," he added, turning on his wife who had shown no sign of saying anything or even being aware of the conversation. "I know my duty, and it doesn't include hypocrisy. Is that right, Mr. — what's your name?"

"Ludlow. Yes, I quite agree with you. I think you're right."

"I know I'm right. Ask me something else."

"You didn't find Mr. Bould very likeable, then?"

"I've just said so. He was a miser, a snob and a bully. He had immoral relations with other women and he treated his wife abominably. Don't tell me I've no proof, because I keep my eyes open," he shouted at his wife, perhaps to point the difference between himself and Bould in this respect.

"I'm sure you are a very careful observer, Mr. Dace."

"I don't miss much that goes on here. Now, what is it that you really want to know?"

"For one thing, I wondered whether you knew anything about Bould's attitude to Mr. Fielding, who lives on the other side."

"Fielding's a waster. He drinks, and he gambles. He and Bould used to get on quite well, and their wives are still friendly. But the men fell out over one thing and another. There were rows about the garden, and about Fielding's dog which is a nasty great brute, if it comes to that. And they say that there was trouble about money. Gambling debts." He lowered his voice as he spoke the last phrase, and looked at his wife as if it were some strange obscenity of which she must never know.

"Yes, I had the same impression."

"Did you now: how much was it for?"

"I really couldn't say," replied Ludlow, resolving not to volunteer any more information to those insatiable ears. He went on, "Do you know Tony Dexter at all well?"

"I've known him since he came to live here, which is nine years ago. The last few months he's been practically living next door. He has a nasty temper."

"Now why do you say that?"

"Because I have evidence of it. What evidence, you ask. The best evidence, the evidence of my own eyes and ears. Two weeks ago tomorrow he was standing out there on the drive and cursing Bould in the most abominable way. I heard him, yes, I myself heard him, threaten to murder Bould. What do you think of that? Threatening to murder your potential father-in-law."

"He must have had a lot of provocation."

"I daresay. Bould did all he could to break the engagement. He was always insulting Dexter. But I still say that young man's got a nasty temper."

"Why did Bould oppose the engagement so much?"

"I'll tell you." Dace leaned forward as if to divulge further dreadful things. "Dexter had been divorced. And don't tell me it was he who divorced his wife, because it comes to the same thing theologically, if it's a question of remarriage."

The last remark had been shouted at the mute Mrs. Dace, but Ludlow decided to take it up.

"Was Bould then a man of strong religious convictions?" he asked.

"Had none at all, that I ever saw. I've been a sidesman at St. Edmund's for over thirty years, and I've never seen him inside the place. Or any of them for that matter, though I suppose she'll be claiming the right to be married there. Young Dexter has a surprise coming, if he thinks he'll get away with that when he has a wife still alive. We shall have some fun. No, I don't know the reason, but Bould had a strong prejudice against divorce. It seemed to anger him. without any sound belief to justify him."

"Had he lived here long?" Ludlow asked.

"Twenty-five years next March. He'd just been married. He didn't live next door then, and I didn't have this house for that matter. But he banked with me from the start, and his account grew year by year. Oh, it grew; you'd be surprised if I told you how it grew . . ."

Ludlow felt thankful that he had not told Dace about hearing the will read, or he would have been required to quote all the details. He said,

"You mentioned Bould's going with other women. Do you know of any in particular?"

"You mean to say you don't know? You're not much of a detective, if you don't know that Bould was carrying on flagrantly with a red-haired woman called June Morland, who fancies herself as an actress. And that wasn't the first, though I admit he's been quieter in the last few years. But at one time I used to hear a good bit of talk at the bank about this one and that one. They say the wife's always the last to know, but she knew about June Morland all right. I was in my little shed, planting bulbs in fibre for the spring, and I could hear her going on at him in their room at the back. She knew all right. I'll say this much, though, they did try to keep it from the girl."

"What do you think of Frances?" asked Ludlow, wondering what scandal Dace would produce about her.

"She's not a bad child, except that she's headstrong and wilful and brought up to have her own way."

"I see. Well, thank you, Mr. Dace. You've been most helpful and I won't disturb you any longer."

"Don't you want to know any more?" asked Dace, looking disappointed.

"Nothing at present, thank you. Perhaps I may call and see you again."

Ludlow was ushered out of the room and into his coat, while Mrs. Dace sat unmoved on her hard chair. At the door, Dace seized Ludlow by the arm and peered up into his face.

"You're a young man," he said.

"Well, not very. As a matter of fact——"

"But you won't always be young. One day you'll find you're ready to retire. Then you'll look round, and you'll get a house in a little place like this."

"I've really no idea where——"

"I'll give you a piece of advice, and you remember it when that day comes. Never start listening to gossip, and never repeat it. A place like this is full of scandals, but keep out of them. Good night."

Bemused but not dissatisfied with his visit, Ludlow stumbled down the neat path and out through the gate. Slipping quickly passed the Boulds' house, he found himself at a gate of rustic work which opened on another well-tended garden. A depressed-looking clay gnome fished without hope in a small lily-pond on the lawn. In the porch of the house, a wrought-iron lantern shielded the electric bulb from perils of wind, and cast light on a painted plaque which announced in a festoon of primroses, "Here live Clifford and Doris Fielding." Thus reassured, Ludlow rang the bell. This seemed to unleash a pack of wolves inside the house. At last Fielding's voice was heard above the furious yelping and Ludlow valiantly decided to stand firm. The door opened and an enormous dog leapt at him with murderous cries. Fielding appeared in the hall-way and peered out.

"Take it easy, Carlos old boy—oh, it's you, Mr. Ludlow — let go of the gentleman's sleeve, Carlos — come in and get warm — let him come in, he's a friend of ours — he's only playing."

Ludlow obeyed his share of these instructions better than Carlos, who continued to jump up and make hungry noises.

"Could the dog be persuaded not to attack me while the process of removing my overcoat prevents me from defending myself?" Ludlow asked politely.

"It's all right, old boy. He won't eat you."

"Perhaps not, but I should prefer not even to be tasted."

Fielding led the way into a room where a good fire helped to make up for the plastic geese and commercial horse-brasses. A plump woman with fading blonde hair was introduced as "the wife" and immediately despatched to the kitchen to make coffee. Ludlow sat down and anxiously watched Carlos take up a position which absorbed most of the warmth from the fire. Except for turning one bloodshot eye at him from time to time, the dog seemed to have accepted the loss of his prey with a fairly good grace.

"This is quite an honour, old boy," Fielding said. "Jolly good of you to look us up. It's the first time there's been a Professor inside our little place. Are you staying here for a long week-end or something?"

Beneath his heartiness there was suspicion and hostility. Ludlow made a quick choice of what manner to adopt.

"As a matter of fact," he said with the light tone that does not come easily to him, "I'm just paying a short visit in pursuit of a little hobby of mine."

"And what's that — bird-watching?"

"Not at any time, and certainly not in this weather."

"Well, there are birds and birds, aren't there, old boy? I heard of a little one that was hopping around trying to get a peck at you yesterday, and took a morning off to fly into London."

"And who told you all that?" asked Ludlow, wondering whether they paid people to be spies in Haleham Green or whether it was all down for amusement only.

"Just another little bird or two. But what's the hobby, then?"

"Murder." Ludlow saw Fielding jerk so sharply that Carlos gave a growl.

"You mean you like slipping weed-killer in people's tea? Jolly idea!"

"I mean that I like to find out why people behave as they do, and what forces can drive one human being to take away the life of another. And I like to find the solution to problems. Old boy," he added, feeling the light touch beginning to slip.

"You've done this sort of thing before, haven't you?"

"I've been able to make some use of my observation and deductive powers to help the police. At present I'm working on my own, though of course Inspector Montero is following his official investigation too. I'm sure you must feel that this unhappy business must be cleared up as soon as possible."

"Can't say I care much. I mean, it's not a nice thing to happen and it meant that a lot of work on that play went for nothing. But if the police can't solve it, then it's not my worry."

"Isn't it the worry of all the innocent people who might be suspected?"

"I always thought that in this country an innocent man has nothing to fear; correct me if I'm wrong."

"You didn't get on well with Bould." Ludlow shot it at him more as an assertion than a question. Fielding started forward again, and got another sympathetic growl in response.

"He wasn't exactly what you'd call a likeable man," he said. "I tried to make a go of it when we came here first, but we were always having rows about things like the garden, and poor old Carlos here."

"Yes, I know," said Ludlow with an anxious glance at poor old Carlos. "And of course it's difficult to like a man to whom you owe a substantial sum of money."

Fielding went white. He was spared any further effort to speak by the appearance of his wife with a tray of coffee and biscuits. For a few minutes they all talked trivialities, until Fielding made it clear by many signs that he wanted to be left alone with Ludlow again. He had recovered his old manner by the time his wife left.

"We were talking about debts and all that. Well, old boy, it's true that I did owe old Bould a few quid. But if people got knocked off for that, there'd be a few more murders than there are."

"Oh, indeed yes. I'd hardly call five hundred pounds a few quid, but I suppose it's a question of comparative values."

"You devil," Fielding said, all his composure destroyed, "are you trying to blackmail me?"

"Certainly not. Besides, I doubt if you would be a very profitable subject for it at present. The debt to Bould is still recoverable, and you lost a good deal today by Sunstream's success in the last race."

Fielding got up and trod on Carlos, who surprisingly took

no notice except to grunt and turn over. If Ludlow had suddenly levitated himself to the ceiling, he could not have caused a greater sensation. Fielding gaped and gasped at him until words somehow formed themselves again.

"What do you want from me?"

"Only a bit of information," said Ludlow, hugely enjoying himself. "As you can tell, I have my ways of getting to know what I want. Your private losses are not my concern. By the way, how did you get Bould to lend you so much money after your frequent quarrels?"

"It was the wives mostly. Doris and his wife have kept pally, and Doris is a good little woman when I'm in a tight spot. And it didn't come all at once. A lot of it was when we were still on fair terms, and he didn't make me sign a paper for the whole lot until fairly recently. Anyway, he could afford it. And he liked having power over people — you heard him that night in the hall, and you obviously know what it was all about. I'd have paid him back all right; I've just had a run of bad luck lately, that's all."

"I sympathise, but as I said it isn't really my concern. What I do want to know is something more about Monday evening. You went to the kitchen, forgetting for the moment that Bould was there, and it seems that you must have been the last person to see him alive."

"Except the murderer, please."

"Oh, of course. But this makes it very important to know how he appeared to you at that time. Was he alert, or did he show any sign of being sleepy and dull? Was he cheerful?"

"He was in fine form. He seemed to have got over his bit of temper, and we chatted away for a few minutes like old pals."

'And that isn't what you told Montero,' Ludlow thought.

"Another question. What do you think of Miss Morland?"

"June?" Fielding looked startled, then relieved and finally leered.

"I thought we'd come back to her soon, old boy. Pretty little thing, isn't she?"

"Perhaps I should have framed my question more carefully. What is your opinion of her character?"

"Character? A pretty girl like that doesn't need to bother about character, what? I tell you, though, I shouldn't be surprised if there was a bit of hearty slap and tickle between her and Bould."

Ludlow showed a look of distaste, which was misinterpreted by Fielding but drove him to further speech.

"She's a decent kid, though. No nonsense about her. She's got a will of her own, and she made a pretty good job of being secretary. At the moment it looks as if she's got her hooks into Donald Hedge — and my bet is that she'll have him up the church path before long. Not that he seems to need much dragging, and I don't blame him either. She's pretty keen on him, actually, and she's loyal. She used to stick up for him whenever Terry Colbert was tearing him up for making mistakes at rehearsals."

"Thank you so much, Mr. Fielding." Ludlow got up with an urbanity that was immediately shattered by a renewed attack from Carlos. This time, however, the dog was more sternly rebuked. Mrs. Fielding emerged from the kitchen to which she had been exiled, was politely thanked for the coffee, and was obviously surprised at her husband's restrained manner. Fielding walked down to the gate with Ludlow. There he stopped and looked grimly at his uninvited guest.

"You'd better be careful, Ludlow," he said. "You seem to find out too bloody much. If you go round here trying to put the screws on people, somebody will do you sooner or later. There was one who twisted Bould's neck, and he might do the same for you if you get across him."

"Really?" said Ludlow with more calm than he felt. "Are you by any chance making a personal threat?"

"I'm talking about whoever it was that killed Bould. Good night."

Fielding walked back quickly to his house, and Ludlow was no less quick in getting back to the lights of the main street. Once there, he decided that Mrs. Fielding's coffee could absorb another drink at the Crown, before Cleopatra was summoned to carry him back to London.

CHAPTER NINE

A Little Prompting is Needed

"And then in 1753 the third baronet gave us land for the headmaster's house, in the part of the grounds where we now have the new science block."

Montero and Springer exchanged glances and then looked in unison at their watches, but Mr. Emberson went on talking. He had now traced the history of Haleham Grammar School from its foundation after the suppression of Haleham Abbey and there were still nearly two hundred years to go before he reached the year that had put it almost entirely under the control of the local Education Authority. Mr. Emberson loved the school of which he was the fussy and devoted headmaster and had spent a great deal of time on research into its development. If the history which he was now writing ever saw publication, it would have little in it that was new to most of the local people or to anyone who had visited the school, for Mr. Emberson would expound to a defenceless traveller in educational supplies with as much enthusiasm as he would address the Haleham Green Historical Society.

The story rolled on, though overhead and all around them the sounds of scraping chairs and pounding feet showed that classes were changing for the last period of the afternoon. A nervous sun dabbed at the puddles on the drive outside and retreated behind another cloud with obvious distaste for the whole scene. Not that it was an unattractive building as grammar schools go. Built mostly a few years before the war but keeping some traces of earlier work, it stood on the outskirts of Haleham Green with its back to the common and its face turned aspiringly in the direction of London. Even in the headmaster's study, the sound of traffic on the main road was muted but not extinguished. Montero sat as upright as he could in a deep leather armchair and waited for an opening.

"It was a few years later than Samuel Hearnshaw came here as a boy. He became a famous actor, you know, and was a great favourite at Drury Lane. I said to Colbert when he was producing one of Sheridan's plays with the local dramatic society——"

"Yes, Mr. Colbert — I've met him," Montero said, looking like a man who has got his grip on a lifeline and is not going to have it dragged away. "I wanted to ask you something about the unfortunate affair that stopped the play from being put on."

"Ah yes, poor Mr. Bould; he was one of our governors. A most unfortunate affair, as you say. Strangely enough, one of the masters at this school was murdered close by the church, about the place where the church hall stands now."

"When was that?" asked Springer, sitting up with interest.

"Let me see, 1809, or was it 1807? It was when Jefford was headmaster, and in fact it was said at the time——"

"What is your opinion of Colbert?" asked Montero, seeing the rapid disappearance of his new hope.

"Colbert? Oh yes, Colbert. He seems to be getting on very well. The head of the English Department is well satisfied with his work. And certainly he has done splendid work for the school play."

"How long has he been here?"

"Just over two years. I hope he'll stay, because he really has the makings of a very good teacher indeed."

"You've had no complaints about him, or his work?"

"No. He seems popular in the common room, and he is

apparently well liked by the amateur society for which he produces."

"I'm glad to hear that, sir. I did have the impression that there had been some trouble here in the school between him and Mr. Bould."

"Oh, I think I know what you mean, Inspector." Mr. Emberson looked embarrassed. "That was nothing at all really. Colbert was taking some boys across to the hall from a classroom, and they got mixed up, as it were, with Mr. Bould."

"What was Mr. Bould doing here at the time?"

"He was a governor," said Mr. Emberson, as if that explained and forgave everything. "He took a great interest in the school, and liked to come and look round sometimes without waiting for an official visit of the Board."

"I bet that made him popular," said the irrepressible Springer.

"My school is always ready for inspection, officer." Springer retired behind his notebook.

"But what happened on this particular occasion?" Montero asked.

"As I said, Colbert was taking some boys across to the school hall, for a rehearsal. They were running round a corner and collided with Mr. Bould, nearly knocking him off his balance. He was not a large man. He was naturally very annoyed and spoke sharply to Colbert who was following them. I'm afraid that Colbert did not reply very tactfully."

"So Mr. Bould came and complained to you. What did you do about it?"

"I think I was able to satisfy him that it was only an unfortunate accident."

"Did you take any action against Colbert?"

"I reprimanded him. He should have been in proper charge of the boys, making them follow him in an orderly manner instead of running ahead. That's what I was taught when I was a young master. But I fear that discipline has sadly deteriorated, and in any case it's not Colbert's strong point. No doubt he will learn."

"There was no question of his dismissal, or anything like that?"

"Oh no. It was not a very serious affair. And I must admit that Mr. Bould was rather prone to make complaints. Though of course he was a great friend of the school, a great friend. I know that he really had quite a good opinion of Colbert, because of his interest in the local dramatic society."

"Do you know any other members of that society?" Montero shot the question unexpectedly.

"Let me see now. There's Hedge of course — the chemist in the High Street, but I know him only by way of business. I think one or two of our sixth form have been used for small parts. And Colbert did bring one of the members to the school, to give a demonstration to the Gymnastic and Boxing Club. His name was Dexter, I think. Yes, that's it, Dexter."

"What did he demonstrate?"

"Some type of wrestling, which he called unarmed combat. No doubt it was all very skilful, but some of it did seem rather brutal. And the effect on the boys was most unfortunate; they were throwing each other about all over the school for days."

"Miss Monica Stafford belongs to the Thespians too, doesn't she?"

"Dear me, yes, I'd quite forgotten. I don't believe she acts though, but helps Colbert in various ways."

"She is your secretary here, I think. Is she satisfactory?"

"Quite excellent. Good secretaries are rare nowadays. She has come to know the school really well, and has given me a lot of help with my private researches. Which reminds me that I have got quite away from the history of the school.

Forgive me for troubling you with these rather sordid modern happenings. I think I was just telling you about the time whan Samuel Hearnshaw——"

"I'd very much like to hear more about the school, Mr. Emberson, but I'm afraid it will have to wait. Sergeant Springer and I must get back to London soon. Before we go, could I possibly have a word with Colbert, and then with Miss Stafford? I won't keep either of them long."

"Certainly." Seeming not at all put out by the interruption of his recital, the headmaster wandered across to an enormous timetable on the wall. "Colbert seems to have a free period now," he said. "I'll send for him."

"That's very kind of you, sir."

"Use this room. I'll take a stroll round the school."

Mr. Emberson left them, with an amiable smile, and the two detectives had time for several deep breaths before Colbert arrived. When he did, he was hardly recognisable as the dishevelled young man who had leapt about in a frenzy of artistic excitement at the church hall a few days before. Yet under the blue suit and the neat silk tie, there seemed to lurk a figure in a sweater and jeans, screaming to get out.

"Sit down, Mr. Colbert," Montero said. "We are just going through some of the statements we took on Monday. Is there anything you would like to add to yours?"

"I don't think so, Inspector." Terry Colbert ran his hands through his hair and immediately began to look more like his real self. "I was so concerned with the rehearsal that I didn't have time to pay attention to anything else."

"You didn't notice anything unusual during the course of the rehearsal itself?"

"No, only June Morland going out and coming back all upset. That wasn't like her—I always thought she was pretty unflappable. It was a bad rehearsal, but no worse than many I've seen."

"I understand that Mr. Hedge was rather off form, if that's the right expression for an actor."

"Donald is always pretty awful. I only use him because we're so short of men — and anyway he is teachable. He hasn't got much acting ability in him, but he does listen to what I tell him. That evening he was really bad; and in the end he lost his temper with me and nearly walked off the stage. After that I more or less let him get on with it. But at the end I simply had to do the screen scene again to lead up to his bit at the end, because that had been simply frightful. That's how Bould's body was discovered."

"But presumably you didn't know at the time that it was there."

"No, of course not."

"Have you any idea why Hedge was so bad that night?"

"It was obvious that someone had upset him. I did wonder whether he and June had had a row, since they were both in rather a state. We've been expecting an engagement there for some time. Anyway, they seem as close as ever now."

"About your own movements that evening, Mr. Colbert. You have told us that you did not leave the main body of the hall at any time after the interval until Bould's body was found behind the screen, except for going on the stage at one point to correct something that Mr. Hedge was doing, or not doing. Do you wish to alter that statement?"

"No. I was in the hall all the time—I had to be, as producer. At one point Donald was so badly out of position that I just had to go up and correct him. That was when he lost his temper, so I went back and stayed pretty quiet. You have to know when to let people alone."

"You didn't go to the kitchen at the back, on your way to or from the stage?"

"No — how could I? I called out to Donald, then ducked

through the curtains and went up on the stage. After he flared up, I came straight back."

"Through the curtains again?"

"No, I vaulted over the front of the stage — it's not very high."

"Thank you, Mr. Colbert. What you tell us is confirmed by other witnesses, so I hope we shan't have to bother you again. You never know, though."

"We're all under suspicion until this is cleared up, aren't we?"

"Let us rather say, you are all of some interest in our investigations. Get in touch with me if you think of anything, however trivial it may seem, which might suggest that anything out of the ordinary was going on in the hall that night. Perhaps you would be so good as to ask Miss Stafford to come in for a moment, if she is in the small office outside."

Monica Stafford came in looking pleased and important. She flashed her not-very-attractive eyes and hair at Montero, and answered his questions so volubly that Springer's notebook was kept busy. She could add nothing, however, to what they already knew. It was only Montero's persistence, and his instinct for a hidden clue, that eventually brought them something important.

"You are quite sure that Mr. Colbert did not leave the hall during the second half of the rehearsal?"

"Quite certain. After Donald Hedge had been so silly, Terry came straight off the stage and stood by my chair all the time. I don't know why you're keeping on at the poor boy. I suppose it's because Mr. Bould tried to make trouble for him here, and you think he wanted revenge. Well, Terry isn't like that——"

"We know all about the little unpleasantness with Mr. Bould, and it doesn't seem at all serious. If it's any comfort to you, we are going just as deeply into everyone's movements that evening, and we are certainly not making any special attack on Mr. Colbert. He is by no means the only one to have had words with Mr. Bould."

"He certainly isn't. I think Mr. Bould was a beast, and I'm not afraid to say so."

"Did you have any personal reason to dislike him, Miss Stafford?"

"No, I don't think he ever spoke to me. But he was horrid — trying to get Terry into trouble here, and the same sort of thing with Arthur Seward, and so nasty to Frances and Tony Dexter, and the absolutely frightful way he behaved to June — oh, perhaps I shouldn't have told you that."

"We know all about that," Montero said reassuringly. "I believe that was why Miss Morland was so upset at one point during the dress rehearsal."

"Yes, it was after she had been to see Mr. Bould and ask him about the letter."

"What letter?" asked Springer, letting down his superior's claim to know everything, but Monica went on unchecked.

"The letter that was sent to Donald Hedge. A horrid, anonymous letter, telling him all about what had been going on between June and that awful man. June was sure Mr. Bould must have written it — that's what she went to the kitchen to try to find out."

"Did Miss Morland herself tell you all this?"

"Yes, we're quite good friends. I knew all about her affair, and how she broke it off when she fell in love with Donald. The day after that terrible evening she told me about the letter. Donald had got it in the morning before the dress rehearsal."

"Which was no doubt why he was so upset that evening?"

"Yes. He knew June had been having an affair, but not who with. It must have been an awful shock for him, because one would rather it were almost anybody than that man. But he's so fond of June that I'm sure it's going to be all right. Love will find a way."

"No doubt it will. Thank you very much, Miss Stafford."

Getting rid of Monica before she could upset him with any more sentimental clichés, Montero looked very pleased with himself.

"Truth is hidden under a great deal of irrelevance, Jack. We have a few grains there that were well worth sifting out. Tell me what you make of it, omitting any reference to the murky history of Haleham Green Grammar School."

"We know," said Springer, "that Dexter is a tough guy; which we knew before. We know that June Morland is a liar; which we had guessed. And we know that Donald Hedge had a thundering good reason for taking a crack at Bould. I must say I'll be sorry if we have to take him in for it. But I don't know whether we're much nearer to knowing which of them did it. Do you, sir?"

"No. But I'm getting an interesting picture of all the tensions and hatreds that were building up round the character of Bould. If we follow each one through, we shall see which snapped first. Come on, let's give the headmaster back his study. We're going to pay a visit to Donald Hedge, before he shuts up shop for the day."

Leaving the school, they drove back to the High Street. Outside the Crown a familiar car was parked, with a tall figure bending over the engine and swearing vividly.

"I'll have to charge you with using obscene language," said Montero, creeping up on Ludlow, who straightened suddenly and hit his head on the open bonnet.

"I was simply quoting to myself to pass the time," Ludlow said. "If you find some sections of English literature obscene, the fault is in your mind and not in the poets."

"It didn't sound very poetical to me. Anyway, why don't you buy a car sometime, and keep your hands and your tongue clean?"

"Cleopatra is something more than a car; she's a character."

"She certainly is. And what are you doing back in Haleham Green?"

"I am in pursuit of truth."

"Really. So are we. Then we are agreed on that at least, and shun the company of those who delight in giddiness and count it bondage to fix a belief, as Bacon says."

"Isn't that the bloke who's supposed to have written Shakespeare?" Springer asked, trying to keep up. The other two turned looks of such disgust upon him that he buried his head in Cleopatra's engine and was soon able to announce success.

"Thank you," said Ludlow. "Now I must get along. I've wasted a lot of time this week. Dashing out here after teaching is bad for my digestion."

"We're just going to have a talk with Donald Hedge. Do you want to come with us, and see if he can mix you something to put your digestion right?"

"You won't get anything out of him," Ludlow said. "I've just been talking to him, but he refuses to say anything about Monday night."

"He'll talk to us," said Montero with grim certainty, "when he hears what we've come to know this afternoon. By the way, Mr. Ludlow, I suppose you did tell us the whole truth about what June Morland told you on Wednesday. Or let's put it this way, which may make it easier for you. Did you materially distort any of the information she gave you?"

"Anyone would think that I was suspected of killing Bould," Ludlow said. "You policemen do get the most extraordinary ideas of your own importance. And how can anything material be done to information, which is abstract? You ought to know better, and I'm sure you do. Where was I? Oh yes. No, I did not change her story; I told it to you as she told it to me. Why should you begin to doubt my integrity now?"

Montero told me what he had learnt from Monica Stafford. Ludlow listened carefully and then asked for a full account of the afternoon's evidence, which seemed to please him greatly. He was unperturbed when Montero, coming back to June, said:

"So you see, your little friend is proved to be a very big liar. Unless Monica Stafford is a bigger one, and I see no reason why she should be."

"I think you can accept as true everything that Monica Stafford has told you," said Ludlow. "I'm sure she hasn't the ability to lie well, and everything in her remarks that has been checked with other witnesses has been proved to be true. But Miss Morland is not a big liar, only an average-sized one. She told a story that seems to have been basically true. She lied only in saying that Hedge heard the whole story of her liaison with Bould from her and not from an anonymous letter."

"Put like that, there's something in what you say. Perhaps it was only face-saving on her part. Or wishful thinking — they had such a row about it that now she wishes she *had* told him first. Still, they seem to have made it up all right now. It's pretty clear that girl is scared about something. Could be that she's afraid of Hedge and is trying hard to get round him again. Let's have a look at him, anyway."

In spite of his earlier refusal, Ludlow's interest was now aroused again and he trotted up the High Street with the other two. Donald Hedge's shop, outside which Ludlow had met him on his first visit to Haleham Green, was small and overcrowded, but had a certain air of quality which still drew custom away from the larger chain-chemists which stood at opposite ends of the street. A bell sounded as Montero opened the door, but Donald was already behind the counter and did not look at all like a man who would have to be summoned from afternoon sleep in the parlour. Indeed he looked as if he had had very little sleep for several nights. He was thinner than when Ludlow had first seen him; and now without the make-up he had been wearing on Monday evening, his face was pale and his eyes seemed to have fallen back more deeply. He glared at Ludlow and braced himself to face Montero. The Inspector, however, seemed to be in no hurry but contented himself with wandering around and looking at various kinds of shaving soap.

"You carry a good stock here, Mr. Hedge," he remarked after a time.

"I try to. It's only by being able to offer a few special lines that I get by."

"You make out of people's vanity what you lose on their diseases?"

"That's about it. The medical side is hardly worthwhile, but the rest makes things possible."

"You're a young man to have your own shop."

"It was my uncle's. It was always understood that I would take over from him — he was a bachelor — as soon as I started to show an interest in this sort of thing when I was a boy. I came here to help him and learn the business as soon as I was qualified, and he died suddenly six months later. I manage on my own, and get a part-time asistant for Saturdays and holidays."

"Do you live here alone?"

"Yes, there's a small flat above."

"A lonely life for you."

"Not really. I'm out a lot in the evenings, with the Thespians and other things. I quite enjoy life here."

Dozens of regular criminals in London could have warned Donald that Montero was busy on what was known as his "old softening-up lark". Now he pounced.

"Mr. Hedge, I am not entirely satisfied with the account of your movements which you gave me on Monday evening.

I'm going to give you a chance now to tell me anything more that you know about the murder of Bartholomew Bould, and I advise you to take advantage of this chance before it is too late."

Donald Hedge tensed himself, and became if possible even paler than before. When he spoke, his voice was firm and controlled.

"I knew on Monday," he said, "and I know now, that you cannot compel me to make any statement. There are laws which can stop you from threatening me, and if necessary I shall make use of them. I have told you the truth, and I shall say no more to you except in the presence of a solicitor."

There was silence in the shop. Springer scowled at an expensive bottle of hand-lotion and Ludlow seemed to be counting the bottles of cough mixture above Donald's head. Only Montero remained unembarrassed as he turned and opened the door.

"Just one thing," he said, his foot poised on the step. "Though you've said that you won't answer me, I can still give you one bit of information. I believe that you are holding a piece of evidence which may considerably help us in our investigations. I shall be coming back with a search-warrant to find it. You can receive me in perfect silence if you wish."

"I've no evidence. What are you talking about?"

"The anonymous letter which you received on Monday morning and which caused you to act so badly at the dress rehearsal. Good afternoon."

"Come here," said Donald, running to the door and thrusting Ludlow and Springer aside. "Don't go. I haven't tried to conceal that — you never asked me about it."

"I was going to, but you assured me that you wouldn't tell me any more. Are you going to now?"

"I suppose so. But how did you find out about it? Did June——?"

Montero came back and sat on the single, high and uncomfortable chair by the counter, leaving the other three grouped round in a tableau that might have stood for an allegory of different degrees of Surprise, in which Donald Hedge would certainly have been the superlative.

"It may comfort you to know," Montero said calmly, "that Miss Morland did all she could to conceal the existence of that letter. Naughty of her, though perhaps understandable in the circumstances. I suppose she did know about it?"

"Yes. I told her as soon as I had got it."

"That was on Monday of this week?"

"Yes."

"Did you go to see her about it?"

"I rang her up at work and asked her to meet me for lunch."

"Was that necessary, as you were going to meet her at a rehearsal that same evening?"

"I knew there'd be no chance to talk there. Anyway, I was too upset to wait."

"It appears then that the revelation of what had been going on between the two of them was a complete surprise to you?"

"I knew that she had been having some kind of an affair, and I had decided not to press her about it. She assured me that it was all over and I believed her. It was certainly a shock to learn that it had been Bould."

"What was your first reaction on receiving the letter?"

"Well—anger, I suppose. Anger against Bould for having taken advantage of her like that. That's what you wanted me to say, isn't it?"

"Who do you think sent the letter?" Montero asked, ignoring Hedge's last question.

"I suppose Bould himself, naturally."

"Why should he accuse himself?"

"He thought he could break it up between us and get June back. I don't think he could understand any woman preferring someone else to him. And he was too conceited and sure of himself to think that anyone might take revenge on him."

"You think that revenge was taken, then?"

"I didn't say that — you're twisting my words. Is this an official statement."

"It is not. Did you keep the letter?"

"You know I did — you said so a few minutes ago, or were you just trying to trap me?"

"I should never think of trapping anybody, Mr. Hedge. Let me see the letter, please."

Donald Hedge hesitated for a moment, then seemed to sag and lose hope as he turned and went up the stairs which led to the upper floor. He returned with a piece of paper which he gave to Montero. The Inspector studied it for a moment, then nodded and put it carefully in his wallet.

"I am keeping it as a piece of material evidence," he said. "You will get it back when this case is solved, or when we decide that it is no help towards solving it."

"I don't want to see it again," Donald said. "I don't know why I've kept it. I just pushed it into a pocket and nearly forgot about it until now."

"Did you show this note to Mr. Bould at any time?" Montero leaned forward over the counter like a persistent commercial traveller as he spoke.

"No, I didn't."

"Or mention it to him at any time?"

"No."

"Not even when you spoke to him in the kitchen at the church hall, on Monday night?"

"I've already told you that he wasn't in the kitchen when I went to get a drink of water."

"Do you persist in that story?"

"Certainly I do."

"But you did go there with the intention of speaking to him, didn't you?"

"All right, I did. I couldn't let it rest any longer, and I slipped out to the kitchen at the end of my part. I was surprised that he wasn't there, and I stood there just feeling empty and miserable until they started calling me to come back on the stage."

"Very well, I'll leave it there for the moment. We shall probably be coming to see you again."

As the two detectives left, Ludlow grinned sympathetically at Donald. Lowering his voice as if he did not want Montero to hear, he said:

"Don't worry too much. I dare say the time will come when you will both be able to laugh about this."

"I doubt it," said Donald, "but thanks all the same. You're on our side, aren't you?"

"Provided you are innocent, I emphatically am very much on your side."

"You're not certain of that, then?"

"I hope that my conversation with Miss Morland made my position clear. She has no doubt repeated it to you."

"Well, yes, she has. She's a wonderful girl, Mr. Ludlow. What happened with Bould wasn't her fault."

"How did you meet her?" asked Ludlow, offering no comment on Donald's last remark.

"She came in here to ask me to stock some theatrical make-up for the Thespians. I'd hardly heard of the stuff then, but it wasn't long before I was in a play and, well — there we were."

"You stock the make-up now, do you?"

"Oh yes, of course. I think it's about the only useful thing I do for the Thespians. I'm not much good as an actor, as you've been able to see for yourself."

Ludlow decided that it was time for him to go, before

he was forced either into rude honesty or into a compromise with his conscience in respect of Donald Hedge's acting ability. With long strides he soon caught up with the other two. Montero looked at him quizzically.

"And what did you find out in that bit of private investigation?" he asked.

"That June Morland tells the truth about most things."

"Except when she's telling lies. Don't forget that she's had plenty of chance to agree on the same story with him, since she saw you. Why did she keep quiet with you about that letter?"

"I don't know. But if what you say is true, why didn't she tell Hedge what story to follow?"

"Maybe she did and we took him by surprise. Anyway, I'm still very interested in Master Hedge. He has both a personal and a financial motive, he behaves strangely all the evening, he takes a chance of being alone with Bould, and there's a piece of paper in Bould's pocket with his name on it. I wish I knew what those figures meant."

"May I see the letter?" Ludlow asked.

Montero handed him a piece of writing paper, inscribed in rough block capitals with a ball-point pen. Its message was terse, brutal and to the effect that June Morland had been Bould's mistress for some months previously.

"Notice anything special about it?" Montero asked as Ludlow handed back the paper.

"Nothing that seems likely to be any use at present. I don't see how even a handwriting expert could make anything out of that."

"Neither do I — though it's amazing what those boys can do sometimes. But I'm pretty sure that piece of paper is exactly the same as the piece that was found in Bould's pocket. It's a common enough type of cheap notepaper and the point wouldn't stand up in evidence. But it does give some confirmation that Bould wrote that letter, and that there was some other link between him and Hedge quite close to the time he was killed. That other piece was clean and hadn't been in his pocket long. I'm getting more and more interested in Donald Hedge all the time."

"There's just one thing though, sir," said Springer, who had been unusually silent for a long time.

"And what's that, my worthy sergeant?"

"He couldn't have done it. I mean, he could have killed him, but he'd never have got the body behind the screen while the curtain was closed. He just didn't have time, before they all came on the stage again, and then he appears out of the kitchen as soon as he's called. It can't be done."

CHAPTER TEN

Some Effective Stage Lighting

They walked along the street, rather put down by Springer's inescapable logic.

"Where are we going now?" asked Ludlow, who seemed to have abandoned his thoughts of returning home.

"We're going to have a talk with Arthur Seward," Montero said. "The shop where he works is at the other end of the High Street."

The shop in fact announced itself from some distance away and left no doubt about its being devoted to wireless, television and electrical appliances. A very bright sign over the window declared that this was the shop of George Ramage. In the window itself two television sets flickered away busily on different channels, as if possessed within by two different groups of clairvoyant gnomes. Lamps, heaters, coolers, washers and dryers stood all around them and stretched away into the well-lit interior of the shop, where it sounded as if several wirelesses were talking all at once. When Montero pushed open the door, his arrival was announced by a musical chime. Mr. Ramage himself proved to be a disappointingly drab figure in the midst of all this splendour. He was small and fat, with a large mouth which flashed prominent teeth when he spoke. Montero introduced himself in a loud voice, and Ramage was thereupon moved to turn down one or two of the wireless sets and make normal conversation possible. Ludlow wandered about like a fascinated but slightly disapproving child while his companions got to work.

"I'd like to have a word with Arthur Seward," Montero said.

"Seward isn't here now, Inspector."

"Doesn't he work for you any more?"

"Bless your heart, yes. He's just out on a job. And I've a pretty shrewd idea of what you want to see him for. Now don't tell me — let me guess. I'll bet it's about that murder that was done on Monday night down at the church hall."

"Quite right. How very clever of you to deduce that, Mr. Ramage."

"Oh, you've got to be shrewd in business. And I keep my ears open and know a thing or two. Pardon me a sec, while I deal with this customer."

Montero and Springer looked round but could see no one but Ludlow, who was pressing all the buttons on an enormous washing-machine and looking severely at it for not performing.

"He's all right," Montero said hastily, "he's with us. Now perhaps you could help us a little."

"Anything I can do, Inspector. It would be a pleasure for me to further the ends of justice."

"Quite so. Tell me about Seward. Is he satisfactory as an employee?"

"From that question, I read between the lines and understand that you suspect him. Well, well, who would have thought it? Arthur Seward a murderer!"

"Please don't understand anything of the sort. I have to make a thorough check on everybody who was anywhere near Mr. Bould on Monday. There is no question of charging anybody yet. What does Seward do for you — I mean, what exactly is his position in your business?"

"Mostly he does the outside jobs, like now. He goes round for repairs — because even the best things will break down sometimes you know. But we give a written guarantee with every article, and I think I can claim to have provided every satisfaction. This is the age of electricity——"

"Yes, I'm sure it is. But I don't want to buy anything just now. Does Seward spend all his time going about to people's houses?"

"Oh no, sometimes he helps here in the shop when we're busy."

"Have you found him satisfactory while he has worked for you?"

"He's a first-rate electrician. I wouldn't be without him for the world."

"He hasn't any faults that you know of?"

"He's got a bit of a nasty temper, and he tends to answer back when he's spoken to. For all that, he's a good workman. He's best really when he's out on a job, working on his own."

"Do you know whether he lives at all beyond his income? I've no doubt that you pay him a very fair wage, but has he ever shown any sign of needing more? Or has he got any obviously expensive tastes?"

"Not that I know of. I gave him a bit of a rise just before Christmas. And he does a few odd jobs for people in the evenings on his own account, which I don't interfere with. He seems all right."

"Does he gamble at all?"

"Maybe he does, maybe he doesn't. If he does, he's never talked about it, and I've never asked. Live and let live, that's my motto."

Montero looked round anxiously to see whether Ludlow was on the point of exploding from all these clichés, but he was now examining an electric hair-dryer and wondering if it was a new kind of vacuum-cleaner.

"I suppose the local drama group took up a good bit of his time," Montero went on.

"Every night of the week sometimes, when they had a

play on. Not all the time, of course, and there was nothing all last summer."

"How long has he been helping them?"

"Must have been about this time last year. It's a good lark, I reckon, all this acting stuff. He seemed to enjoy it — said they were a nice crowd of people to work with."

"I suppose you don't know how he came to be interested in them in the first place?"

"That I do. As I said, it was about this time last year. Arthur Seward was over at Mr. Bould's place, doing a job on his cooker. The young girl there — Frances her name is — got talking to him out in the kitchen and told him he ought to join their drama lot. Said they needed a good electrician. So he goes along one night to see what's what, and likes the look of it. He built a new switchboard for them — smashing job, I must say."

"May I guess that it was then that Mr. Bould made a complaint to you against Seward?"

"It was," said Ramage, looking a trifle disconcerted.

"And may I guess further that Seward was accused of familiarity with Frances Bould?"

"You're a shrewd one, Inspector; you ought to be in business. Yes, he said that Seward had been flirting and making suggestions as it were, instead of getting on with his job."

"What did you do about this complaint?"

"I mentioned it to Seward, but careful like, because he isn't the sort of man you can afford to lose. He said there was nothing in it, and anyway he was going to talk to who he liked."

"You didn't yourself take it very seriously?"

"Can't say as I did. That Bould, he was a terrible snob. And jealous of that daughter of his — wouldn't allow anyone was good enough for her. Mind you, I don't say she isn't a nice girl."

"So Seward couldn't have felt he was in any danger of dismissal as a result of Mr. Bould's complaint?"

"Course not. All I was hoping was that he wouldn't walk out on me. I wouldn't have done anything, not even after I got that letter."

"What letter?"

"Ah, so there's something you don't know, Inspector. Never mind, we're none of us perfect. I'll make no secret of it. In fact, I'll tell you all about it. The letter that came on Tuesday morning. I'd just finished reading it when Arthur walks in. 'Bould's dead,' he says, just quiet, and goes over and starts getting out his tools. And there was I standing with a letter from Bould in my hand, and he was dead. Must have posted it just before he went to the rehearsal. It didn't half give me a funny feeling. I mean, one day a letter is something you can answer back and go and argue about. Next day, there's nobody to answer. The letter don't seem to belong anywhere. It's a queer world."

"But what was the letter about?"

"Give me time, I'm just coming to that. It was another complaint about Arthur Seward. Said he had shown familiarity to Frances again and had been rude to Bould himself. Said he wouldn't come near my shop again unless I got rid of Seward. Cheek! I ask you, who does he think he is — was? Is it any concern of mine what people get up to when they're off duty?"

"None at all, I'm sure. Did you keep the letter?"

"No, I burned it and never said a word about it to Seward or anyone. I couldn't bear to have it near me, when he that had written it was dead before I ever got it."

"Thank you very much, Mr. Ramage. Can you tell me where I'd be likely to find Arthur Seward?"

"He's down at the hall, doing a job."

"Something wrong with his switchboard there?"

"No, this is something wrong with the lights. The Vicar sent for him to go down."

"What time will he be back here?"

"Probably won't come back. He finishes work at half five, and it's not far off that now. When he's out on a job right up to time, he goes straight home?"

"You trust him to do his full time, then?"

"He's never let me down yet, that I know of."

They collected Ludlow from the far corner of the shop and took him out with a bemused expression. After the glowing wonders of Ramage's electrical appliances, the street seemed particularly gloomy in the new-fallen darkness. Many of the shops were already shut and Donald Hedge's window was dark when they went by. They turned up the side road to the church hall, and Ludlow gave a shiver that did not come from the rising wind which curled round the corner to greet them. Arthur Seward had got the lights working again and was packing up his tools when they entered. The yellow pools of light on the bare floor seemed more depressing than darkness. This was no place for light and the pretence of goodness. All three of them looked involuntarily towards the curtains drawn across the front of the stage and could half believe that a dead man still lay there. Seward, however, did not seem to be troubled by the shadows. He glared at Montero and made it quite clear that he was not in the mood for being kept any longer from his own fireside. A few of Montero's velvet-sheathed threats reduced him to truculent obedience. Rolling a cigarette for himself, he leaned on the stage and waited for the questions.

"Going back to your movements on Monday night," Montero said, "do you still maintain that you did not move from your switchboard during the second part of the rehearsal?"

"I told you, I had to go out sometimes to pull the curtain across the middle of the stage."

"The traverse; quite so. But apart from that, you did not leave your place at the side of the stage?"

"I've told you, no."

"You did not look behind the screen at any time?"

"Why should I?"

"Did you?"

"No."

"It seems incredible to me that a body should have been dragged or carried on to the stage and placed behind the screen, yet you heard nothing."

"I can't help that, it's the truth."

"Surely your attention would have been drawn by any noise behind the main scene, however slight, while a rehearsal was going on."

"I've got all my work cut out to watch the lighting and the curtains. Anyway, I wouldn't take much notice, because somebody might have come up to do a bit with the scenery or arrange the furniture. That wouldn't surprise me."

"Not during another scene, surely."

"Terry Colbert's that fussy, he's quite likely to change his mind half-way through about where a table ought to be."

"You don't care for him?"

"For God's sake, stop twisting what I say. Terry's a fine fellow, and don't try to make out I said different. He was down there in the hall all the time——"

"Yes, we know that; don't get excited. You prefer him to some of the other members?"

"I certainly do. He's not a snob like some of them."

"Like the late Mr. Bould, for instance?"

"You've said it."

"How familiar were you with his daughter, exactly?"

Seward started up from his lounging posture, threw his cigarette on the floor and stamped on it with as much viciousness as if it had been Montero's face.

"So you've picked up that story too, have you?" he said. "Let me tell you, I never said a wrong word to her."

"Mr. Bould seemed to think you did."

"He'd think anything. Just because she made herself pleasant to me, and got me to join this society, and didn't treat me like a dog, he thinks there must be something going on. Ask her if you don't believe me. Ask Dexter, who's engaged to her — he ought to be the one to make a fuss, if anybody had given him cause, which I never did."

"All right, we'll leave it at that for the moment. You can go. Leave the lights on — we're going to have a look round."

Seward hesitated, and looked cunning.

"There isn't anything more you want to know?" he asked.

"Have you got anything more to tell us?"

"Suppose I had, would it be worth my while?"

"It certainly wouldn't be worth your while to conceal it."

"That's as may be. You can't find out everything without a bit of help, you clever detectives. Think it over. I don't do work for nothing, you know. If you hear from me, a few people round here are going to get some shocks."

He heaved up his tool-case and walked away. Springer made as if to go after him, but was restrained by a glance from Montero. Ludlow was apparently playing with the curtain which separated the main part of the hall from the passage leading back to the kitchen.

"We carried out experiments on every bit of equipment in the place," Montero said. "So stop climbing up the curtain, come and sit down and tell us what you think."

Springer pulled out three of the uncomfortable chairs and they sat down, with their backs to the stage.

"What did you find out in your experiments?" Ludlow asked.

"That it seems to be impossible for anyone to have done it. We tried it out with a sack the same weight as Bould, and I can't see how any of them could have knocked him out, broken his neck and carried his body up to the stage in the time that we know he had. There must be an answer, since the man was killed, but I haven't found it yet."

"I still wonder if he wasn't killed behind the screen. There'd be time for any of them to do that," Springer said.

"But why should he have gone there? And could he have been killed so silently that Seward didn't hear anything?"

"*If* he didn't hear anything. I'd like to have a few more words with that one."

"So you shall, Jack, so you shall. And in fact he's probably the only one who had time to go down to the kitchen, kill Bould and bring him back on the stage. It would take careful timing, but it could be done. What do you think, Mr. Ludlow? You've been very quiet, for you."

"I haven't had much chance to get a word in, and anyway I've been thinking. It is a useful exercise, and needs concentration. One of the distinguishing marks of the academic mind is the ability to keep strictly to the point. Now I take it that your suspects are still Dexter, Fielding, Hedge and and Seward, with the possibility of Mrs. Bould and June Morland being somehow concerned. Now let us take Seward first. He is known to have a bad temper and has a reputation for violence. On the other hand, he does not seem to have a strong motive, since his employer clearly thinks too highly of him to dismiss him for any complaint made by Bould. What a fascinating shop that was. Though I get impatient with the praise that is lavished on the works of science, I must say that it does in some respects make life easier and give us more leisure for civilised things. I certainly wouldn't be without my refrigerator, which I refuse to refer to as a fridge. Anyone would think that there was a danger of choking over any word of more than two syllables——"

"I've no doubt you are keeping strictly to the point, in your academic way, Mr. Ludlow," Montero said with a smile "but perhaps we could get back to Seward and the others."

"I was just saying when you interrupted me that Seward had the temperament and the opportunity but seems to lack motive. The others have fairly strong motives, and if we can solve the difficult problem of timing, any of them might have done it. Hedge seems to be most closely linked with the dead man, by that mysterious piece of paper. Fielding and Dexter are the more likely types to be physically capable of doing it."

"And what about the ladies?" asked Springer.

"Do you really think that either Miss Morland or Mrs. Bould would be physically capable of breaking a man's neck and then carrying his body up a flight of steps?"

"Don't forget that the two of them were together in the kitchen at the end of the rehearsal, and we still don't know why Miss Morland went there instead of on the stage. If they did it between them, it would be possible."

"Not much time, though, Jack," Montero reminded him, "and one of them had to find time to wash up the cups as well. Blowed if I can see why, since we know for certain that he wasn't poisoned. Still, it's got to be one of those few. Colbert and Monica Stafford give each other alibis that in any case are confirmed by everybody in the hall, and all the rest were in each other's company the whole time. Still, we haven't entirely wasted the afternoon. We've learned a bit about the history of Haleham Green Grammar School, and we've had a pleasant chat with Mr. Ludlow. We also know that Hedge was in the right mood for killing on Monday night and that Seward has more cards up his sleeve than he's yet chosen to play. Come on, it's cold in here. Let's leave Haleham Green to its own devices for the week-end and hope that they don't go on murdering each other. There seems to be enough scandal here to stir up all the crimes in the calendar."

Scandal, Ludlow thought after they had separated and he had turned Cleopatra's cold nose towards London. It had been going on ever since Sheridan satirized it on the stage, as it had started long before. But where his elegant intrigues had ended in reconciliation after the moment of shocking truth, these sordid affairs had started a circle of violence and mistrust that was still widening. Dexter and Frances would be pursued by it, to taint the freedom and the money that Bould's death had brought them. Fielding was still desperately in debt, and shown up as a reckless gambler and a liar. Seward clutched his secret grudges in sour passion, as Mrs. Bould clutched her sorrows and betrayals. Donald Hedge could not sleep at night, and June Morland — the image of Bould rose palpably, grossly in Ludlow's eyes and seemed for an instant to fill all the road in front: spread out, obscene, waiting for death under the wheels. Was there any glimmer of tenderness in that dreadful relationship? Had either of them, even for a moment, felt the wonder and terror of passion that is shared? Or could not even June's submission have broken Bould's selfishness?

The hints that had been chasing each other in Ludlow's brain began to slow down and take a recognisable shape. His face was thoughtful and unhappy by the time he reached his flat and could close his door against the world.

CHAPTER ELEVEN

Interval for Tea

The next day was bright and clear, a late winter stirring that gave some promise of spring not too far away. As it was a Saturday, Ludlow set out to do his shopping. He was in the corner devoted to the more exotic foods in his local Supermarket and, clutching his wire basket, was thinking about the relative claims of frozen camel steaks and crocodile meat in butter when he let out a cry. "Fool," he exclaimed, "ignorant and slow-witted fool." A fat woman who was trying to balance a handbag and two children as well as her basket looked threateningly at him. A number of other shoppers, equally unfamiliar with his occasional moods of vocal self-depreciation, stared and waited for the fight to start. Ludlow ambled away towards the tinned fruits, unconscious of having done anything remarkable. "It will be easy to confirm it," he announced to the queue which he joined at the cash-desk on the way out.

When he got back and unloaded his purchases, he re-read the letter which had come by the first post. It was from Mrs. Bould, declaring her disappointment that Ludlow had been in Haleham Green again, and had even called on the Daces and the Fieldings, but had not favoured her with a visit. She longed to meet him again, and begged him to name the first possible day when he could come to tea. 'In other words,' thought Ludlow, 'she's desperate to find out exactly what I'm up to, and how much I know. In the process of finding out, she may give something away.' He looked at his diary. Nothing was going to drag him out to Haleham

Green on a Sunday afternoon. Monday he had a late class and the probability of several students needing to be seen after it. He wrote a polite acceptance for Tuesday.

By Tuesday the weather had reverted to its seasonal habit, and little flurries of rain jumped out at Cleopatra all along the road, without ever turning into a real shower. Ludlow drove into the road where the Boulds lived and stopped outside their gate. As he locked the doors, a series of urgent squeaks from behind him made him turn round and see the small figure of Mr. Dace dancing up and down on his doorstep. Taking the squeaks and signs as a demand for attention, Ludlow left the Boulds' gate and went up the neat path of the neighbouring house.

"I've been waiting for you," said Dace with an aggrieved air.

"As a matter of fact, I'm going to tea with Mrs. Bould."

"I know that, so I've been looking out for you."

"How on earth did you know?"

"I heard them discussing it, when I was in my little shed in the garden yesterday. They were glad you were coming today. They're all waiting for you now — Dexter's there too. He sent an excuse to be away from his office. Oh, you've got them frightened all right."

"I don't want to frighten anyone. I'm just trying to get information."

"I dare say. But don't think you can fool me, just because I'm an old man. You're playing a clever game, and I know who you're working for. Well, here's some information if you want it. Arthur Seward was round to see Fielding last night, on the other side of the Boulds. They had a terrible row, and when Seward went away Fielding was shouting threats at him, and Seward was shouting back. I could hear them right inside my house with the windows shut and the curtains drawn. There's your information — make what you like of it. Now be off, I can't stand here in the cold all night, like you young fellows."

Ludlow made his way back down the path and stood thinking for a moment or two before going back to the Boulds' gate. Then he nodded, not without satisfaction, and went to fulfil his invitation. Whatever strange notions Dace might have of Ludlow's activities and employers, he was certainly well-informed on local affairs. Mrs. Bould and Frances were waiting to greet Ludlow, who feared an inquisition on his defection in going next door first. Mrs. Bould, however, was either less observant or more discreet than her neighbour, for she welcomed him gushingly while Dexter hovered like an anxious mastiff in the background.

The house left no doubt that Bould had been a rich man. Although it did not from outside look much bigger than the others in the road, it stretched back farther and was planned inside in a more ample way. The room to which Ludlow was conducted was large, and expensively furnished. Tea was laid out in the traditional way, with a variety of breads, sandwiches and cakes which few young wives would have known how to organise. Balancing a cup and a plate, Ludlow waited for the purpose of his invitation to be revealed. It gradually became clear that the intention was not to offer him any information, but to find out what he already knew. He therefore applied himself manfully to trivial conversation. The atmosphere was not lightened by Dexter, who sat heavily in his chair, giving the erroneous impression of a man weighed down by a heavy overcoat, and alternately glowered at Ludlow or looked lovingly at Frances. Small talk is not Ludlow's strongest gift, especially with people he does not know well. With Dexter keeping mostly on the spectators' side of the touchline, the conversation was rather a curious one; Mrs. Bould and Frances were too well aware of their duty to force Ludlow into a direct answer, but they did their best.

"It was nice seeing you at the Crown the other evening," said Frances.

"Yes, indeed, a pleasant meeting. I hardly expected to see anyone I knew during a brief pause for warmth and refreshment."

"You ought to have come to us," said Mrs. Bould. "We should have been delighted to see you. At least, I should because Frances was out, as you saw. You must have thought it very strange of her, Mr. Ludlow, at such a time."

"Not at all; I can quite understand her wish to get away for a time."

"Yes, at a time like this, one doesn't want to be too much alone. Other people can have different ideas if they like, but we've always tended to go our own way. It would have been a kindness in you to have called."

"I hardly felt that I knew you well enough. After all, we had scarcely met."

"But, Mr. Ludlow, we all felt we knew you so well after that wonderful lecture you gave us," Frances said, with an admiring look that made Dexter glower more darkly than ever.

"It's very kind of you. I should certainly have followed up such a pleasant occasion, if I had felt that that was so," Ludlow said, lowering his guard a little before the assault of flattery.

"You called on Mr. Fielding, however," said Mrs. Bould taking quick advantage.

"Well—yes, I did have a little matter to discuss with him."

"You called on the Daces as well," Dexter said, breaking his silence. "You can't have had any business with them, because they don't belong to the Thespians, and you'd never heard of them before I told you about them in the pub. As soon as you heard that they knew everyone's business, you ran off to see what you could find out."

"Really, Tony, don't be so rude. Mr. Ludlow can call on

who he likes," Mrs. Bould said cheerfully. "You see, Mr. Ludlow, everything is known round here soon after it happens."

"So I've noticed. Reverting to my little talk, I'm glad you enjoyed it, Miss Bould. I hoped it helped a little with the production — that is to say, would have helped — I mean——"

"We learned such a lot from it," said Frances, "and I'm sure it would have helped us a lot. We talked about it between then and the dress rehearsal. What did you think of the rehearsal itself?"

"It was promising," said Ludlow cautiously, wondering how on earth to approach this family who were talking as calmly as if the cancellation of the play had not been caused by the murder of one of them.

"I hope we shall put it on again, when all this is over. It seems a pity to waste so much hard work. Don't you think it would be worth doing again?"

"Oh, certainly. Of course, the comedy of manners puts a heavy burden on the amateur company. It is so artificial that it needs precision and perfect timing if it is to succeed. I well remember a so-called professional production——"

"What did the Daces fill you up with?" Dexter asked abruptly.

Ludlow reflected that most of the men in this case seemed to be ruder than the women, or perhaps less well able to contain their fears. He decided that it was time to edge round towards an open attack, dropping a few pieces of bait first.

"Mr. Dace told me never to listen to gossip," he said.

"You'd have to keep well away from him to obey that," Dexter said.

"Oh come now, Tony," Mrs. Bould said, "I'm sure Mr. Ludlow quite enjoyed his little talks with Mr. Dace, both last week and this afternoon."

'Careful,' thought Ludlow. 'Perhaps she's a lip-reader as well.'

"Mr. Dace was not quite himself this afternoon," he said. "He had been rather upset by what happened yesterday evening."

The other three looked at each other, and Mrs. Bould seemed to flash a warning at Dexter. Frances spoke and obviously regretted her question the moment it was out.

"What happened yesterday evening?" she asked.

"Apparently there was some disturbance in the road outside, between Fielding and Seward. I thought you might have heard it."

"We were out. We — went to Tony's place." Frances blushed and showed herself again to be a very pretty girl but a bad liar.

"I wonder what they can have been quarrelling about," Mrs. Bould said innocently.

"I've no idea. Of course, I don't know about the local feuds and rivalries."

"It might be anything, if it's those two," said Frances. "They've both got nasty tempers."

"Yes, so I believe. In fact, your father had trouble with both of them at different times."

"Well, you know about the row with Mr. Fielding. It wasn't much really, and Doris is rather sweet — that's his wife. I don't think there was any trouble with Mr. Seward."

"Didn't your father make some complaint of him to his employer?" asked Ludlow, wondering whether Montero would approve of his methods of interrogation.

"That was some time ago. There was no quarrel — I mean, nothing actually happened."

"Bartholomew had very high standards," Mrs. Bould said primly. "He could never put up with slovenly work."

"Indeed? I had no idea that there was any dissatisfaction

with Seward's work. I thought the whole thing centred on Miss Bould."

"What the hell do you mean?" Dexter leapt to his feet, shaking with anger. "Frances, what's been going on?"

"Nothing at all, darling. Daddy got annoyed when Arthur Seward came here first, because he talked to me while he was supposed to be mending something. That's how I got him to come to the Thespians, and a good thing for all of us when you think of the work he's done with the lighting."

"But there was a more recent occasion for complaint, wasn't there? Didn't your father write a letter to Ramage the very night he — the night of the dress rehearsal?"

"He said he wasn't going to. I thought I'd talked him out of it but perhaps he changed his mind again. I wish I'd never told him."

"What did you tell him?"

"Seward tried to make a bit of a pass at me one night while I was waiting to go on. I told him off properly, and he apologised. It was nothing."

"The swine, I'll break his neck for him!" shouted Dexter, who had stood silent but with growing anxiety during the last few exchanges.

There was a long pause while they all looked at Dexter, Frances with pride and concern, Mrs. Bould with thin-lipped irritation and Ludlow with a bland curiosity that seemed to hope for more. Dexter sat down very slowly and clenched his hands while he stared into the fire. Ludlow took out his pipe and prodded it, saying at last to no one in particular:

"Do you mind if I smoke?"

"Oh, please do," said Mrs. Bould with relief. "Frances, try to find an ash-tray. Neither of us smokes, Mr. Ludlow, and Bartholomew smoked only cigars, and seldom outside his own study."

There was silence again while Ludlow got his pipe going and looked benevolently at the others through the smoke. Mrs. Bould made a vague gesture towards the teapot, then thought better of it and subsided again. Ludlow, looking a picture of perfect innocence, started to talk about the weather and praised the warm coal fire by which he was sitting. He managed to pass ten minutes almost in a monologue, which is in itself nothing unusual for him but is a fair achievement if he keeps off English literature for the whole time. At last he got up and said that he must go, an assertion which none of them attempted to deny. Dexter grunted something but did not come out to the hall. While Frances was helping him on with his coat, Ludlow said:

"Did your father at any time suggest that he himself might like to act in a play?"

Frances looked surprised. "I don't think so," she said. "He was keen on my doing it, and he seemed rather proud of the parts I took. I never heard him say that he wanted to try, and I don't think he'd have been much good."

Mrs. Bould made no comment, and did not seem to have heard the question. Ludlow thanked her politely for his tea and went off down the path, conscious that more than one pair of eyes, from more than one house, followed him to the gate. No eyes could follow him once he had driven away, and there was no witness to the unhappiness in his face. This was a thoroughly unsavoury business, he thought. Why should he go asking people about their most intimate affairs, raising enmity and causing embarrassment instead of devoting himself to the passing-on of knowledge and critical values to which his professional life was supposed to be dedicated? What reason had he to interest himself in the death of a man whom he had scarcely met and had heartily disliked? The trouble was that he could not help knowing what he knew and understanding what he understood. He wished that Montero would understand it as well, without any more help from him. But to stand apart now would be part of the great betrayal which the artists and scholars of one generation had already committed. To shrug the shoulders at one violent death was to join those who had refused to believe in the existence of Dachau, who had preferred not to hear the name of Guernica. He had to go on. Meanwhile, there was a question to be answered, and if Bould's daughter did not know the answer, he had to seek someone who might.

Ludlow remembered where Terry Colbert lived, from having taken him home on the evening of the lecture. It was a flat over a small shop, and a little practical research on nameplates and bells soon found what was wanted. A tousled head was poked out of a first-floor window and said:

"Who's that?"

"It's Ludlow. I was going past and remembered that you lived here. Could I possibly come in for a minute? There's something I'd like to ask you."

The head withdrew, and in a few moments reappeared in the doorway attached to the whole body of Terry Colbert, who led the way upstairs. In a small room, Ludlow's coat was pushed out of sight behind a curtain and Ludlow himself was offered a chair.

"A pleasant little flat," Ludlow said.

"I'm afraid it's a bit untidy."

Ludlow privately marked this as the understatement of the year, but he looked with approval at the well-filled bookcases and at the pictures, cheap but framed and hung intelligently, on the rather grubby walls.

"Would you like some tea?" Terry asked. "Or would you rather have beer? I haven't been back from school very long, but I'll be cooking a meal fairly soon if you'd care to join me."

"I have just had rather a large tea with Mrs. Bould and her daughter, so I won't have anything now, thank you.

I must apologise for coming in unexpectedly like this, and I promise not to keep you long."

"Please don't apologise, Mr. Ludlow. It's splendid to see you again. I enjoyed your lecture and the little chat we had afterwards when you were kind enough to drive me back here; I only wish it could have been longer. It's not often I get any decent conversation nowadays."

"You find the company in Haleham Green a little inadequate?"

"You can say that again. They're not a bad lot, I suppose, but they haven't got many ideas among them. Cigarette?"

"I'll have a pipe, if you don't mind. Isn't there anybody at your school worth talking to?"

"Not really. The Head's all right, but he's so wrapped up in the history of the school that he hasn't much else to talk about. There aren't many others who interest me — it's a school that's pretty strong on the science side."

"Ah, yes." For ten minutes they both went on very happily about the iniquities of scientists.

"What did you do before you came here?" Ludlow asked eventually.

"I was teaching somewhere else for a bit. Before that, I was at the Institute for my education year; after I'd done my degree at Queen Adelaide's."

"Yes, I remember having a chat with you about my worthy colleague Professor Pigeon. Who was your particular tutor there?"

"Bassalt, most of the time. Is he still there?"

"Indeed he is. We actually found ourselves on the same side at the Board of Studies a few weeks ago. The pretensions of these pure philologists are getting as bad as those of the scientists, with whom they seem anxious to group themselves. Bassalt remarked, very rightly—— But I mustn't weary you with academic politics."

"I find it very interesting. I wish I was in your sort of

job, instead of trying to teach boys who don't want to be taught. It's rather a comfort to know that you have your trouble with your colleagues too."

"You enjoyed your time at the university, then?"

"I did, because I loved the subject I read. To tell the truth, I was always disappointed at not going to Oxford."

"Oxford is delightful, certainly; I'm glad I went. But it's not a lifelong tragedy not to have been there."

"I don't know. You miss an awful lot by not going there, and not only academically. I had an offer of a place there, but I just couldn't afford to take it. In London you can starve in your own way and be left alone, but there you have to live up to the right standard all the time."

"Not really, you know. Oxford absorbs everyone, and makes very little distinction amongst her children once they are accepted. Of course, money is always useful."

"I'll say it is. With more money I might have got on better. Sorry, that's probably just conceit. But I do get a bit fed up with this dump."

"School-teaching must have its compensations, surely?"

"Oh yes, many of them. There's a certain spontaneity about boys that is very refreshing — once you can get them to sit quietly and listen to you. They're capable of wonderful performances on the stage, because they aren't either shy or conceited. They are content to be someone else, without wondering how they can best show off themselves."

"Your Headmaster spoke very appreciatively of your work with the boys for the school play."

"I didn't know you'd met him."

"I haven't, but I heard about it from Inspector Montero."

"You're keeping in touch with him then — about the murder? I'd almost forgotten about that."

"I'm sorry to bring your mind back to it, but that is my main reason for being here. Can I ask you one or two questions, and also ask you not to speak of them to anybody?

As we are colleagues in the same field of teaching, I believe I can."

"It's nice of you to put it like that," said Terry, with a sheepish grin. "I'm not anywhere near your mark, and I know it. You mustn't take too much notice of me — I get a bit fed up sometimes, that's all. And I was really very disappointed at the play having to be called off after all the work that had gone into it. I'd like to track down Bould's murderer, if only for spoiling the play. Sorry — is that too flippant? It's no good pretending I liked the man himself. Ask me anything you like, and of course I'll keep it all quiet."

"Thank you. Then tell me, did Mr. Bould show any personal interest in acting, apart from his honorary office? He was quite proud of his daughter's acting I know, but did he himself ever want to act?"

Terry looked at Ludlow with surprise and admiration.

"How extraordinary that you should ask me that," he said. "I was amazed when Bould came up to me at one rehearsal and said he'd like a part in one of the plays. He'd never shown the slightest inclination before. I don't think he mentioned it to anybody else."

"I don't think he did." Ludlow looked severely at his pipe, which was making rebellious bubbling noises. "Do you think he'd have been a good actor?"

"I'm pretty sure he wouldn't. I tried to put him off as politely as I could, but he kept on asking me about it, and wanting tips on how to prepare himself for a part. It would have been a bit of a problem, if he'd lived. I mean, I couldn't afford to get the Thespians in the wrong with him, but he could never have been anything but a nuisance on the stage. I've no doubt he was shrewd enough in business, but he was essentially a stupid man. Do you remember the way he mishandled your lecture when he was supposed to be taking the chair?"

"I certainly do," said Ludlow with feeling. "Now, please tell me what you think of June Morland. And don't leer or look knowing, or I shall go berserk and break up this comfortable room of yours."

Terry laughed. "June's all right," he said. "You saw for yourself that she's a good actress, though she was a bit off form the night of the dress rehearsal. Usually she's as steady as a rock. She's a good girl, though she does have rather a high opinion of herself. But she's a joy to produce, except that occasionally she takes ideas into her head and won't have them put out — she can be terribly impulsive. The best thing about her is that she's loyal, even when she hasn't much cause for it. She stood up to the Boulds all right, I can tell you."

"What have the Boulds been trying to get her to do?"

"You may as well have all the dirt, if you don't know it. June told Donald Hedge, and Donald told me when I dropped in for some soap on my way home. They went down to see June last evening — Mrs. Bould and Frances, with Tony Dexter tagging along as well. They — or rather Mrs. B. — tried to get her to say what she had got out of Bould when he was alive. They seemed to think that he had handed over a lot of cash to her, or that somehow she was going to get more than had been left her in the will. But she wouldn't tell them a thing."

"Was the affair between Bould and her generally known?"

"A lot of people put two and two together, and got various answers. Of course, it's common property now. I can't say I was ever terribly interested, so long as it didn't interfere with her acting. She never appealed to me in that sort of way, though Donald seems to be pretty well hooked."

"Thank you. Now I mustn't keep you any longer from your evening meal."

"Don't go yet. Stay and have a bite with me."

"I must get back, but thank you all the same. You've been most helpful."

"Have I really? I can't see that I've told you anything useful. Do you know who the murderer is?"

"Perhaps. Tell me, would you like a chance to prove that your work on the play was not entirely wasted?"

"Of course. But how——?"

"Reconstruction is sometimes a help in solving a murder—or any other mystery."

"You mean like Hamlet and the Players?"

"In a sense. What I have in mind would be a more direct re-enactment. Never mind for the moment. I must get a few things more clearly first. And if anything is to be done, let us do it in the name of abstract justice. I shan't be such a hypocrite as to pretend that there are great reasons of affection for learning who killed Bould. You for one can have no love for him."

"Because he made a fuss to the Head?"

"I was thinking rather of the nuisance which he made of himself at rehearsals. After all, in a modern school under the local authority, a teacher's position is protected. He can't be sacked just because a bad-tempered Governor makes one complaint about him."

"That's true. But it still doesn't do to get in badly with the Governors and the Head. They may not be able to sack you, but they can hold you back. There are special allowances, and posts of responsibility, and so on. And sooner or later there's always the question of a testimonial for another job."

"Very well. I'll include that in the counts against Bould, if you like."

"Do that. As long as you don't think that bit of bother made me kill him."

"I know it didn't. So will you still help with my little reconstruction, if it becomes necessary?"

"In the name of abstract justice? You can count on me."

"Thank you. Now I really must go."

"But I still don't know what exactly it is that you want me to do."

"Nothing at present. I'll let you know soon. If not directly, then through an intermediary who will be coming to see me soon."

"You're very mysterious, Mr. Ludlow, but I promise I'll do all I can. And I really have enjoyed talking to you. Let's hope it won't be too long before we meet again."

"It won't—probably before the end of the week. Is the scenery for the play still standing in the church hall?"

"Well yes, it is. We were to have run till Saturday, and it's only the Tuesday following now. I expect we ought to do something about it, but nobody's had the heart to go near the place."

"Keep it up for as long as you can."

"They may want the hall for a whist drive or something."

"They needn't play whist all over the stage. Good-bye. I'll remember you to Pigeon and Bassalt when I see them."

"Yes, please do. And thanks for calling."

So, as urbanely as if there had been no murder, Ludlow ended a fruitful and depressing visit to Haleham Green. He drove Cleopatra back to London at what was, for her, literally a rattling speed.

CHAPTER TWELVE

Ludlow Calls a Rehearsal

Next day Ludlow was rather late into college, though anyone who had been keeping watch on him might have seen him leaving his flat at an earlier hour than was usual for him. When he arrived in time for his first hour of teaching he looked puzzled and not very happy. His mood had not improved when the time came for a meeting of the Library Committee, on which he represented his department. He sat in silence through the first items of business, grunting assent to the minutes and apparently withdrawn into deep hostility against all books and their readers. After forty minutes he suddenly hit the table with his fist and let out an exclamation. Nobody took much notice, because the member from the Economics department had just said:

"A disamenity is being suffered, due to the non-availability of certain periodicals."

It was generally understood that Ludlow was protesting against a new abuse of the English language, and indeed he relapsed into silence again for the rest of the meeting. What exactly had caused his exclamation will appear later.

He went back to his room to find June Morland and Donald Hedge standing outside the door.

"Do you want to see me?" he asked somewhat unnecessarily.

"You told me to come back this week," said June, "but you weren't here."

"It is always advisable to make an appointment before calling," Ludlow said. "However, come in."

He ushered them into his room, saw them into chairs and sat behind his desk waiting for one of them to begin.

"I hope you don't mind Donald coming with me—it's his half day and the only time he could get away from the shop."

"I'm delighted to see both of you, of course. Now, what do you want to tell me?"

"We hoped you were going to tell us something," Donald said. Seeing no sign of response he went on: "I mean, you've been going around Haleham Green asking questions, and you've been with the Inspector. Do you know who was responsible for the crime?"

"Do you mean, have I found the murderer?"

"Yes."

Ludlow pressed his fingertips together and looked hard at the opposite corner of the ceiling. He studied the configuration of the plaster while the others waited. When he spoke, it was to June and not to Donald.

"Last week, you came to see me in this room and asked me to try to find the murderer. Your confidence in my ability to do so was flattering, though I was by no means sure at that time whether I could fulfil it. I did, however, make two important conditions of which I must now remind you. First, I should not be able to withhold from the police any information which might be relevant to the case. Secondly, if I started to investigate I should have to carry it to the end, no matter who wanted me to stop. These conditions still hold. I started to ask questions, as Mr. Hedge has put it, at your request. I may add that I have wasted a great deal of time that might have been better occupied and that I am heartily sick of the name and sight of Haleham Green."

"But you will go on, won't you?"

"I have already tried to explain that I must go on, whether I want to or not. Are you sure that you want me to follow this thing to the end?"

"Yes, of course."

"With whatever pain and distress may be caused to anyone?"

"I'm not afraid."

"We must get this cleared up." Donald burst out with unusual vehemence. "It's hanging over us, over the Thespians, over the whole of the district. Nobody can feel any safety until we know the answer. Perhaps any one of us, without realising it, knows something that would point to the murderer. He may strike again — at June, at me, at anybody at all. We can't know a minute's happiness together until everything is cleared up."

Ludlow turned a benevolent eye on him and spoke as if they had just dropped in for a social call in passing.

"Ah yes," he said, "I don't think I've had a chance to congratulate you on your — ah — unofficial engagement to Miss Morland. May I ask when it is to become official?"

"As soon as this business is over."

"And what will you do then?"

"Well — get married, of course."

"And stay in Haleham Green?"

"We haven't decided that. I might sell the shop and start again somewhere else. Life wouldn't be easy for us there. You've simply no idea how much gossip there is in a place like that."

"I've noticed something of the kind. It certainly makes a detective's work easier. Well, I wish you every happiness. But there is work to be done first. Once again, you're sure that you want me to go on with it?"

"Yes," said June. Donald gulped and nodded.

"Very well. Miss Morland, will you arrange a rehearsal of *The School for Scandal* for Friday of this week?"

"But — I don't understand, Mr. Ludlow."

"The play you were rehearsing for production. Surely you haven't forgotten. We'll make it a dress rehearsal, I think, and hold it in the church hall as usual. Let me see, what time — when do you usually start?"

"Eight o'clock. The costumes have gone back," June said helplessly while Hedge stared with his mouth open.

"Never mind, we can do without the costumes. I have learned from Mr. Colbert that the scenery is still in position, and that is the important thing. Be sure that everyone is on time. I'm sure that on this occasion Mr. Colbert will not object to a small audience, consisting of myself, Inspector Montero and Sergeant Springer. No one else outside the cast is to be admitted. We shall need Seward, of course. And Mrs. Bould must come. Will you arrange that, please?"

"But — but, what do you want us to do when we get there?"

"As I have said, I want a dress rehearsal without costumes. To be precise, I want to repeat the rehearsal which ended so unhappily on Monday last week. That one posed a lot of questions: I hope that this will answer them."

"I don't know that I'm very keen on going through all that again," Donald said. "What kind of a game is this you're playing with us?"

"Let us say, if you like, that I am indulging my love of the drama and renewing the pleasure of seeing you all act. If Miss Morland has the confidence that she seemed to have in me last week, she will understand and do as I ask."

"I don't understand, but I'll do it," said June. "But I'm sure a lot of them will feel just like Donald and not want to come. What happens then?"

"Tell anyone who is inclined to be recalcitrant that absence from this rehearsal will be taken as a sign of guilt. A sign of guilt, Mr. Hedge," he added, looking at Donald.

Hedge shrugged and got up as if there were no more to be said. June rose too and they both went, bewildered, to the door which Ludlow politely held open for them.

"Eight o'clock on Friday then. I shall look forward to seeing you. Good afternoon, Miss Morland. Good afternoon, Mr. Hedge."

When they had gone, Ludlow no longer looked his usual urbane self. He went back and sat down at his desk. Twice he stretched his hand towards the telephone and drew it back. The third time he picked up the instrument and spoke to the college operator. His voice was the voice of a man who hates what he is going to say.

Neither June nor Donald ran a car, and they were glad to find an empty compartment in the train back to Haleham Green. It was the dead time of late afternoon, before the terrifying rush and scurry out of London has begun. The north-west suburbs had already given way to patches of open country before either of them spoke. Then June clutched Donald Hedge's sleeve and said:

"I'm so terribly frightened."

"But why?" asked Donald, putting his arm round her. "It looks as if everything will be cleared up soon. I don't know what that fellow Ludlow is playing at, but I think he's on to something. I shouldn't be surprised if he gave us the answer on Friday."

"I know — that's what I'm afraid of."

"I don't understand you. Whatever happens, it can't hurt us?"

"Are you sure of that — Donald, are you quite sure?"

"Of course I am. What a funny girl you are. As long as we've got each other, everything else is unimportant. You do trust me, don't you?"

"Of course."

The train stopped at the station before Haleham Green. A few doors banged as returning shoppers and schoolchildren got out under the lamps that had just been lit to break up the dusk of the platform. June and Donald were silent in their compartment, isolated from the world outside, forgotten by its troubles and its pleasures. They could have consented to be carried on for ever in the train, never having to leave and face the other people who knew things that were better forgotten. When the train started again, June said, hysterically:

"We'll never be free of him."

"What do you mean? Who are you talking about?"

"Bould — he'll always be there, between us. Because he was killed like that, he'll have power over us. I know that I shall never be able to lose him."

"June, do you still care for him at all?"

"Oh, Donald, how could you? I never cared for him. But he has power over us. You feel it too — you feel it, don't you?"

"I don't feel anything of the kind. Pull yourself together, my own dear girl. We're together, and nothing else matters. Nothing can touch us."

"Will you always feel that? Don't you fear him coming between us? You'll always have that to hold against me."

"I'll never hold it against you."

"But you'll feel it, won't you. You'll think about it and remember what he was like and what happened to him."

"Perhaps I will," Donald said slowly.

"Donald, he was the only one, you must believe that. You do believe it, don't you?"

"Yes." Donald's answer was a fraction too late and hesitant.

"You don't believe. We can't go on like this. How can we get married if you're always wondering how many men I had before I met you. He was the only one, and I've told you many times how it came about. If you don't trust me, it's an empty thing to talk about loving me."

"I do trust you, and I love you, but — oh, June, how could you have done it, how could you?"

Now it was Donald's turn to plunge tearfully for comfort, which June gave him until the train jerked to a stop at Haleham Green and he had to extricate himself. So the shadow of Bartholomew Bould, known to have done little good in his life, seemed to spread even darker after his death. And if June and Donald did quarrel and make it up in the phrases that have been worn out in life and in novels until they are threadbare, yet they were no less truly under the shadow for that. As they came out from the station, June red-eyed and Donald heavily blowing his nose, each clung to the other yet did not want to be alone together. They needed light, company, public places to force them to cover their doubts with the veneer of convention.

"Let's go to the Crown for tea," Donald said, and June was more than ready to agree.

As they walked up the main street, they met Terry Colbert on his way back from school.

"Nice to have time to run around on Wednesday afternoons," he said cheerfully.

"It's Donald's early-closing day, and I had a day coming to me anyway," June said. "I thought you didn't have school on Wednesday afternoon, so you needn't talk about running around."

"I go Saturday mornings, so there. But today was my day on duty, so I had to stay and look after the boys in detention — little horrors. Where did you go?"

"We went to London."

"To look at the Queen, like the pussy-cat?"

"Actually, it was to look at Mr. Ludlow. And to talk to him. Terry, can you imagine, he wants us to have a rehearsal of the play."

Terry Colbert did not seem particularly surprised.

"I thought he was up to something," he said. "We had a talk yesterday. When does he want it?"

"This Friday. And he says that everyone must be there. otherwise it will be taken as a sign of guilt."

"That ought to fetch them," Terry said with a laugh. "It will probably bring them there exactly on time, which is more than I've ever managed to do. Is Ludlow going to unmask the murderer in the middle of a scene?"

"He didn't say exactly, but he is going to have those detectives there."

"Does he want us to do the whole thing? The costumes have gone back."

"I told him that, but he said it didn't matter about the costumes, so long as we still had the scenery. He said he wanted us to repeat all that happened at the dress rehearsal last week."

"In every detail? That'll be a bit difficult, but we'll try. So I'll have to have a row with you again, Donald, and you'll have to threaten to walk out, as you did then."

Donald Hedge, who had been looking sulkily at the ground during this conversation, stopped kicking one foot against the other and said, smiling:

"I think he's mad."

"Don't you believe it, my boy. I've conceived a great respect for old Ludlow. If he wants us to go through these antics again, it's for a good reason. Will you contact the members, June? I'll tell Monica, and the couple of lads from school."

"All right. We'll see you on Friday, then."

"It's a silly pantomime," Donald said as June took his arm and led him off in the direction of the Crown.

"It isn't, darling — it's an eighteenth-century comedy, and you've got to be a good boy and act your best."

"That doesn't seem good enough for Colbert. I don't want to go on that stage again, after what happened."

"Do you think I do? No, let's not start arguing again.

We must go through with it. Remember, he said that not to be there would be a sign of guilt."

"I wish I'd never heard of the Haleham Green Thespians."

"Then you'd never have met me, you silly thing."

Donald Hedge was not the only one who could have done without the Haleham Green Thespians. At the same moment, Montero in his office at Scotland Yard was glaring at the piece of paper on which was written the name of Donald Hedge, followed by three numbers. Springer watched him patiently, ready to administer respectful attention or humorous comment as the mood required. Only a single desk-lamp gave light where the two men were working, and threw their shadows on the wall as if there were a pair of twisted, giant detectives standing behind them. The traffic on the Embankment was building up to its peak now, and the roar gave an unending background to that room high above the river.

"It must be one of them, Jack — and don't tell me that none of them had time to do the whole job, because I know that. You still think one of the women is in it as well, don't you?"

"There doesn't seem to be any other way out of it, sir. If we can find the woman, that ought to show us which man actually did it."

"If you say, '*Cherchez la femme*' I shall do something that I'll regret."

"I wouldn't say anything rude. But are we sure it must be one of those four?"

"If it isn't, there's been a tremendous conspiracy to provide alibis, which I find hard to believe."

"But what about somebody from outside — somebody we've never seen. He could have been let in through the back door, hidden down in that dressing-room and got away after he'd done it. The key was always in the back door, inside, so nobody need have let him out."

"It sounds too easy, in a way, but we may have to come to it. I still think we can look much nearer home. There are some perfect motives, and at least three of the men seem to be the sort who would use violence."

The telephone rang and Springer, at a sign from Montero, picked it up.

"It's Ludlow," he announced.

Montero took the telephone. The traffic outside had got itself into a solid jam, and the room seemed strangely silent all of a sudden. Montero, glad of the break, spoke genially. Springer listened on an extension earpiece.

"This is an unusual concession to the world of science, isn't it?" Montero said. "I thought you didn't like the telephone."

"I detest it." Ludlow's voice came thinly over the wire, as if he were a thousand miles away. "It is sometimes necessary. I've wasted an appalling amount of time on this case, travelling about, sitting in cold halls, talking to dull and unsavoury people, drinking strong tea ——"

"You didn't ring me up just to tell me your troubles, did you?"

"If you will allow me to get in a single word, I was about to say that I have some important information for you, and I simply have no time to come and see you. I suppose it's all right to tell you by means of this thing?"

"Security's good at this end. What about yours?"

"I think the operators here are too busy to listen. They wouldn't understand what it was about, anyway. But I may be too late. Have you solved the matter which interests us?"

"No. Have you?"

"It would seem so. It's just like Falstaff."

"Like what?"

"Falstaff, at Shrewsbury. Only he got credit for it. You follow me?"

"Yes. But who's our Falstaff, and who's the Prince?"

"There are one or two things I want you to do," Ludlow said as if Montero had not spoken. "It might be a good thing to have men following our suspects, in case any of them does something silly — or has something done to him."

"Of course. I've got men to spare — as many as you like. We're only a few thousand short. You wouldn't like me to put a man on every single inhabitant of Haleham Green, would you?"

"No, thank you. If it's difficult, there's one who might be really dangerous — I'll tell you in a moment. The second thing is, will you come to a dress rehearsal on Friday?"

"Will I what?"

"Come to a dress rehearsal on Friday. Eight o'clock at the church hall. There won't be any costumes, but we still have the scenery. Bring Sergeant Springer with you. I think I can promise you both an interesting evening."

"If I didn't know you pretty well — all right. Anything else?"

"Yes. I've been doing some research."

"How fascinating."

"It was. As I said, I've really been very busy over this case of yours. I was out in the small hours of this morning getting information. It can't have been a minute after nine when I left my flat. Now I want you to do some — you have the resources for digging into things that I might find difficult."

"Don't tell me there's anything that you find difficult."

"None of us is omniscient. Now listen carefully."

Ludlow spoke for some time. Montero's deceptively innocent eyes grew rounder and rounder, while Springer's face seemed to get longer and longer. At last Ludlow said:

"Is all that quite clear?"

"More or less."

"You understand what I want you to do."

"Yes, but it's a bit irregular, some of it. Are you sure you're right?"

"Can you see any way in which I'm wrong?"

"No. All right. We'll see you there on Friday. Do you want a lift out there?"

"Thank you, I have my own car."

"Is that what it is? I never knew. Good-bye, then."

"Wait a moment. There's something that I forgot to tell you — something very important."

"Yes?"

"It gets very cold in that hall. Bring warm coats."

"We haven't forgotten the last time."

Montero put down the telephone and looked at his assistant.

"Well, strike me pink," Springer said cheerfully. "Do you get it, sir?"

"More or less. There are a few blanks to be filled in, but he must be right."

"What did all that lark about Falstaff mean?"

"Oh that," said Montero, "that's easy."

CHAPTER THIRTEEN

The Last Scene

In spite of Ludlow's gloomy prophecy, the church hall was a great deal warmer than it had been on his previous visits. Arriving a few minutes before eight, he found the cast all assembled, complete with producer, prompter and stage-manager. Mrs. Bould was in her old place by the radiator, knitting away furiously as if her husband was still waiting outside in the kitchen. Frances and Dexter clung together in one corner, June and Donald Hedge in another. Terry Colbert paced about anxiously, while Monica watched him with adoring eyes. The whole thing seemed like an uncanny repetition of the last rehearsal, but now the disaster was foreseen and only one of them knew whom it would strike. In their ordinary clothes they now seemed pathetic and more vulnerable, cloaked by no unreality from the sordid affair into which they had all been plunged. A casual arrival would have found no way of discovering Ludlow's secret. The faces were bored, resentful, excited or nervous according to the temperaments which they covered, but there was no apparent sign of guilt.

Montero and Springer arrived almost immediately after Ludlow, and relieved the atmosphere by some ironical comments on Cleopatra's speed. Montero took Ludlow aside and whispered to him while the others watched with curiosity. Montero then thanked them all for coming to assist the police, and asked them to do exactly what Ludlow wanted. For once ill at ease at being in a prominent position, Ludlow asked Colbert if he was ready to start.

"As soon as you like," Terry said, cheerful now that he could get back to his beloved rehearsal even under these conditions. "The scenery is in position just as it was last week. Do you want us to go from the beginning of the play?"

"There is no necessity for that," Ludlow said. "Will you start from the point where Mr. Bould went out to warm himself? That was just after the library scene, I think — the scene which you repeated at the end when Bould was — ah — discovered."

"Shall we have to do that bit again?" June asked with a little shudder. "I don't think I could bear it."

"Whether that will be necessary will emerge in due course," said Ludlow calmly. "For the moment we shall go from the point in the main rehearsal where Bould went out. Just one other matter. Mr. Seward, would you be kind enough to keep the main curtain open the whole time, so we can see everything that happens on the stage. All of you, please do exactly as you did at the dress rehearsal."

"Including the mistakes?" Donald Hedge asked.

"Everything. Now I'm quite ready, so let's start."

Ludlow went and sat on one of the uncomfortable chairs at the back of the hall, where he had sat before, and looked benevolently at the company as if encouraging them to start reading their essays aloud. There was a long pause while everyone fidgeted and looked at the floor. Montero coughed, and said diffidently:

"Would it help if Sergeant Springer went out and followed Mr. Bould's actions to start you off?"

"A very good idea," said Ludlow. "Please do that, Sergeant."

Springer, overcome by the theatrical nature of the occasion, and perhaps with reminiscences of impressions of Dickens at an old police concert, assumed a Scrooge-like attitude and stood in the middle of the hall exclaiming: "Oh it's cold, it's horrible cold. I can't stand it. I'm going out to sit in the kitchen and get my poor old body warm."

"That will do, Sergeant," said Montero severely. "Just go."

The chastened Springer went, and disappeared behind the curtain at the side of the stage.

"There were a few words after he'd gone," Colbert reminded them. "Do you want us to remember what we all said?"

"That is hardly necessary," Ludlow said. "The important thing is that, during that short conversation, Miss Morland followed Mr. Bould out to the kitchen. Will she please do that now, but stay just inside the curtain and come back at the same point as she did before?"

June went out, looking sullen and rather frightened. The actors in the next scene took their places on the stage and started the rehearsal. Terry Colbert criticised and bullied them as he had done before, and this seemed to encourage them so that the scene took on some semblance of life. Then June Morland came back and sat down near Ludlow, at whom she looked angrily.

"I think that last time I rather forgot myself and broke down," she said. "Do you want me to do it again? It wouldn't be at all difficult, as I feel now."

"Please don't distress yourself," Ludlow said cheerfully. "I will announce the point when your lachrymose noises broke off the action, and then we must all try to do what we did before."

After a minute or two he said: "That was it." He got up and stood by June, while those who were not on the stage came and joined him. Montero impassively watched them.

"Now we can go on," Ludlow said. "Mr. Colbert, please be sure to get your next interruption at the right time."

The scene went on, more half-heartedly for the pause. Donald Hedge again forgot his words as before, but at different places and obviously not from any attempt to repeat his previous performance. Towards the end of the scene, Colbert shouted:

"Donald, you're out of position again. Is that exactly what I said before?"

"The exact words don't matter. Go on as well as you can remember."

"I'm in the right place," Donald Hedge said feebly.

"No, you should be more downstage."

Terry Colbert hurried through the side-curtains and on to the stage, where he started to push Hedge forward.

"Do you want to push me over the front?" Hedge asked.

"You must open up the stage. And try to be more lively when you get the letter."

"If you're not satisfied, I may as well go home. It isn't quite the thing to interrupt so much at a dress rehearsal."

"All right, I'm sorry. Let's try to finish without any breaks."

Terry vaulted over the footlights and took up his position by Monica Stafford with her prompt-copy.

"I'm afraid that wasn't quite right," he said anxiously to Ludlow.

"Never mind," said Ludlow, "you got the same sentiments. We're getting along very nicely. Are you in the picture, so to speak?" he added to Montero, who reluctantly shook his head.

The scene soon ended, and Seward appeared to draw across the traverse curtain for the next one. First he carefully picked up the screen and put it back into place. Some of the actors for the next scene went across the stage and into the wings on the far side. Tony Dexter stayed with Frances.

"You will understand," Ludlow said to no one in particular, "that at the dress rehearsal the front curtain was drawn between scenes. We are now able to see all that took place on the stage. Please notice that, so far, the screen has been in view all the time, but is now hidden by the traverse. Go ahead."

The scene began. After a short time, Tony Dexter went through the side-curtains to await his entry. Ludlow kept his eyes on Fielding, who did not move. Eventually Dexter came on.

"Please stop," Ludlow said. "Mr. Fielding, you should be there by now."

"What do you mean?" asked Fielding, red-faced. "I haven't got anything in this scene."

"Quite so. That is why you went for your little talk with Mr. Bould. You were in the kitchen by the time Mr. Dexter came on."

"Hell's bells," said Fielding, "I thought you wanted a rehearsal. You don't need all the private bits, surely."

"Unfortunately nothing is private in an affair like this. Can we go back a few lines, please?"

They did so, and Fielding slouched off to the kitchen. The scene was played through to its end without interruption. Then the stage emptied again and Seward came on to draw the traverse back and reveal the screen for the last scene.

"We must stop again," said Ludlow. "Get Mr. Fielding out of the kitchen, please."

Fielding was fetched, and Ludlow looked severely at the whole company.

"I am afraid," he said, "that some of you have not played your parts properly. We have failed to achieve a replica of what happened up to this point at the dress rehearsal. You for one, Mr. Seward, will understand me."

"What d'you mean," asked Seward indignantly. "I've done every bit the same as before, and not missed a cue. Only thing different is not to pull the front curtain, like you said."

"Quite so. And if we had had the front curtain open at

the rehearsal, we should have seen what you saw when you drew the traverse and revealed the screen."

"And what do you reckon I saw?"

"Clifford Fielding, moving away from behind the screen and making some excuse for being there."

"I've never denied it, not straight out," said Seward.

"You bastard, Ludlow," said Fielding.

Montero seemed to look reproachfully at Ludlow before saying: "Clifford Fielding, I am going to ask you to accompany me——"

"Stop, stop," said Ludlow. "You mustn't rush to conclusions so easily. Didn't I tell you it was like Falstaff? If you remember your *Henry IV*, Prince Hal kills Douglas and leaves his body on the battlefield, where Falstaff comes and carries it off and gets the credit for a deed of valour. That's what Fielding did, but he nearly got anything but credit for it."

"You mean that Bould was already dead when Fielding found him?" asked Donald Hedge.

"Precisely. Fielding had his own reasons for not wanting the body to be discovered too soon."

"Then I'm all right—I'm cleared. I didn't go out alone until after this scene." Donald hugged June, who still looked dazed by all that had happened.

"That is so," said Ludlow. "Now we can clear those who did not leave the hall alone before this point. We are left with Miss Morland, who went out immediately after Bould; Dexter, who waited alone for his entry; Seward, who could have been out during the scene. Also the producer, Terry Colbert."

All looked at Terry, who laughed.

"You're wrong there, Mr. Ludlow," he said. "I never left the hall during the time we've been considering."

"But you did," said Ludlow. "We all saw you up there on the stage."

"Oh come, really, do you think I could have killed a man in the time it took me to go through the curtain and up a few steps?"

"Of course not. But you had plenty of time in fact. Taking advantage of the disturbance caused by Miss Morland's return, you slipped out just as the scene recommenced."

"That's a lie!" Terry was pale now and no longer laughing. "I was watching the scene the whole time. Why did I go on the stage at all, except to correct Donald who was out of position?"

"That was your clever move, which nearly let you get away with it. We all assumed, myself included, that your shout of admonition to Donald Hedge came from outside the curtain. In fact it came from inside."

"What do you mean?"

"You had made your exit unobserved in the semidarkness, thanks to the diversion and general milling about. You did not want to be seen slipping back, now that all was calm again, without any explanation of why you had been out. So you worked an illusion, and a clever one. You took care that everyone should see you come *back* to the hall, in such a way that we assumed you had left it only for a moment, to go on the stage. You shouted to Hedge, because you were certain that there would be something to correct in his acting. You have often said, and he has admitted, that he needed continual instruction; so he was a safe one on whom to pick. By doing that, and then coming back very openly over the front of the stage, you made us all think that you had been in the hall right up to the time when you shouted. But by that time, Bould was already lying dead in the kitchen, with his neck broken."

Ludlow looked at Montero and raised an eyebrow. Montero came forward and said:

"Terence Bould, otherwise known as Terence Colbert, I have here a warrant for your arrest ——"

Terence turned and rushed through the side-curtains. First Donald Hedge, then Tony Dexter, started after him. They were forestalled by the return of Springer, holding his prisoner firmly by the arm.

"I thought you might try to get out that way," Montero said cheerfully. "That's why I sent the Sergeant out there. Perhaps we'd better go and get through the formalities outside in the car."

There was not a sound in the hall until they had gone out. Then Monica Stafford began to cry, in great noisy gulps.

CHAPTER FOURTEEN

After the Curtain

"When did you first realise that he was Bould's son?" Montero asked.

Montero and Springer were in Ludlow's flat, having seen their prisoner charged and lodged in Cannon Row for the night. Ludlow had given them coffee and brandy to drive the cold of the night from their bones and was now looking ready to talk at great length, given the least encouragement. As the two detectives were just as anxious to listen as he was to speak, all three were well satisfied at the moment. Ludlow leant back, pressed his fingers together, and refused to be hurried.

"Let us take things in their proper order," he said. "One of the flaws in your line of investigation, if I may be permitted to say so, is that you look too hard for motives at the beginning. For my own part, drawn unwillingly into this wretched affair as I was, it became increasingly clear that one man was guilty. The question of his real motive had to be resolved eventually, but I was not over-troubled by it at the beginning. Very recently, when I was sure that he was guilty, he told me that the only motive that you and I knew about — his quarrel with Bould over a matter of school discipline — was not strong enough for murder. I told him that I believed him, and I meant it. No, it was apparent almost as soon as Bould's body was discovered that at least three people knew more about it than they should. Those three were Fielding, Colbert and Miss Morland."

"I'm not sure that I follow you," Montero said.

"Of course, you weren't there at the time," Ludlow conceded kindly, "though I did tell you what had happened and you might have guessed. Let me take first the reaction of Colbert, as I suppose we'd better continue to call him. It is rather like the situation at one of the more complicated Elizabethan plays, where nearly all the characters have been assuming different names during the action and are revealed in the last scene. You will no doubt recall the most interesting example in ——"

"All right, we'll call him Colbert," Montero cut in desperately. "What did he first do to arouse your suspicions?"

"I was about to tell you when I was led off the track. Yes, he reacted violently to the discovery of Bould's body when the screen was thrown down. It seemed for a moment as if he was going to be sick. Yet there was no reason for great alarm or disgust — there was no blood, no immediate sign of violence, no way in fact of being sure that the man was dead and not merely unconscious. So I naturally wondered why he was so upset."

"And what about the other two?"

"I'll come to them later. The next thing was the cigarette."

"What cigarette?" asked Springer, who had been looking very much out of his depth and brightened up at the mention of something with which he might be able to help.

"The one which was picked up by one of your colleagues just inside the kitchen."

"I don't remember showing you that," said Montero.

"You didn't. You described it to me as being of a common make, and completely unmarked. As you said at the time, most of the people in the play seemed to smoke occasionally. What you failed to remember that this was a dress rehearsal. Almost everybody in that hall was wearing full make-up. If you've ever smoked, or drunk a cup of tea, when you were made up for the stage, you will know that it is impossible to avoid leaving a trace of paint. If the cigarette was unmarked, it must have been smoked by one of a very few people. Apart from myself, the only people in the hall who were not made up were Mrs. Bould and Monica Stafford, both of whom would probably have worn some lipstick of their own anyway, Seward, Bould himself, and Colbert. I remember Colbert smoking a lot during the rehearsal, and there can be no doubt that he threw down and crushed that cigarette just before attacking Bould. Later investigations showed that Bould smoked only cigars, Mrs. Bould did not smoke, and Seward rolled his own."

"That's very ingenious," Montero said slowly, "and I hand it to you. But you know, we can't go around arresting people for things like that. I'm sure you're right, but the cigarette could have been dropped there by someone before they were made up."

"I am aware of that: it was an interesting pointer, nothing more. No, Colbert's guilt became apparent only as a combination of factors. Chiefly, perhaps, by an elimination of the others, who could not have done the whole job in the time. For several days, I must admit that I did not see my way clearly. However, Colbert's very suspicious behaviour at that dress rehearsal made me concentrate on him, and at last I had the answer. This was something of an exercise in dramatic criticism, a play within a play, as it were. By studying the behaviour of some of the characters, it must be possible to enter into their minds and thence to discover what had motivated them. As an intellectual adventure, it was really most stimulating. A pity that so much more had to be at stake."

"So Colbert made you suspicious by his reaction to the discovery of the body and then you had this bright idea about the cigarette?" asked Springer, who always liked to get things straight.

"Yes, but Colbert's behaviour was odd in every way.

After running about the hall and making a thorough nuisance of himself, he made this dramatic appearance on the stage and then suddenly subsided. He attached himself firmly to Monica Stafford, and was never away from her side until the body was discovered. Once he had convinced us that he had made only a very brief exit from the hall, it was in his interest to secure a perfect alibi for the rest of the time."

"But he didn't know the body was behind the screen," Montero said.

"Precisely. And this is the dramatic situation to which I referred. Let us try to enter into the minds of the three people who gave themselves away when Bould's body was found. Can we imagine what anxiety, what frantic worry alternating with relief, must have been vibrating in that cold and shabby hall. First, there was Fielding, who had gone to the kitchen and found Bould there dead. I knew Fielding was lying when he gave two different accounts of Bould's reaction to his presence. From that it might have been deduced that Fielding was the murderer, but I remained unconvinced. Fielding is not an intelligent man, but he would not have taken such a risk when Dexter had just seen him go into the kitchen, only a few minutes after a violent quarrel with Bould. In fact it was these circumstances that made him panic and do what he did. If Bould's body were found, suspicion would point to him very strongly. I am not sure whether it occurred to him then, though I think it probably did, that this was also a wonderful opportunity to get back that document which put him in debt to Bould for five hundred pounds. He thought that Bould would keep it at home and that it could be got back that very night before the attachment of all Bould's papers."

"We thought that was what he was after," Montero said. "So he had the best possible reasons for delaying the inevitable discovery of Bould's body until next day."

"He might have got away with it too, if they hadn't done that scene over again," said Springer.

"Yes," Ludlow agreed. "A search might have been made in the hall, but it is unlikely. They would have assumed that Bould had got out through the back door and perhaps met with an accident outside. There was no reason to suppose that the screen would be disturbed until the following evening. Unfortunately for Fielding, he was discovered by Seward just when he had stowed the body away. I doubt whether Seward realised at the time what he was doing — he must have got Bould concealed just in time. Later, however, Seward was able to put two and two together ——"

"And make five by assuming that Fielding was the murderer," said Montero. "That's what he was trying to hint to us. And that's why you wanted a man put on Fielding for the last couple of days."

"Yes. Seward was trying to blackmail Fielding, who had no money after his heavy losses. I feared that Fielding might become violent in desperation, before everything was cleared up. Now where was I? You put me off."

"I'm so sorry," Montero said humbly. "You had just got to the placing of Bould's body behind the screen."

"Just so. And there it stayed until what should have been the end of the rehearsal. Now this is where we have to pay great attention to the performances of our actors, if we are to arrive, as I did, at their motives. Consider how Colbert must have felt at this point. Hedge had just come back from the kitchen, Mrs. Bould had gone out there. No uproar, no suggestion that anything was wrong. What on earth had happened to the body? Colbert had been at great pains to build up an alibi for himself. The body simply *had* to be discovered before they left the hall, while his movements were fresh in all memories. So, stalling for time as it were, he decided to do the screen scene again. It was one that he had every excuse for repeating, but he didn't know that it was going to reveal the body in the most dramatic way."

"So one of them wanted the body to be found and didn't know where it was, and the other knew where it was and didn't want it found. It must have been a bit of a giggle," Springer said.

"As you say. Remember too that Colbert had a key to the hall and would tend to fall under suspicion if they all went away and the body was found later. But can we imagine Fielding's state of mind? After he had so carefully prevented discovery, here he was faced with immediate exposure. He protested violently about doing that particular scene again, thereby proving how much *he* knew. He recovered well by the time of discovery — too well, for he pretended to think that Bould was playing a joke on them. As I said, there were no immediate signs of violence, but no man could have supposed that Bould had gone there for fun."

"We still don't know why June Morland wasn't the first to find the body," Montero remarked.

"My dear Inspector, we do: she was. Suspecting nothing, and anxious to get the thing over after a day which had been particularly trying for her, she went to the stage while the others were still arguing, looked behind the screen and saw Bould. Now various people, chiefly Colbert, have told me things about June Morland to back up my own observation. She has good nerves — 'unflappable' was the word used, I think — tends to be impulsive and is very loyal. All day she had been worried about the note which had told Hedge of her affair with Bould. Now she finds Bould dead, after Hedge has just come from the kitchen. Her mind rushes ahead, hysterical and yet calm. Hedge has killed Bould for revenge; Hedge is a dispensing chemist, therefore he used poison; the poison must have been slipped into Bould's cup of tea during the interval, and Hedge has just gone and moved the body after the poison has taken effect.

She must go and wash up all the cups before the police get there and examine them. It was obvious, even when she came to see me the day after the inquest that she still feared that Hedge had done it. She thought she could — ah, work on me, to divert my inquiries away from him. But she really gave herself away when she was called out of the kitchen after the body was found. She took the news of Bould's death quite calmly, but reacted with doubt and then relief when she heard that his neck had been broken. Thus she too showed what *she* knew — and what she thought she knew."

"Women!" said Springer with deep disgust.

There was silence while Ludlow poured some more coffee.

"I suppose it was Colbert who sent that anonymous note to Hedge," Montero said at last, "to give a motive that might turn suspicion on to him."

"I doubt it. I think it was probably Mrs. Bould, who showed a curiosity about my investigations which was rather out of keeping with her obvious lack of feeling after her husband's death. The note which she sent to me asking me to come to tea was written on the same paper as the letter we got from Hedge. That's not conclusive, of course, but it seems almost certain."

"And that paper was the same type as the piece that Bould had in his pocket, with Hedge's name and those figures on it," Springer said excitedly. "So she wrote that too."

"I'm sure Bould wrote that himself," said Ludlow, "borrowing a piece of paper from his wife who had her writing-case with her at the hall."

"Have you solved what that means too?" Montero asked.

"I think so; but let us try to keep to a chronological order. It was clear to me that Colbert needed more motive for a murder than a minor upset at his school. Now suppose you tell me what you discovered in that little piece of research into public records which I set you. I could have done it of course, but you and your colleagues in other parts of the country have readier access than I to these things."

"Of course," said Montero. "We found that Bould had been divorced by his first wife, the present Mrs. Bould being cited as co-respondent. That was not very long before he came to live in Haleham Green, where his daughter Frances was born. There was one child by the first marriage, a boy called Terence who passed into his mother's custody. Bould must have had a good lawyer, and his first wife must have been either very humble or very proud, because she got ridiculously small alimony. She must have had a struggle to bring up the boy, whom we know as Terence Colbert, and to send him to the University. She died, probably before her time, a few months before he came to live in Haleham Green with a post at the Grammar School. Whether he came there looking for revenge, or whether it was a coincidence and he only discovered Bould's identity later is yet to be found out. Not that it matters. But in the bit of talk I've had with the boy this evening, it's become clear that he did this for the sake of his mother's ill-treatment and the poverty that he himself has had to go through because of it. I think he may have had hopes of a bit of legacy as well. He might have known better, since Bould had never taken any trouble to get news of him all those years and had no idea who he was. But on the whole his motives seem to have been fairly pure, if that isn't a funny word to use in this connection. But may I now ask you again, when and how did you realise that he was Bould's son?"

"You may, and now I will answer you because the question comes in its logical place. Already heavily suspecting Colbert, I wanted to check up on him. I soon proved in conversation that he was telling the truth about his time at the University. I thought I might find some records of him there which would tell me what kind of man he was, and perhaps give me the real motive. I did, but not as I expected. I went to call on the Registrar of Queen Adelaide's, who is a friend of mine, and asked if I could look through the files of students for the period when Colbert must have been there. I could find no record of any Colbert having been registered. Puzzled by this, I went carefully through the degree-lists in English and found — no Terence Colbert, but a Terence Bould. It all fell into place. The records of Terence Bould showed that his mother had been his legal guardian. I remember Colbert's desire to have gone to Oxford, his conviction that lack of money had held him back. And I remembered something else. Bould's opposition to Dexter's engagement to Frances had been based on the fact that Dexter had already had a marriage dissolved. It appears that he was what is known as the 'innocent party', though whether there can ever be complete innocence on either side in such a tragic affair can perhaps be determined only by those who take their morality from records of conduct and not from consideration of attitudes and motives. However, innocent or not, there were valid theological objections to Dexter's remarriage. But it seemed that Bould had no theological beliefs on this, or indeed any other matter. Now it is a fact for which my psychologist colleagues no doubt have a long name, but which is clear to anyone who understands human nature, that people often strongly condemn those faults in others of which they are aware in themselves. I was sure that there was something in Bould's life to do with divorce, and I was right. Then there was Mrs. Bould's reactions to the reading of the will, to which I drew your attention at the time. As well as her natural indignation with June, she was anxious to know whether there were any other legacies of large sums. She too thought that Bould might have left something to the woman she had supplanted — or to the son of that marriage. She had no idea that the son was in fact well known to her and had effectively broken her husband's neck."

"A trick which he learned from Dexter's little demonstration of unarmed combat at the school." Montero looked reflectively at Ludlow. "It seems we're in your debt again," he added.

"No doubt you would have solved it in time," Ludlow said encouragingly. "I of course had the advantage of being there and seeing all the different reactions for myself. That almost convinced me, but I was still puzzled about the timing. Once I realised that Colbert had been out for longer than we all thought, covering himself by shouting at Hedge from inside the curtain, the rest was fairly easy. If he hadn't insisted so much on how bad an actor Hedge was, I might not have realised how safe it was for him to give a correction without actually being able to see the stage. And as the screen was exposed all the time he was out, someone else must have moved the body. Fielding's reactions made it pretty certain who it was."

"And now," Montero said after a respectful pause, "*please* tell us the meaning of that note in Bould's pocket —'Donald Hedge, 5, 9, 25.' It was that which made me suspect Hedge for so long, and the cipher boys are still going round the bend about it."

"There would be no need for any going around bends," said Ludlow with a smile, "if they had any experience of the stage. I ought to have understood much sooner than I did. I am rapidly becoming old and useless. However. Yes, 5 and 9 are the reference-numbers for the two basic colours used in a straight male make-up for the stage; 25 is the stick for lines and shadows. After learning that Hedge stocked make-up, I found out from Colbert that Bould had been showing some desire to act. He had been getting particulars that same evening when he was killed and had written them down on a piece of paper borrowed from his wife. It shows the insensitivity of the man that he was quite prepared to go and do business with Hedge for his own convenience, in spite of all that had happened."

Montero nodded, then got up and signed to Springer that it was time for them to go. At the door he thanked his host again, but Ludlow shook his head and looked bewildered.

"I don't know," he said. "There seems to have been no merit in Bould, who lived selfishly all his life and caused a great deal of unhappiness. Colbert is an intelligent and decent young man, yet I've hunted him down like an animal. Why do we do it?"

"Don't worry," Montero. said. "You've certainly helped us a lot, but he'd have been found out in the end even if you hadn't come into it."

"Why do we do it?" Ludlow repeated.

"I wouldn't like to answer that, Mr. Ludlow. I'm just a simple copper, and my job is to deliver the goods. Isn't there an answer in all these books you've got here?"

"Yes, I think there is," Ludlow said slowly.

"And isn't it something to do with respect for life, and a love that doesn't depend on individual merit? You're making me use some funny words. I'd better say good night."

They shook hands and parted. Ludlow went to the window and looked out into the street that was now quiet and almost deserted. A thin rain was beginning to fall, a reminder that the winter still had several weeks in which to have its way with the world. There was no satisfaction in his face as he stood there, but the look of a man who disliked the way he had trodden but knew that he could tread no other. And when he did not think of the man in the cell, he thought too long of some red hair and a little nose that tilted provokingly. It was a long time before he slept.

Montero and Springer did not sleep early either, but returned to their office for another hour's work.

"Well, that's that," Montero said at last. "All the loose ends tied up and an easy day tomorrow. In court in the morning, ask for a remand in custody, and all we have to do the rest of the time is nearly two weeks' work that's been accumulating while we've been tasting the heady delights of Haleham Green."

"I reckon it was a lucky thing that Mr. Ludlow went out to give them a lecture," Springer said. "We'd still be scrambling, if he hadn't got himself mixed up in it because he can't say no to a silly bit of skirt."

"You do violence to our amateur colleague's motives, which are as mixed as those of most men. By the way, I wonder how long that affair will last — I mean the attachment between June and Donald Hedge. Want to bet on it, Jack?"

Springer was still pensive. "You know, sir," he said, "there were an awful lot of offences in this case besides murder. Concealing evidence, interfering with evidence, blackmail, sending annoying letters — I don't know what else."

Montero switched off the reading lamp and yawned.

"We'd better leave those to Inspector Belling and the local division to deal with if they want to," he said. "But somehow I think they've had enough scandal round there for the time being."

THE PERENNIAL LIBRARY MYSTERY SERIES

Ted Allbeury

THE OTHER SIDE OF SILENCE P 669, $2.84
"In the best le Carré tradition . . . an ingenious and readable book."
—*New York Times Book Review*

PALOMINO BLONDE P 670, $2.84
"Fast-moving, splendidly technocratic intercontinental espionage tale . . . you'll love it." —*The Times* (London)

SNOWBALL P 671, $2.84
"A novel of byzantine intrigue. . . ."—*New York Times Book Review*

Delano Ames

CORPSE DIPLOMATIQUE P 637, $2.84
"Sprightly and intelligent."
—*New York Herald Tribune Book Review*

FOR OLD CRIME'S SAKE P 629, $2.84

MURDER, MAESTRO, PLEASE P 630, $2.84
"If there is a more engaging couple in modern fiction than Jane and Dagobert Brown, we have not met them." —*Scotsman*

SHE SHALL HAVE MURDER P 638, $2.84
"Combines the merit of both the English and American schools in the new mystery. It's as breezy as the best of the American ones, and has the sophistication and wit of any top-notch Britisher."
—*New York Herald Tribune Book Review*

E. C. Bentley

TRENT'S LAST CASE P 440, $2.50
"One of the three best detective stories ever written."
—Agatha Christie

TRENT'S OWN CASE P 516, $2.25
"I won't waste time saying that the plot is sound and the detection satisfying. Trent has not altered a scrap and reappears with all his old humor and charm." —Dorothy L. Sayers

Andrew Bergman

THE BIG KISS-OFF OF 1944 P 673, $2.84

"It is without doubt the nearest thing to genuine Chandler I've ever come across. . . . Tough, witty—very witty—and a beautiful eye for period detail. . . ." —Jack Higgins

HOLLYWOOD AND LEVINE P 674, $2.84

"Fast-paced private-eye fiction." —*San Francisco Chronicle*

Gavin Black

A DRAGON FOR CHRISTMAS P 473, $1.95

"Potent excitement!" —*New York Herald Tribune*

THE EYES AROUND ME P 485, $1.95

"I stayed up until all hours last night reading *The Eyes Around Me,* which is something I do not do very often, but I was so intrigued by the ingeniousness of Mr. Black's plotting and the witty way in which he spins his mystery. I can only say that I enjoyed the book enormously." —F. van Wyck Mason

YOU WANT TO DIE, JOHNNY? P 472, $1.95

"Gavin Black doesn't just develop a pressure plot in suspense, he adds uninfected wit, character, charm, and sharp knowledge of the Far East to make rereading as keen as the first race-through." —*Book Week*

Nicholas Blake

THE CORPSE IN THE SNOWMAN P 427, $1.95

"If there is a distinction between the novel and the detective story (which we do not admit), then this book deserves a high place in both categories." —*New York Times*

END OF CHAPTER P 397, $1.95

". . . admirably solid . . . an adroit formal detective puzzle backed up by firm characterization and a knowing picture of London publishing." —*New York Times*

HEAD OF A TRAVELER P 398, $2.25

"Another grade A detective story of the right old jigsaw persuasion." —*New York Herald Tribune Book Review*

MINUTE FOR MURDER P 419, $1.95

"An outstanding mystery novel. Mr. Blake's writing is a delight in itself." —*New York Times*

THE MORNING AFTER DEATH P 520, $1.95

"One of Blake's best." —Rex Warner

Nicholas Blake (cont'd)

A PENKNIFE IN MY HEART P 521, $2.25
"Style brilliant . . . and suspenseful." —*San Francisco Chronicle*

THE PRIVATE WOUND P 531, $2.25
"[Blake's] best novel in a dozen years. . . . An intensely penetrating study of sexual passion. . . . A powerful story of murder and its aftermath."
—Anthony Boucher, *New York Times*

A QUESTION OF PROOF P 494, $1.95
"The characters in this story are unusually well drawn, and the suspense is well sustained." —*New York Times*

THE SAD VARIETY P 495, $2.25
"It is a stunner. I read it instead of eating, instead of sleeping."
—Dorothy Salisbury Davis

THERE'S TROUBLE BREWING P 569, $3.37
"Nigel Strangeways is a puzzling mixture of simplicity and penetration, but all the more real for that."
—*The Times* (London) *Literary Supplement*

THOU SHELL OF DEATH P 428, $1.95
"It has all the virtues of culture, intelligence and sensibility that the most exacting connoisseur could ask of detective fiction."
—*The Times* (London) *Literary Supplement*

THE WIDOW'S CRUISE P 399, $2.25
"A stirring suspense. . . . The thrilling tale leaves nothing to be desired."
—*Springfield Republican*

Oliver Bleeck

THE BRASS GO-BETWEEN P 645, $2.84
"Fiction with a flair, well above the norm for thrillers."
—*Associated Press*

THE PROCANE CHRONICLE P 647, $2.84
"Without peer in American suspense." —*Los Angeles Times*

PROTOCOL FOR A KIDNAPPING P 646, $2.84
"The zigzags of plot are electric; the characters sharp; but it is the wit and irony and touches of plain fun which make the whole a standout."
—*Los Angeles Times*

John & Emery Bonett

A BANNER FOR PEGASUS P 554, $2.40
"A gem! Beautifully plotted and set. . . . Not only is the murder adroit and deserved, and the detection competent, but the love story is charming." —Jacques Barzun and Wendell Hertig Taylor

DEAD LION P 563, $2.40
"A clever plot, authentic background and interesting characters highly recommended this one." —*New Republic*

THE SOUND OF MURDER P 642, $2.84
The suspects are many, the clues few, but the gentle Inspector ferrets out the truth and pursues the case to its bitter and shocking end.

Christianna Brand

GREEN FOR DANGER P 551, $2.50
"You have to reach for the greatest of Great Names (Christie, Carr, Queen . . .) to find Brand's rivals in the devious subtleties of the trade."
—Anthony Boucher

TOUR DE FORCE P 572, $2.40
"Complete with traps for the over-ingenious, a double-reverse surprise ending and a key clue planted so fairly and obviously that you completely overlook it. If that's your idea of perfect entertainment, then seize at once upon *Tour de Force.*" —Anthony Boucher, *New York Times*

James Byrom

OR BE HE DEAD P 585, $2.84
"A very original tale . . . Well written and steadily entertaining."
—Jacques Barzun and Wendell Hertig Taylor, *A Catalogue of Crime*

Henry Calvin

IT'S DIFFERENT ABROAD P 640, $2.84
"What is remarkable and delightful, Mr. Calvin imparts a flavor of satire to what he renovates and compels us to take straight."
—Jacques Barzun

Marjorie Carleton

VANISHED P 559, $2.40
"Exceptional . . . a minor triumph."
—Jacques Barzun and Wendell Hertig Taylor, *A Catalogue of Crime*

George Harmon Coxe

MURDER WITH PICTURES P 527, $2.25
"[Coxe] has hit the bull's-eye with his first shot."
—*New York Times*

Edmund Crispin

BURIED FOR PLEASURE P 506, $2.50
"Absolute and unalloyed delight."
—Anthony Boucher, *New York Times*

Lionel Davidson

THE MENORAH MEN P 592, $2.84
"Of his fellow thriller writers, only John Le Carré shows the same instinct for the viscera." —*Chicago Tribune*

NIGHT OF WENCESLAS P 595, $2.84
"A most ingenious thriller, so enriched with style, wit, and a sense of serious comedy that it all but transcends its kind."
—*The New Yorker*

THE ROSE OF TIBET P 593, $2.84
"I hadn't realized how much I missed the genuine Adventure story . . . until I read *The Rose of Tibet*." —Graham Greene

D. M. Devine

MY BROTHER'S KILLER P 558, $2.40
"A most enjoyable crime story which I enjoyed reading down to the last moment." —Agatha Christie

Kenneth Fearing

THE BIG CLOCK P 500, $1.95
"It will be some time before chill-hungry clients meet again so rare a compound of irony, satire, and icy-fingered narrative. *The Big Clock* is . . . a psychothriller you won't put down." —*Weekly Book Review*

Andrew Garve

THE ASHES OF LODA P 430, $1.50
"Garve . . . embellishes a fine fast adventure story with a more credible picture of the U.S.S.R. than is offered in most thrillers."
—*New York Times Book Review*

THE CUCKOO LINE AFFAIR P 451, $1.95
". . . an agreeable and ingenious piece of work." —*The New Yorker*

A HERO FOR LEANDA P 429, $1.50
"One can trust Mr. Garve to put a fresh twist to any situation, and the ending is really a lovely surprise." —*Manchester Guardian*

MURDER THROUGH THE LOOKING GLASS P 449, $1.95
". . . refreshingly out-of-the-way and enjoyable . . . highly recommended to all comers." —*Saturday Review*

NO TEARS FOR HILDA P 441, $1.95
"It starts fine and finishes finer. I got behind on breathing watching Max get not only his man but his woman, too." —Rex Stout

THE RIDDLE OF SAMSON P 450, $1.95
"The story is an excellent one, the people are quite likable, and the writing is superior." —*Springfield Republican*

Michael Gilbert

BLOOD AND JUDGMENT P 446, $1.95
"Gilbert readers need scarcely be told that the characters all come alive at first sight, and that his surpassing talent for narration enhances any plot. . . . Don't miss." —*San Francisco Chronicle*

THE BODY OF A GIRL P 459, $1.95
"Does what a good mystery should do: open up into all kinds of ramifications, with untold menace behind the action. At the end, there is a bang-up climax, and it is a pleasure to see how skilfully Gilbert wraps everything up." —*New York Times Book Review*

FEAR TO TREAD P 458, $1.95
"Merits serious consideration as a work of art." —*New York Times*

Joe Gores

HAMMETT P 631, $2.84
"Joe Gores at his very best. Terse, powerful writing—with the master, Dashiell Hammett, as the protagonist in a novel I think he would have been proud to call his own." —Robert Ludlum

C. W. Grafton

BEYOND A REASONABLE DOUBT P 519, $1.95
"A very ingenious tale of murder . . . a brilliant and gripping narrative."
—Jacques Barzun and Wendell Hertig Taylor

C. W. Grafton (cont'd)

THE RAT BEGAN TO GNAW THE ROPE P 639, $2.84
"Fast, humorous story with flashes of brilliance."
—*The New Yorker*

Edward Grierson

THE SECOND MAN P 528, $2.25
"One of the best trial-testimony books to have come along in quite a while." —*The New Yorker*

Bruce Hamilton

TOO MUCH OF WATER P 635, $2.84
"A superb sea mystery. . . . The prose is excellent."
—Jacques Barzun and Wendell Hertig Taylor, *A Catalogue of Crime*

Cyril Hare

DEATH IS NO SPORTSMAN P 555, $2.40
"You will be thrilled because it succeeds in placing an ingenious story in a new and refreshing setting. . . . The identity of the murderer is really a surprise." —*Daily Mirror*

DEATH WALKS THE WOODS P 556, $2.40
"Here is a fine formal detective story, with a technically brilliant solution demanding the attention of all connoisseurs of construction."
—Anthony Boucher, *New York Times Book Review*

AN ENGLISH MURDER P 455, $2.50
"By a long shot, the best crime story I have read for a long time. Everything is traditional, but originality does not suffer. The setting is perfect. Full marks to Mr. Hare." —*Irish Press*

SUICIDE EXCEPTED P 636, $2.84
"Adroit in its manipulation . . . and distinguished by a plot-twister which I'll wager Christie wishes she'd thought of." —*New York Times*

TENANT FOR DEATH P 570, $2.84
"The way in which an air of probability is combined both with clear, terse narrative and with a good deal of subtle suburban atmosphere, proves the extreme skill of the writer." —*The Spectator*

TRAGEDY AT LAW P 522, $2.25
"An extremely urbane and well-written detective story."
—*New York Times*

UNTIMELY DEATH P 514, $2.25

"The English detective story at its quiet best, meticulously underplayed, rich in perceivings of the droll human animal and ready at the last with a neat surprise which has been there all the while had we but wits to see it." —*New York Herald Tribune Book Review*

THE WIND BLOWS DEATH P 589, $2.84

"A plot compounded of musical knowledge, a Dickens allusion, and a subtle point in law is related with delightfully unobtrusive wit, warmth, and style." —*New York Times*

WITH A BARE BODKIN P 523, $2.25

"One of the best detective stories published for a long time." —*The Spectator*

Robert Harling

THE ENORMOUS SHADOW P 545, $2.50

"In some ways the best spy story of the modern period. . . . The writing is terse and vivid . . . the ending full of action . . . altogether first-rate." —Jacques Barzun and Wendell Hertig Taylor, *A Catalogue of Crime*

Matthew Head

THE CABINDA AFFAIR P 541, $2.25

"An absorbing whodunit and a distinguished novel of atmosphere." —Anthony Boucher, *New York Times*

THE CONGO VENUS P 597, $2.84

"Terrific. The dialogue is just plain wonderful." —*Boston Globe*

MURDER AT THE FLEA CLUB P 542, $2.50

"The true delight is in Head's style, its limpid ease combined with humor and an awesome precision of phrase." —*San Francisco Chronicle*

M. V. Heberden

ENGAGED TO MURDER P 533, $2.25

"Smooth plotting." —*New York Times*

James Hilton

WAS IT MURDER? P 501, $1.95

"The story is well planned and well written." —*New York Times*

S. B. Hough

DEAR DAUGHTER DEAD P 661, $2.84
"A highly intelligent and sophisticated story of police detection . . . not to be missed on any account." —Francis Iles, *The Guardian*

SWEET SISTER SEDUCED P 662, $2.84
In the course of a nightlong conversation between the Inspector and the suspect, the complex emotions of a very strange marriage are revealed.

P. M. Hubbard

HIGH TIDE P 571, $2.40
"A smooth elaboration of mounting horror and danger."
—*Library Journal*

Elspeth Huxley

THE AFRICAN POISON MURDERS P 540, $2.25
"Obscure venom, manical mutilations, deadly bush fire, thrilling climax compose major opus.... Top-flight."
—*Saturday Review of Literature*

MURDER ON SAFARI P 587, $2.84
"Right now we'd call Mrs. Huxley a dangerous rival to Agatha Christie." —*Books*

Francis Iles

BEFORE THE FACT P 517, $2.50
"Not many 'serious' novelists have produced character studies to compare with Iles's internally terrifying portrait of the murderer in *Before the Fact,* his masterpiece and a work truly deserving the appellation of unique and beyond price." —Howard Haycraft

MALICE AFORETHOUGHT P 532, $1.95
"It is a long time since I have read anything so good as *Malice Aforethought,* with its cynical humour, acute criminology, plausible detail and rapid movement. It makes you hug yourself with pleasure."
—H. C. Harwood, *Saturday Review*

Michael Innes

APPLEBY ON ARARAT P 648, $2.84
"Superbly plotted and humorously written." —*The New Yorker*

APPLEBY'S END P 649, $2.84
"Most amusing." —*Boston Globe*

THE CASE OF THE JOURNEYING BOY P 632, $3.12
"I could see no faults in it. There is no one to compare with him."
—*Illustrated London News*

DEATH ON A QUIET DAY P 677, $2.84
"Delightfully witty." —*Chicago Sunday Tribune*

DEATH BY WATER P 574, $2.40
"The amount of ironic social criticism and deft characterization of scenes and people would serve another author for six books."
—Jacques Barzun and Wendell Hertig Taylor

HARE SITTING UP P 590, $2.84
"There is hardly anyone (in mysteries or mainstream) more exquisitely literate, allusive and Jamesian—and hardly anyone with a firmer sense of melodramatic plot or a more vigorous gift of storytelling."
—Anthony Boucher, *New York Times*

THE LONG FAREWELL P 575, $2.40
"A model of the deft, classic detective story, told in the most wittily diverting prose." —*New York Times*

THE MAN FROM THE SEA P 591, $2.84
"The pace is brisk, the adventures exciting and excitingly told, and above all he keeps to the very end the interesting ambiguity of the man from the sea." —*New Statesman*

ONE MAN SHOW P 672, $2.84
"Exciting, amusingly written . . . very good enjoyment it is."
—*The Spectator*

THE SECRET VANGUARD P 584, $2.84
"Innes . . . has mastered the art of swift, exciting and well-organized narrative." —*New York Times*

THE WEIGHT OF THE EVIDENCE P 633, $2.84
"First-class puzzle, deftly solved. University background interesting and amusing." —*Saturday Review of Literature*

Mary Kelly

THE SPOILT KILL P 565, $2.40
"Mary Kelly is a new Dorothy Sayers. . . . [An] exciting new novel."
—*Evening News*

Lange Lewis

THE BIRTHDAY MURDER P 518, $1.95

"Almost perfect in its playlike purity and delightful prose."

—Jacques Barzun and Wendell Hertig Taylor

Allan MacKinnon

HOUSE OF DARKNESS P 582, $2.84

"His best . . . a perfect compendium."

—Jacques Barzun and Wendell Hertig Taylor, *A Catalogue of Crime*

Frank Parrish

FIRE IN THE BARLEY P 651, $2.84

"A remarkable and brilliant first novel. . . . entrancing."

—*The Spectator*

SNARE IN THE DARK P 650, $2.84

The wily English poacher Dan Mallett is framed for murder and has to confront unknown enemies to clear himself.

STING OF THE HONEYBEE P 652, $2.84

"Terrorism and murder visit a sleepy English village in this witty, offbeat thriller." —*Chicago Sun-Times*

Austin Ripley

MINUTE MYSTERIES P 387, $2.50

More than one hundred of the world's shortest detective stories. Only one possible solution to each case!

Thomas Sterling

THE EVIL OF THE DAY P 529, $2.50

"Prose as witty and subtle as it is sharp and clear. . .characters unconventionally conceived and richly bodied forth . . . . In short, a novel to be treasured." —Anthony Boucher, *New York Times*

Julian Symons

THE BELTING INHERITANCE P 468, $1.95

"A superb whodunit in the best tradition of the detective story."

—August Derleth, *Madison Capital Times*

BOGUE'S FORTUNE P 481, $1.95

"There's a touch of the old sardonic humour, and more than a touch of style." —*The Spectator*

Julian Symons (cont'd)

THE COLOR OF MURDER P 461, $1.95

"A singularly unostentatious and memorably brilliant detective story."
—*New York Herald Tribune Book Review*

Dorothy Stockbridge Tillet
(John Stephen Strange)

THE MAN WHO KILLED FORTESCUE P 536, $2.25

"Better than average." —*Saturday Review of Literature*

Simon Troy

THE ROAD TO RHUINE P 583, $2.84

"Unusual and agreeably told." —*San Francisco Chronicle*

SWIFT TO ITS CLOSE P 546, $2.40

"A nicely literate British mystery . . . the atmosphere and the plot are exceptionally well wrought, the dialogue excellent." —*Best Sellers*

Henry Wade

THE DUKE OF YORK'S STEPS P 588, $2.84

"A classic of the golden age."
—Jacques Barzun and Wendell Hertig Taylor, *A Catalogue of Crime*

A DYING FALL P 543, $2.50

"One of those expert British suspense jobs . . . it crackles with undercurrents of blackmail, violent passion and murder. Topnotch in its class."
—*Time*

THE HANGING CAPTAIN P 548, $2.50

"This is a detective story for connoisseurs, for those who value clear thinking and good writing above mere ingenuity and easy thrills."
—*The Times* (London) *Literary Supplement*

Hillary Waugh

LAST SEEN WEARING . . . P 552, $2.40

"A brilliant tour de force." —Julian Symons

THE MISSING MAN P 553, $2.40

"The quiet detailed police work of Chief Fred C. Fellows, Stockford, Conn., is at its best in *The Missing Man* . . . one of the Chief's toughest cases and one of the best handled."
—Anthony Boucher, *New York Times Book Review*

Henry Kitchell Webster

WHO IS THE NEXT? P 539, $2.25
"A double murder, private-plane piloting, a neat impersonation, and a delicate courtship are adroitly combined by a writer who knows how to use the language." —Jacques Barzun and Wendell Hertig Taylor

John Welcome

GO FOR BROKE P 663, $2.84
A rich financier chases Richard Graham half 'round Europe in a desperate attempt to prevent the truth getting out.

RUN FOR COVER P 664, $2.84
"I can think of few writers in the international intrigue game with such a gift for fast and vivid storytelling."
—*New York Times Book Review*

STOP AT NOTHING P 665, $2.84
"Mr. Welcome is lively, vivid and highly readable."
—*New York Times Book Review*

Anna Mary Wells

MURDERER'S CHOICE P 534, $2.50
"Good writing, ample action, and excellent character work."
—*Saturday Review of Literature*

A TALENT FOR MURDER P 535, $2.25
"The discovery of the villain is a decided shock." —*Books*

Charles Williams

DEAD CALM P 655, $2.84
"A brilliant tour de force of inventive plotting, fine manipulation of a small cast and breathtaking sequences of spectacular navigation."
—*New York Times Book Review*

THE SAILCLOTH SHROUD P 654, $2.84
"A fine novel of excitement, spirited, fresh and satisfying."
—*New York Times*

THE WRONG VENUS P 656, $2.84
Swindler Lawrence Colby and the lovely Martine create a story of romance, larceny, and very blunt homicide.